T0276910

DEATH STRANDING 02

DEATH STRANDING
Volume One

DEATH STRANDING
Volume Two

DEATH STRANDING 02

BY HITORI NOJIMA

BASED ON THE GAME BY HIDEO KOJIMA

TRANSLATED BY CARLEY RADFORD

TITAN BOOKS

Death Stranding: Volume Two
Print edition ISBN: 9781789095784
E-book edition ISBN: 9781789096590

Published by Titan Books
A division of Titan Publishing Group Ltd
144 Southwark Street, London SE1 0UP.
www.titanbooks.com

First edition: February 2021
10 9 8 7 6 5 4 3 2

Death Stranding by Hideo Kojima/Hitori Nojima
Copyright © 2019 Sony Interactive Entertainment Inc.
Created and developed by KOJIMA PRODUCTIONS.
All rights reserved.
Cover illustration by Pablo Uchida
Original Japanese edition published in 2019 by SHINCHOSHA Publishing Co.,
Ltd.
English translation rights arranged with SHINCHOSHA Publishing Co., Ltd.
through The English Agency Japan Ltd.
English translation copyrights © 2021 by Titan Publishing Group Ltd.

A CIP catalogue record for this title is available from the British Library.

Printed and bound by CPI Group (UK) Ltd, Croydon, CR0 4YY

CONTENTS

CHARACTERS

Sam Porter Bridges - A "porter" who has rejoined Bridges for the first time in ten years. He is heading west as Bridges II.

Amelie - The leader of Bridges I, who went out west to rebuild America. She is currently being held in Edge Knot City.

Bridget Strand - The last President of the United States of America. She has devoted herself to rebuilding the UCA to reconnect a broken world.

Die-Hardman - The director of Bridges, an organization created specifically to rebuild America. A close associate of Bridget.

Deadman - A member of Bridges and an ex-coroner. He is in charge of BB maintenance among other things.

Mama - A mechanic from Bridges involved in the development of the Q-pid and Chiral Network.

Heartman - A member of Bridges who hopes to unravel the mysteries surrounding the Death Stranding and the Beach.

Fragile - The young, female leader of the private delivery organization Fragile Express.

Higgs - A member of Homo Demens who is trying to prevent the rebuilding of America and accelerate human extinction.

Unger - A mysterious man who wants the BB.

VOCABULARY

Bridges - An organization created by the last President of the United States of America, Bridget Strand, for the sole purpose of reconnecting all of the disjointed cities and people across the ex-USA and rebuilding America.

Death Stranding - A mysterious phenomenon that affected the entire world. When antimatter stranded from the world of the dead comes into contact with the living, it causes a voidout.

BB - Bridge Babies. Artificially created "equipment" that allows its users to sense the presence of the dead.

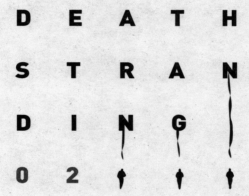

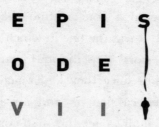

EPISODE VIII

DEADMAN
(continued)

Once the winds calmed, the force of the snow flurries finally weakened. The black clouds that hung in the air all around Sam, that had seemed close enough to touch, had dissipated, but the sun was still nowhere to be seen. It had been four days since Sam had left Mountain Knot City and he had finally reached the highest peak in the mountain range. Despite the detour, he was relieved to discover that his path would indeed lead him over the summit. Yet once he reached the top of the peak that stood thousands of meters above sea level, he still found he could not see beyond the pale veil that covered the sky and obscured the world on the other side. It seemed impossible to him that a vast blue sky stretched out just beyond the clouds, slowly fading into the jet-blackness of space.

Sam remembered a conversation that he had with Bridget as a child. It was the one in which she told him all about their ancestors' expedition toward the western frontier. About how once they had reached the western frontier, they then carried on and aimed for the next frontier—space. Finally, once they had conquered the last physical frontier, they embarked upon a quest for the electronic frontier of networks and cyberspace. "Listen, Sam," Bridget started. "The Strand family all come from a single ancestor, who was among the first to reach America. Cultivating new places and building the infrastructure to give other people a future is in our blood. It was our ancestors who were the first to build a bridge to the island of Manhattan. That's why I want you to build bridges, too."

How naïve Sam Strand had been back then as he obediently nodded and promised her that he would.

But the path to space was now closed and the bridge they were now trying to build was to the world of the dead. Was that the new final frontier?

The Chiral Network was an amalgam of a network and the world of the dead. Lockne had told him all about it. A member of Bridges, she was the younger twin sister of the theoretical physics expert Mama and the co-developer of the Q-pid.

"I don't think it's meaningless for the Chiral Network to

access the world of the dead and bring back the past we lost and everything that went with it," Lockne had once explained. "We need to reclaim the knowledge that the Death Stranding stole from us, but if that's all we do, then what are we doing but staring down memory lane? We run the risk of becoming bound by the past, just like Målingen and I were bound by our daughter.

"Mountain Knot City may now be a knot on the Chiral Network, but that doesn't mean I want to go back to Bridges. I need some time to think," Lockne told Sam. Now that Lockne and Mama had managed to untangle themselves from the estrangement caused by the misunderstanding about their dead daughter, Lockne had new paths open to her. Sam wondered what kind of options he had now.

He looked down at the empty void on his chest.

Lou, the BB whose pod normally occupied that area, was with Deadman for repairs. All that was left was empty space. Even when the repairs were complete, the pod that would be returned to Sam would no longer contain Lou, but a blank BB with no memories. There had been no other choice. And now, on top of that, Sam found himself dwelling on Deadman's news about the shadier side of Bridges. What was he supposed to do about the fact that Bridget had carried on the BB experiments in secret? What about the past of Die-Hardman, who served her? It seemed that for now, the only option open to him was to pretend like he hadn't heard anything and carry on with his task of transporting goods and reconnecting the Network as he went west in search of Amelie.

That was why he had battled the winds and traipsed all the way up the sides of these snow-capped peaks.

While Deadman was busy repairing Lou, Sam was to summit the mountains and head west from the direction of Mountain Knot City, to deliver some chiral allergy medication to the Geologist's shelter. As the people stationed there continued to excavate the land, they had reported early symptoms of chiral contamination. Sam had DOOMS, so contamination didn't bother him too much, but for normal people it could easily become deadly. Luckily, the symptoms that the Geologist was experiencing appeared to be on the milder side, but they still needed dealing with fast.

<Sam! Sam Bridges!>

A codec call came through his cuff links and jolted Sam out of his thoughts. The tone was peculiar, in that it was restless yet aloof.

<It's me, Heartman. Can you hear me?>

Even within Bridges, Heartman knew the most about the Beach by far, but Sam had only ever been able to talk to him via wireless means or as a hologram.

<Sam, I heard that you're currently en route to visit some old acquaintances of mine. So if I'm not mistaken, that means that you'll be heading to my

place soon after, right? I'm still not connected to the Chiral Network, but I do fall under the operational area of the network installed at Mountain Knot City, so I should be able to relay through the wireless and voice call with you even when you're high in the mountains. Of course, once the Chiral Network is connected, I'll be able to speak to you as a hologram too.>

Heartman was speaking at such a pace that Sam wondered if he was even closing his lips between sentences.

<My friends may be stationed out in the shelters, but all of them are experts in their own fields in the natural sciences. I don't know if you've been told this, Sam, but the area that you're heading to is very unusual. It's full of fossils from the late-Cretaceous Period. Now, that might not seem so strange since we know that the dinosaurs went extinct 65 million years ago, but in reality there isn't that much fossil evidence left behind that shows them living all the way to the end of that period. So, what we have under the soil there is a record of extinction. I've been told that the shelter that you're heading to now is the Geologist's base. Now, he's made quite an interesting discovery. You may not be able to imagine this, and I've only heard about it, so I'm not even sure that I quite

believe everything myself, but they say he's found
a fossil Beach. That's why he has started
experiencing symptoms of chiral contamination.

<I'm sure he'll recover once you deliver him the
medicine. But remember, he's not the only one
involved in this research and investigation. There's
a paleontologist digging up fossils of extinct
creatures and an evolutionary biologist out there
waiting for you, too. Everyone is looking forward
to your arrival and the activation of the Chiral
Network, when they can recover the past research
data that was lost in the Death Stranding and
access the memories and records directly from the
time of the extinction itself. I am too, for that
matter. Oh, Sam, I do hope you get here quickly.>

It was just as Heartman had described. The plan was to
drop by their shelters and activate the Chiral Network for
them. But first, he needed to deliver the medicine to the
Geologist. Once he had done all that, he would need to
drop by Deadman's place to pick up Lou. Heartman may
have been very talkative and extremely quick-thinking, but
he would have to wait.

<Sam, are you still there? I would love nothing
more than to keep this conversation going, but I'm
afraid my time is almost up.>

Sam wanted to point out that their call had been more

like a monologue than a conversation, but before he could say anything, a robotic voice interjected with `<One minute remaining.>`

`<Sorry about this, Sam, but I need to borrow you so I can verify their discovery in detail. So, please hurry up and get the Chiral Network up and running at their places and mine. You're not just connecting places and people here. Let's talk in more detail next time. See you, Sam.>`

Heartman disconnected the call with the same urgency that he had originally rung with. The phrase "a fossil Beach" echoed around Sam's head. He wondered if it had anything to do with the fossils they were finding of the dinosaurs that had managed to cling on until the very end. He wondered what fossilization of the Beach even meant. He couldn't even fathom it. But, just like Heartman said, none of this was confirmed, so there was no point thinking about it yet. Sam stood up, looked up at the sky, and readjusted his hood. The snow was beginning to fall again.

Black clouds once more obscured the heavens. Something sounded like an animal howling in the distance, but on further listening, Sam realized that it was the sound of the violently blustering wind. Gusts battered Sam, crying like countless invisible beasts, which threatened to topple him over. He braced himself against the land, but he couldn't withstand the weight of his cargo and fell backward.

The violent, beast-like wind rushed over Sam as he became buried in snow. The flurries swirled and groaned and blocked out his vision. As he struggled back to his feet, cursing, the wind knocked him back down. Standing had become impossible.

There was nowhere to shelter from the wind on this blizzard-battered mountain peak. Sam grabbed a climbing anchor out of his backpack and thrust it into the bedrock beneath the snow. He tied the strand around his waist and secured himself to the other end.

All he could do was lie face down and wait for the winds to calm. He clung to the snowfield on his belly. If there was any space between himself and the ground, the wind would get in and blow him away. He wondered just how far his body would be carried in weather like this. Would it be just like when he was taken by the supercell before?

Sam could feel his body heat draining away as he was rendered immobile. He couldn't stop the ringing sensation in his back teeth. The feeling of being cold had already disappeared and now the only sensation running through Sam's body was pain. But that pain would eventually disappear, too. Then it would be the end. He tried to muster all his strength into his limbs, but his fingers and toes only continued to grow more and more numb. The snow gradually concealed the outline of his body from the waist down, making it look as if his body was gradually dissolving away into particles. *Just like a BT.* That thought felt like part-hallucination and part-dream. It was a bad omen. He couldn't look inwards at a time like this, he had to look outwards. He had to bind both body and mind back to earth.

After a while, Sam realized there was a rhythm to this wind. It didn't stop blowing, but there was a little bit of a calm after the more violent gusts. If he could predict when the calm would come, he might be able to move. If he stayed here, he was going to succumb to frostbite.

The wind weakened. Sam gripped the strand that was tied to his waist with both hands, and began to move forward as he kept his center of gravity low to the ground. Once he reached the summit it was all downhill. He concentrated his strength into his hand, which gripped the strand. The feeling in his palms and fingertips was returning. Perhaps it was because of the change in terrain, but the wind seemed to be losing strength. The snow continued to come down in droves and Sam still couldn't see anything, but he was sure that even at this pace, he was slowly making his way down the mountain.

He kept telling himself that it was just a little farther. He didn't think about anything else, he just put one knee in front of the other like a machine. If he could just keep doing that then he would escape this blizzard and make it back to the real world.

Something suddenly made Sam nervous. He could hear

a sound. It was like the groan of a BT. It was getting closer and louder. He could hear it from overhead, from the peak of the mountain he had just ascended.

But it was no BT. It was only after something hit Sam hard, flinging him down the mountain like a rag doll, that he realized what it really was. It was a rockfall. He had barely avoided being hit head-on, but had still been grazed by the falling rocks. The earth and sky switched places over and over and Sam was plunging through the black clouds. One of his backpack straps snapped and cargo was sucked into the sky.

He was completely disorientated. All because of some stupid rockfall, Sam was tumbling all the way down the snow-covered slope. He was groping for something, anything, to grab onto to stop his fall, but there was nothing.

It felt like his *ka* had disappeared from his *ha*. Just like it did at the Seam. Even though he felt like he was falling through the sky, he could hear the sound of waves. A baby was crying.

It was calling out for Sam. A wave had rolled onto the shore and was trying to drag the naked baby into the sea. Sam broke into a run and jumped into the water. Lou was still crying out for him. The waves tossed Sam around helplessly as he stretched out his right arm and barely grasped onto the BB's umbilical cord. He used it to reel the BB in and take it safely into his arms. As he cradled it to his chest, he realized that the baby was Målingen and Lockne's daughter. But Sam didn't question it. A BB was a bond, both shackle and anchor. The BB gave meaning and direction to Sam's life, a bridge from a fixed start to its end, whenever that may be.

Once he realized that, he broke down and wept. He couldn't see anything through the never-ending stream of tears. That's why he didn't notice the red suit approaching him in the distance. The baby cried out and tried to break free of Sam's embrace. It was a joyous cry from the heart that Sam had never heard before.

Mama!

The BB—the baby—cried.

The woman in the red suit held out her slender arms and took the baby from Sam. Or rather, the baby escaped to her arms of its own volition. It was Amelie.

Amelie's eyes were overflowing with tears, too. Tears that were black. As soon as her tears hit the baby nestled to her chest, it began to collapse in on itself, breaking down into countless minute particles. It was just like the way Sam's blood returned the BTs to the other side. Amelie's tears returned the BB back to the place where it was meant to be.

Wait! Stop! Give that kid back to me!

Sam's voice didn't reach her. (*Well, I am being held very far away in Edge Knot City, aren't I?*)

Sam kept screaming in vain until his own shrieks woke him up.

He was lying face up on the snowy slope and it took him a moment to realize that he must have been out cold and having a nightmare.

The winds had died down, the snow had stopped, and the clouds had disappeared. Sam propped himself up and wiped away his tears. But they were no longer tears of sadness. Sam's nostrils filled with a familiar odor. He was right in the middle of BT territory.

He sensed a strong BT presence. It was so strong that the tears wouldn't stop flowing. He felt his body break out into goosepimples and his muscles began to spasm and tremble. He broke into a fever. Then came the alternating chills and nausea. He felt like he could hear the breathing of the dead next to his ear, but without a BB, he shouldn't have been able to hear anything. A handprint appeared right beside him. It formed only one of a trail of black handprints across the pure white snow. The stench of the dead grew overpowering. Sam covered his mouth with his hands and curled up in an attempt to conceal his presence as much as possible, but the trembling didn't stop. Sam couldn't tell if he was trembling from the cold or the fear.

The handprints around Sam multiplied, all different sizes and all going in different directions. Multiple BTs were searching for him. He was surrounded on this snowy mountainside. He felt like an offering being made to them in atonement for some past sin. What an ego. If Sam caused a voidout here, he would be back. But the energy from that voidout would reduce Mountain Knot City to nothingness, along with Deadman and Lockne and Lou. What kind of offering brought such destruction and calamity to the world? Offerings were supposed to be given to maintain peace.

Although Sam could identify the handprints and presence of the BTs, his heart was still tormented with speculation and suspicion. He never thought being unable to see them would frighten him this much. The empty area on his chest that was usually occupied by Lou felt heavier than ever.

He grew light-headed as his body begged for oxygen. He couldn't hold his breath any longer. But the handprints were still circling. Sam used his numb hand to remove the glove on his right. The tips of his fingers had turned dark and bruise-like. It was a sign of frostbite. He sank his teeth into his wrist, felt the warmth of his own blood spurt forth, and spread it thickly over his face. Even though it had been coursing through his own veins, it still smelled foul and only made him feel even more wretched. Still, he sensed the BTs flinch.

The handprints stopped moving.

Sam removed one side of the cuff link, exposing the cutter. It was the same cutter that had sliced through Mama's umbilical cord. Normally, a unit attached to a blood bag would be inserted into a broken blood vessel to maximize the amount of blood drawn. Sam felt a pain like his heart was exploding. Steam rose from the cutter as blood trickled out. Sam groped around for his backpack with his left hand and removed a hematic grenade. It was connected to a full blood pack. Sam had no idea how many BTs there were, or where they were prowling.

He closed his eyes. If he couldn't see them in the first place then there was no point in looking. He prayed to his absent BB.

Protect me, Lou.

He thought that he heard Lou's voice in response. Even if he was just hearing things, all he could do was believe in it. Sam threw the grenade, like a separate heart filled with his own blood, overhead toward the voice.

There was a small explosion and blood rained back down on Sam. The blood hit the BTs, revealing the outlines of their bodies and where they were. They soon broke down into particles, but Sam knew that he would have to do more to get rid of them all.

Sam stood and advanced forward, brandishing his blood-covered cuff links like a whip. The BTs shrunk back. Sam's vision began to spin until he could no longer tell what was up and what was down.

Maybe it was because of all the blood he had lost that all the color began to drain out of Sam's world, turning it monochromatic. He kept moving forward as black blood scattered across the white snow. He was like a saint, parting tempestuous seas and walking between them toward the promised land. But there were no living people following in his footsteps behind him.

By the time Sam was sure that he was out of BT territory, he no longer had the strength to stand. He barely had any energy left at all. He used the last of his strength to stem the bleeding from his wrists and stitch himself up with a medical stapler. He followed up by throwing some blood replacement supplements and smart drugs into his mouth, and chewed. He even appreciated the cryptobiote that he found in the bottom of his backpack.

The cuff links picked up a weak radio signal, telling him he was close to the Geologist's shelter. Once he had descended the slope, it would be around three kilometers away, but at that very moment that distance felt almost impossible. Sam found himself some exposed bedrock, thrust in a pile, and tied his strand around his waist. He descended the rest of the slope depending on a literal lifeline.

The Geologist's shelter lay a distance away that Sam would normally have been able to cover on foot within thirty minutes, but he needed much more time than that now. Thankfully, oxygen levels had increased and the snow had stopped falling once he had descended down the mountainside. Since he took a break partway down, he found some of his strength had returned as well.

The Geologist was a Bridges scientist, and even on the hologram you could see how emaciated he had become. When Sam finally handed over the medicine he had brought, the Geologist was overcome with joy and tears, and could only thank Sam over and over again.

"Thank you, Sam Bridges. I can't tell you how grateful I am. I was feeling giddy or getting majorly depressed over the smallest of things. I've never experienced anything like it. I thought that all these haywire emotions were because I was out here all alone at first, but it turned out that wasn't the case. It was because of chiral contamination. I always knew that it was a possibility, but I never thought it would actually happen to me. It was a sign that the chiral rays the chiralium was giving off were having an effect on both my body and mental state. It presents very similarly to stress, so that's what I thought it was at first. At this rate, I probably would have started contemplating suicide, but thanks to you I'm going to get better."

Sam could see some slight effects of the chiral contamination in the speed and breathlessness in the Geologist's speech. Sam wanted to tell the Geologist to just hurry up and take the medicine, but he couldn't get a word in edgeways.

"It was approximately 3.8 billion years ago when life first emerged on this planet, and ever since then we have seen repeated mass extinction events of varying scales. Out of all these events, the largest ones are known as the Big Five. They each occurred at the ends of the Ordovician Period, the Devonian Period, the Permian Period, the Triassic Period and the Cretaceous Period respectively, wiping out most of the life on the Earth's surface.

"But why does a phenomenon that eradicates all life on this planet occur in the first place? By what mechanism does it take place? And was the Death Stranding the sixth mass extinction event? I've been trying to get to the bottom of all these questions together with Heartman and my colleagues, but the only result that we've turned up so far is the discovery of a fossil Beach. Do you understand what that means? When an earthquake occurs, frictional heat at the fault line forms a stratum called pseudotachylyte. They're known as fossilized earthquakes, therefore making this a fossilized Beach. We were looking at strata from the end of the Cretaceous Period, when we found this strange thing mixed in with dinosaur and ammonite fossils. But it's not something that can be seen with the naked eye. The term 'fossil' is more of a metaphor here. We detected the chiralium and that chiralium is what first caused these symptoms.

"Speaking of chiralium, chiralium was only found after the Death Stranding occurred. It was brought here via the special dimension that we call the Beach. Some of us think that it always existed somewhere, just like the Higgs Particle and dark matter, and we just hadn't found it yet. This fossilized Beach proves that. It also proves that this isn't the first time the Beach has appeared on this planet. At the very least, there's a chance that it also appeared during the extinction event that took place at the end of the Cretaceous Period. We haven't been able to accurately verify this yet, but we can assume that there is at least some kind of relationship between the occurrence of the Beach and extinction events. By investigating the strata formed during other periods of extinction, we might find other fossilized Beaches, meaning that the Beach is involved in mass extinction events. Are you following me?

"Look, I don't really understand the Beach. I know that it is linked to the spirit of each person and that it can be used as paths on the Chiral Network, and I kind of get that it is something that can't be physically touched, but whenever I listen to the stories of people like you with DOOMS, it almost feels as if the place actually exists."

That impression was correct. Sam knew that even he couldn't explain his experiences on the Beach to other people. The words that people with DOOMS and people without DOOMS used to describe death were different. The way they imagined death was different.

The syntax they used to describe the Beach itself was different. A gap in perspective that Sam knew couldn't be bridged.

The one thing that Sam had followed in the Geologist's ramblings was that the likelihood that the Death Stranding was the sixth mass extinction event had increased dramatically. If the reward for finally solving the eternal mystery known as death was extinction, would everyone just roll over and accept that? Did death use the fate of extinction as a gag for those who found out its truth?

"Hopefully, we'll be able to further clarify the relationship between the Beach and extinction, but that all hinges on you activating the Chiral Network for this area."

Sam took out the Q-pid in response to the Geologist's remarks. He pressed it to the receptor fitted onto the delivery terminal and activated the network. *If the Beach had been connected to all those past extinction events too, then didn't that mean that the Chiral Network, which used it as an intermediary, could have yet another use?* Sam questioned as he replaced the Q-pid inside the breast pocket of his suit.

Immediately after Sam left the shelter, a call registered on Sam's cuff links. It was Deadman.

<Thank you for waiting, Sam.>

There was no way that Deadman could have known about all the crap that happened within the BT territory back there, but his cheery tone still annoyed Sam.

<I'm all done. I managed to reset the BB without any problems at all. Now all I have to do is test whether it still functions properly, whether the

amount of stressors it can withstand is up to
spec, etcetera, etcetera.>

So, the new BB was complete. And Lou was gone. Maybe
he should treat it as the new Lou. But just as parents could
not replace their children, or other people could not replace
lovers or friends, there was no replacement Lou. (*Hey, Sam,
is that true?*)

<I'm going to take it out and test it. The
Mountain Knot City staff are going to be helping,
so there's no need to worry about me. This whole
area is covered by the Chiral Network now, thanks
to you, so we'll know where the BT territory is and
we'll be able to predict the weather. We should
even be able to detect the movements of those
beasts to some extent. So, once you're finished with
your job, all you need to do is come and pick the
BB back up.>

Sam wanted nothing more than to punch the cuff link,
but he couldn't cancel the call from his end. That made him
even more annoyed.

<We're going to be testing out the BB in an area
southeast of the Geologist's shelter. It's right
next to the distribution center near Mountain Knot
City. I know that you already went out west, and
I'm sorry that I have to call you back this way,
but at least you won't have to climb over the big

mountain this time. With your legs you should be
able to make it in a day. Plus, once you've taken
back the BB, you'll be able to rest up in a private
room at the distro center.>

Sam even felt annoyed at how Deadman was trying to
make it sound like it was the most thoughtful suggestion
ever. Sam was the one out here busting his ass, delivering
the cargo and rebuilding America. What was he doing?
Sam held back his tirade and simply switched the codec
itself off. Then he proceeded down the gentle slope alone.

It was getting colder now that Sam had entered the long
shadow cast by the high peak, but after the extreme cold of
the blizzard that he encountered before, this was nothing.

Once he had climbed this slope he would be able to see
Lou again. Or rather, the BB previously known as Lou.

Complicated feelings welled up inside him as he looked
up at the ridge of the mountain. To put it bluntly, it hurt to
think that even though he would be creating new memories
with the BB, he would have to let go of the old ones.

Once he had climbed the slope, he could see the
distribution center in the distance. He was almost there.

<Sam, can you hear me? Watch out!>

Lockne's voice suddenly cried out from the codec
transceiver on his cuff link.

<It's happening again. The chiral density is
rising.>

Sam scanned his surroundings to try and figure out what she was talking about, but there was nothing unusual to be seen.

The Q-pid that Sam was using was the one that Lockne fixed. Had there been some kind of mistake? As Sam questioned himself, a vivid upside-down rainbow appeared in the southern sky. Even though it was an evil omen that signified a bridge between the world of the living and the world of the dead, it was undeniably beautiful. Sam must have seen it a hundred times, so he was surprised by this feeling he was having. In reality, it was a terrible thing, but he was so captivated by it. He was feeling something that he couldn't put into words. He wasn't quite in awe of its beauty, nor was he fearful; it was something else entirely. Just as he found it impossible to describe his feelings, he couldn't stop his tears either. This wasn't his usual allergic reaction. For some reason he was really moved.

The transmission from Lockne cut out. Sam tried reaching her again, but no matter how many times he tried, no sound came from the transceiver. Even though he was in an area covered by the Chiral Network, he couldn't connect. All of this seemed to back up what Lockne had said about the sudden rise in chiral density. Or maybe something had happened back at Mountain Knot City.

He felt a sudden warmth on his chest, and when he pulled out the Q-pid, its six shards were emitting so much heat it felt like they might burst into flames. What was happening? Sam tried to rip the Q-pid away from his neck, but the Q-pid began to float away as if it was a creature with a mind of its own. It floated off into the air as if it was taunting him.

The second that Sam stepped forward, led on by the Q-pid, the scenery around him transformed in an instant.

An unbelievable gale was blowing at Sam from behind. He lost his balance and almost fell forward. He tried to cover his head with both arms to brace for the impact, but it was useless. His body floated. Gravity was gone and Sam was flailing through the air. Next to him, a huge whale was flying as its body rotated around like a drill. The debris of buildings, ships, and cars of varying sizes that Sam had only even seen in picture form, and faceless people that had appeared out of nowhere, were swallowed up in a giant whirlwind and sucked into the sky.

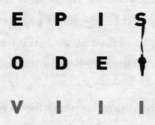

EPISODE VIII

CLIFFORD

When Sam woke up, he found himself in a dilapidated town that he didn't recognize. It was the kind of town that was built from stone and brick, not the kind of town you would find in America. The area was inundated with the sounds of shells and gunfire, together with the hum of heavy machinery that sounded like some kind of growling beast. The enormous bird that was tearing through the sky and causing the deafening roar above was an airplane. It was defying gravity. It was flying. Sam knew of planes that flew through the sky, but this was the first time he had seen one with his own eyes.

Sam fled to the nearest ruins to avoid the crossfire. The transceiver switched on and communication was established. It was Deadman.

\<Is that you, Sam?\>

Sam heard the worry in Deadman's tone before he had even finished addressing him.

"What's the matter? Where are you?" Sam asked.

\<I don't know. It seems like we were sucked up into that storm as well. Since we can contact each other wirelessly, that hopefully means that you're close by. Me and the BB are fine. We're in some kind of sewer system. I don't think anyone has spotted us yet.\>

An explosion went off somewhere in the distance, shaking the ruins. Debris began to fall from the ceiling.

\<When I came to my senses we were by the entrance to a sewer, so I ran in there and now we've been lost for a while. I saw a guy who looked like the one you described last time. He was with the skeleton soldiers, so I'm sure he was the same one. He had a doll of a baby with him.\>

Deadman seemed to be more talkative than usual. Maybe it was to distract himself from his own feelings of anxiety.

\<This is probably a battlefield from World War Two. It'll be somewhere in Europe. When I was running away I caught a glimpse of some tanks and fighter craft.\>

"How do you know?"

<Did I never tell you how much of a World War
Two nerd I am?>

Without even commenting, Sam launched into a new
line of questioning.

"Are there any landmarks nearby? I'm coming to get you
and Lou. And then I'm going to kick that guy's ass. Then we
should be able to go home."

But Sam wasn't certain of that. That just happened to be
how events transpired last time, but he had to do something
or they would never get out of here.

<There's a Gothic-style building. It's half
rubble, so I can't be sure, but it doesn't look so
old. It looks like it might be from the Gothic
Revival period. It has a forest-like silhouette.
There are a couple of pointed turrets coming out
from the roof that look like trees. It's a tall,
huge building.>

Sam only understood about half of what Deadman said.
"Is he some kind of architecture nerd now, too?" Sam
muttered, heading outside.

Sam picked up an abandoned rifle that lay in the ruins
of the building. It was lighter than the one he had picked up
in the last battle and looked easier to use. It had been over a
hundred years since World War Two, but Sam couldn't
believe how refined guns had already become. Come to
think of it, it was around this time when nuclear weapons

had first been developed as well. Humans had been creating tools to destroy each other for a long time, it seemed.

Sam soon found the building that Deadman had described. The one that had the silhouette of a forest. If Sam had understood correctly, then this was it.

It was indeed half rubble, just as Deadman had said, but the entrance wasn't blocked.

Sam passed through the hallway and headed down the stairs into the basement. As Sam looked at the bulletins posted along the wall, he realized this must have been some kind of public building, but none of the postings were in English, they were all in German, so he couldn't be sure.

All of a sudden, Sam was almost knocked to his feet by a powerful crash and violent tremors. He was left barely standing with a hand on the wall for support. Just as he thought it had calmed back down, he began to hear the intermittent explosions of shells followed by screams. It seemed like the location of the battleground had shifted.

He pushed on an iron door in the corner of the basement that was partially covered in green rust, and entered a tunnel. The space was filled with the stench of stagnant water and the tepid air seemed to coil around his body. In the background he could also faintly smell the scent of blood and gunfire. Sam heard another explosion and the tunnel shook once more.

"Deadman! Where are you?!" Sam's voice echoed loudly.

It was like he was surrounded by a thousand invisible Sams, shouting in unison.

"Sam! Over here!" Deadman shouted.

Sam continued down the tunnels, following the sound of Deadman's voice, and eventually found him clinging tightly to an iron grille, calling out Sam's name. Under one of his arms was the pod.

"Sam! Over here! Quick!" Deadman urgently beckoned.

Sam calmed the agitated Deadman and shifted his gaze to the pod. Regaining some composure, Deadman held the pod out to him through the iron bars.

Sam couldn't help but murmur Lou's name as he took the pod back, but there was no response from Lou, who seemed to be asleep. Sam said Lou's name once again, but the BB only cried out in displeasure after having its sleep interrupted.

"The little one should be working again. Let me see." Deadman grabbed the pod back. Sam thought he was going to make some adjustments to the pod or something, but Deadman simply cradled it in his arms and gently swayed. He was rocking the BB. The BB stopped crying and Deadman looked at Sam triumphantly, but Sam didn't say anything. Luckily, the awkwardness of Sam's displeasure at how Lou had forgotten him and become attached to Deadman was dispelled by the sound of an explosion. It sounded like a bomb had been dropped. The whole tunnel shook, and fragments of brick fell from the ceiling. Nearby,

Sam heard soldiers asking someone to identify themself.
Deadman held the pod close as if to protect it.

"Maybe this is a special Beach for soldiers who died in
battle. A maelstrom of their bitterness and regret," Deadman
muttered, handing the pod to Sam. "If this is the same place
as last time, then maybe the key to getting home lies with
the same man you met last time."

Sam mounted the pod on his chest. A nostalgic weight
returned.

"You should wait here," he told Deadman.

Sam connected the cord to the pod.

"So? Do you still share memories?" Deadman inquired.

Sam silently shook his head at Deadman's question. The
BB inside the pod had an innocent expression on its face,
like it had just been born. It seemed this kid had forgotten
everything after all.

The Odradek booted into life with a groan. The sensor
was spinning rapidly and soon formed into a cross shape.

That man's face flashed across Sam's mind.

The kid may have forgotten Sam, but it still reacted to
the man. The Odradek was pointing in his direction.

"You know, Sam, I'm starting to understand why BB is so
important to you," Deadman said, looking at the pod. "It's
just a tool. Life and death are supposed to be irrelevant. But
we've got attached to each other all the same… Haven't we?"

"Kid's not just a tool. Name's Lou," Sam replied curtly.

Even if the BB had forgotten all about Sam, its name was still Lou. Sam stroked the pod and began to walk in the direction of the sewer exit.

Bells were ringing. They sounded like church bells.

But as they rang out across the battlefield, their purpose wasn't to return the souls of the dead back to heaven, but to inspire them to fight and bring them back to life.

The bombers that controlled the skies dropped bomb after bomb after bomb, but the church spire remained unscathed. Like devoted followers fearing the wrath of God, each time the bombs fell anywhere near the spire, the bombers changed course. All the missiles and shells being thrown through the skies completely missed it. It was like someone had commanded that the bells weren't to be silenced until all the dead, with their lingering attachment to this world, had been resurrected.

All those people had died before they even had a chance to realize it, at the hands of weapons designed to kill en masse. If life was a sentence, theirs had been interrupted partway through and left without a period to wrap everything up neatly at the end. And they were coming back to look for it.

Numerous filthy dolls in the shape of babies hung from a giant spider's web that spanned the spire below the swaying bells. Some had their heads caved in, others were missing limbs, and some had bellies that had burst open. One of the dolls began to shake as if it was having a fit. With each spasm, a single eyelid jerked open and closed. It was like the doll was frantically pleading for something but unable to cry.

In response to its silent wailing, the man who lay across the center of the web awakened.

He had found the period at the end of his sentence.

The thread coiled around him unraveled, and the man gracefully descended out of the web.

And now it begins again. Someone was speaking. *It's finally time to put an end to this story of yours that was so cruelly interrupted.* Flames erupted overhead as if to celebrate the man's awakening, and the spider's web began to go up in an inferno. Embers poured down like rain. The man placed a cigarette between his lips and let the rain light it. He breathed the smoke in deeply before letting it all back out and smirking.

Cliff had found him.

As the tobacco smoke diffused and disappeared, four soldiers took their place around the man. All were fleshless. Only bone. The man flicked the cigarette away and raised his arm up high.

Then he brought it back down, silently commanding his soldiers. *Go forth. Take back the period that was snatched away from you.* The man watched the soldiers move out. *Capture the child and bring the man who won't let go of it back here.*

Once Sam had escaped the sewer, he was immediately greeted by bombs. They were showering down from the bombers above. They were still a distance away from the spot were Sam was standing, but the thundering sound of explosions still pierced his eardrums and the tremors shook his insides. He had to find that man. When he checked the direction that the Odradek was pointing in, he could see a church-like structure.

It had a strange appearance. Despite the fact that its foundations had been mercilessly decimated, the spire thrusting up into the sky wasn't damaged in the slightest and stood firm. Sam didn't know a lot about the structure of buildings, but even he knew that was unusual. The foundations were dust, yet the spire alone was still standing there. He wasn't close enough to get a good look, but he couldn't make out a single chip or crack. There wasn't even any soot from the flames all around. In this place where anything and everything was an offensive target, destroyed and defiled, this tower alone was sanctified and protected.

And the Odradek was pointing right at it. That was where the man was.

But Sam had no idea how to get there. Bullets were flying all around him and there was no end to the bombing in sight. Flames scorched the sky and the shrieks of soldiers were constant. This was just like the time before. Sam was on a battlefield where the dead killed their fellow dead. Where the means of the massacre was on an even grander scale than the original battleground.

When Sam gazed up at the silhouettes of the bombers and checked the weight of his rifle, reality hit him.

Sam flitted from shadow to shadow, between broken barricades, disorganized sandbags, toppled-over tanks, and ruined buildings that dotted the cobbled streets, paying careful attention so as not to get caught up in the battle. Even though he could hear the final wails of agony from soldiers on all sides, he hardly actually saw any of them.

The thought of nuclear weapons suddenly crossed his mind. How just one bomb could kill countless people en masse and wreak destruction over an absurdly large area. Maybe this battlefield was far away from other people. Maybe it was a battlefield that didn't involve humans, it was just one they died on. Where people killed one another at a distance, rather than staring their opponents in the face as they fought toe-to-toe with fist or gun. Where they died without the opportunity to understand their own deaths. It was a battlefield where all that remained was the never-ending absurdity of it all, stagnating like sediment.

The battlefield was an endless, absurd cycle.

The only way to put a stop to that cycle would be to make the dead aware of the fact that they were dead. Just as people in the world of the living incinerated the bodies of the recently departed, to deprive their soul of a place to wander back to and give them their period at the end of their sentence.

If this war and this battlefield really had existed in the past, then humans had been mass-producing BTs for a long time. Maybe voidouts and the Death Stranding were disasters of mankind's own making.

Sam's footing slipped as the thought distracted him. He placed a hand on the wall of the building and steadied himself. When he looked down at his feet, he found that puddles had formed in the empty spaces left by missing cobbles. Sam tutted at his own clumsiness and carried on forward. That's when he realized that what had pooled at his feet wasn't water, but blood. Sam wondered how many people's blood it took to form a puddle this deep. He was submerged up to his ankles.

Sam tried to pull his foot back out, but someone's hand was clamped around his ankle. It was trying to drag him back into the puddle.

Sam slapped at the hand that was now pawing at the barrel of his rifle, and used all of his might to yank his foot free.

—*BB*.

A voice calling out for the BB resounded within his head. The puddle of blood began to swell and something appeared. Its helmet was slick with blood, its hands stained red, and blood was gushing from the end of its rifle. A skeletal soldier had shown itself. Without a moment's hesitation, Sam sprayed bullets at it with his rifle. As it shattered to dust it was engulfed in flames and disappeared.

—*BB*.

Instead of wails of agony, Sam heard the voice of the man.

Then he felt a sharp pain shoot through his right leg. He had been shot. When he turned around, three skeletal soldiers were lying in wait. All three of them were pointing their rifles at him. The next one to fire was Sam. He may not have hit any of them, but at least they flinched, and while they did, he was able to make his escape into the shadow of a truck. There was a burning pain in Sam's leg where he had been shot, and it felt like it had swelled to several times its normal size.

The moment that Sam peeked out to see if the coast was clear, he was met with gunfire. It was the same soldiers as the time before. The Odradek's sensor backed up his theory as it flashed from white to orange. He could tell from Lou's uneasy jerks, as well. It might not have been the time or place, but Sam felt relieved. This kid might not remember him anymore, but they were still able to connect like always.

—*BB*.

The top of the truck began to burn alongside the sound of the explosions. Hand grenades were being thrown inside.

Dragging his wounded leg behind him, Sam mustered all his strength to escape. Trucks exploded one after another. He could feel hot winds and impact tremors on his tail. Lou was terrified and crying out. Choked by the black smoke, Sam searched for a place they could hide. The buildings lining the road were all piles of rubble, and didn't look like they would be able to conceal them at all.

Driven forward by the bullets, Sam finally found a building with a red-brick facade. The glass was shattered and only the frame remained, but the original entrance still stood. Sam entered its dim interior. Part of the wall had collapsed, shelves had fallen down and several pieces of furniture were toppled over. There was no sign of anybody. A coffee cup and a cracked plate sat on the table. The open newspaper featured a black-and-white picture of a town ablaze and a headline in large German letters.

Sam sensed a presence outside the window and hid in the shadow of the table. It was one of the skeletal soldiers. Luckily, the soldier didn't seem to have realized that Sam was in there. As Sam decided to just let the soldier pass, an explosion shook the building.

Fine rubble fell from the ceiling, making a clattering sound as it collided with the cup on the table below.

The radio in the bay window suddenly switched on.

Somewhere over the rainbow, way up high—

It was an English song. An old song that Sam had a

feeling he had heard somewhere before.

There's a land that I heard of once in a lullaby. Oh, somewhere over the rainbow—

As if it heard the song, the skeletal soldier turned back and looked in Sam's direction. It didn't have any eyeballs, but those empty sockets saw Sam. From where Sam was hidden under the table it should have been impossible for their eyes to meet, but still, they saw each other. Sam immediately shot at it.

Then he turned on his heel and ran out of the exit at the back, finding himself in a narrow alleyway just wide enough for one person.

He could see the church spire in the sky, which was punctuated by tall buildings on both sides of him. The Odradek was still pointing in that direction. There was no way Sam could get lost now, so he began to run. It sounded like the aerial bombing campaign was still in full swing as several bombers darted by, streaming bombs out of their bellies, and vanished. Explosions sounded all across the town as it crumbled into rubble and went up in flames. This confusion was a good opportunity for Sam. It could have hindered the movements of the skeletal soldiers somewhat. The church spire was almost upon him. It was just a little farther until a gap in the path. A soldier flew out from the buildings, and when Sam turned around he could see one standing behind him, too.

He was cornered. He dropped low and tackled their legs as he dodged their fire. Even though they were only made of bones, each one of them felt like they weighed just as much as an adult human. Sam snatched up a handgun from one of the fallen soldiers and shot it in the chest. Several ribs shattered into dust and a small flame blew out from where the heart should have been. As Sam looked on, the flames spread, engulfing the rest of the skeleton.

Next, he shot at the soldier approaching from the rear as it charged forward, firing without pause. Every bullet went wide as the gap between them shrank. Sam's opponent seemed to have run out of ammunition as he tossed away his rifle and brandished an army knife. Sam aimed at his undefended chest but missed. That was his last bullet. All he could do was dodge the flailing knife and lunge at the soldier's chest. Their bodies entangled, but the moment they hit the floor, the soldier's helmet slipped off with a clunk onto the cobbles below. More than half the soldier's skull had been blown off. It was strange enough that these skeletal soldiers were able to move in the first place, but for them to be so animated in such a broken state felt even more ominous to Sam. The very bone that should have held their brain in place was missing, yet they fought as if still alive. As he held the soldier down, Sam saw his chance.

Skeletal arms pounded Sam's back. It felt like he was being hit with steel. In fact, the pain was so bad that it knocked the wind out of him. His grip slackened for a moment, and before he knew it, their positions were reversed. The soldier was straddling Sam with one hand around his neck and the other balled into a fist, attempting to rain punches down on him. Sam dodged the fist as he rammed the ammunition clip clutched tightly in his hand into the soldier's chest. Another rib broke.

The soldier stopped moving. Sam thrust the clip at it once more with all the strength he could muster. The bones crumbled and disintegrated into fine particles. The particles gave off the red light like embers, eventually setting fire to the soldier's chest.

It let out an inhuman scream of agony as the flames engulfed it and it disappeared.

Sam brushed away the fallen sparks and stood back up, before leaving the alleyway and continuing toward the church.

The church bells were ringing to an insane rhythm.

Unlike the exterior of the church, its interior was in a sorry state. The arched roof was riddled with holes and the heaven depicted there broken. The stained glass had melted muddily and the pews that had once seated the churchgoers were charred black from all the fires. The air was filled with the stench of decay, which quickly enveloped Sam. On the altar right in front of him lay an offering of a small whale on its back. That was where the smell was coming from.

The Odradek showed that the man was here. It had

formed into a stiff cross shape and stood unmoving. Lou wasn't crying, but still seemed to be trembling with fear.

Something fell on the altar. It bounced off the whale's exposed belly and rolled to Sam's feet.

It was a doll. But its eyelids were opening and closing furiously as if it was having a fit.

—BB.

Sam turned in the direction of the voice to find the man standing there.

"Give me back my BB," he said.

As soon as the man opened his mouth, the sound of a gunshot rang out. The bullet grazed Sam's shoulder before lodging itself in the altar directly behind him. The bullet had still caught him with enough force to throw his balance, and he crashed backward with it. Blood trickled out from the tears in his uniform.

Sam clutched the pod containing Lou with both arms, as if to hide it. The blood from his shoulder wound trickled down his arm, dirtying its exterior. The man looked down at the unsightly form of Sam, clumsily sat on his ass against the altar. The man's expression seemed to flicker for a moment. Sam thought he could see a flash of sadness, but it soon disappeared.

"Give me back my BB," repeated the man, almost as if muttering deliriously. He slowly lifted his arm and pointed the gun toward Sam. But for some reason, Sam didn't feel the same bloodlust that he had felt right after the man first appeared.

"Let it go…"

The man's tone was vague. It was like he was remembering something. Sam glared at the barrel of the gun and shook his head. He couldn't leave the BB. He had no reason to hand it over. Lou didn't belong to this man.

The man was slowly tightening his finger's grip on the trigger. Sam thrust out a single hand and tried to cover the barrel. Even if he had to lose this hand, he would never leave Lou behind.

The man's face once again contorted into a sad expression. His focus was no longer on the pod, but on Sam's hand. The man was trying to remember something. That much Sam was sure of.

Who the hell was this man? He didn't belong to *this* battlefield. He wasn't like the other soldiers, who simply continued to slaughter one another as apparitions of this warzone.

The man had something in his head, but it seemed like he couldn't express it.

There was a crash of thunder, and the stately wooden doors to the chapel blew open before shattering into pieces and bursting into flames. When he saw it, the man screamed something. It was an animalistic roar full of anger and fear. He was howling at the entrance.

Perhaps he was enraged that the pristine spire had been broken, or scared this holy ground was about to be defiled. The only thing Sam could be sure of was that the man was confused. Sam mustered the last of his strength, got back up, and sprang forward. But the man was quicker as he turned and blocked him.

Arm crashed into arm and shoulder rubbed against shoulder. At that moment, a shard of metal jutted out from near the man's collarbone.

It resembled Sam's Q-pid and was attached to a chain around the man's neck. The force of the collision toppled the man over backward.

The shard around the man's neck burned red. Sam's own Q-pid emanated heat, almost like it was responding.

Somehow, the fallen man seemed to have lost the will to fight, but as Sam looked into his eyes, they weren't those of a man who had given up completely and was ready to surrender. If Sam finished him off now, then he would be able to return to his own world. But his confidence was shaken. This man wasn't dead like a BT.

Defeating him wouldn't send him back anywhere. This man was after a different kind of funeral.

"BB…"

He wanted Lou. But there was no way Sam would hand Lou over. If this child was neither born nor dead, then there was no reason to hand Lou over. Sam only wished he could have done something so that Lou could have been properly born into the world of the living.

The man reached out. He was riddled with injuries, yet still staggered to his feet and began to step toward Sam. Sam readied his gun with his left hand and defended the pod with his right. But that was all he could do. He couldn't move forward, nor could he move back.

The man frowned and squinted at Sam as if blinded by light.

"BB. BB… This is all my fault." The man tried to touch the pod. "I should… I should never have put you in that prison, BB…"

The man was crying. Black tears rolled down his face. The man mustered strength into his arms and pulled the pod toward him. He was so surprisingly strong that Sam toppled forward. The two became entangled and writhed on the church floor. Sam grabbed the man's neck as he tried to tear himself away, but something coiled around his hand.

Time seemed to flow extremely slowly. The man's bangs swayed and Sam could see everything in minute detail, from his fine movements and ensuing flying specks of mud to the chain from which the metal shard hung as it broke and flew away from the man's neck. Sam pushed the man away and attempted to stand. The man was face up and made another grab for the BB.

Sam's eyes met those of the man. It was like he was being

sucked into them. He felt that he would drown in those eyes, which were deeper than any sea. He felt like he was being dragged down eternally, slowly crushed to death by the water pressure of this ocean, never to return to the surface again. Sam closed his eyes as fear took hold.

MOUNTAIN KNOT CITY

He was drowning.

He had been swallowed up by the sea, the source of all life, and now Sam was drowning.

This universe came from a bang. This planet from another bang. When life eventually emerged, what nurtured it was the sea that had cooled down this molten rock. Eventually, life crawled out of the sea and onto the land, where it became a slave to gravity on the frontier known as the earth's surface and formed new chains of existence.

Then the scorned mother ocean became a vengeful goddess and drowned all the life on that earth. The Beach was her pathway to exact her revenge.

Sam saw a faint light in the distance above. But even as he made frantic attempts to reach it, he couldn't escape the ocean. No matter how much he struggled, he didn't get an inch closer to the surface. It was getting harder and harder to breathe. Sam could feel himself becoming light-headed.

When at last he knew that the ocean was about to kill him, he realized he was inside a nightmare.

When Sam woke up, he was in a subterranean private room.

It was an artificial room built to protect and conceal a human race who had been betrayed by the sea and rejected by the earth's surface.

The cuff link that was linking him to the bedframe automatically released, and Sam sat up. He wiped away his tears and checked on the BB pod that was set inside the incubator. The display on the monitor told him the BB was once again functional.

"Lou," Sam called, disconnecting the pod's connection to the incubator. He cradled the lukewarm pod and called out Lou's name again. Lou was curled up, eyes closed and mouth tightly shut.

There was no reaction to Sam's voice. It was like the little one couldn't even hear him.

"Lou," Sam repeated.

Lou's eyes eventually opened at the sound of Sam's voice. Lou, or rather the Bridge Baby now, looked up at Sam blankly with eyes that still couldn't quite see yet. *Maybe it's not fully awake from its long sleep yet?* Then Sam remembered. No, that wasn't it. Sam had prepared himself for this. He knew he had to face the facts. At the very least, he had been able to prolong this little one's life. That was one of the reasons he had taken this mission in the first place. To stop this child dying in vain. And that he had accomplished.

"How's little Lou doing?" Deadman's voice came from behind Sam. It seemed they had both returned unscathed from the battlefield. Sam knew he should be happy about that, but he wasn't quite feeling it right now.

"No response." Sam knew he was clinging on to lost hope, but he still passed the pod to Deadman to have it examined.

But the pod slipped right through him. The BB seemed to react to that. It looked at Deadman's hologram and laughed. Or maybe that too was all in Sam's head, because by the time Sam had glanced at the pod, the BB's eyes were already closed.

"You saved us. Whatever you did back there returned us to our own world. Lockne and the others found us out cold near Mountain Knot City. It seems like only a minute had passed in this world. You and the BB were brought back here. You've been dead to the world for near enough twenty-four hours. You slept for a whole day, you know. Slept like the dead. I'm already back in Capital Knot. Fragile's Beach has been coming in handy, although I have to say that I don't like using it anymore. I keep worrying that I'm going to end up back there."

A small metal plate set on the table caught Sam's eye. Deadman noticed and changed the subject.

"Oh, that. You were holding it. It's an old dog tag. US issue. Wasn't easy prying it out of your hand."

That was the metal Sam had spotted around that man's neck. He couldn't be sure, but he must have brought it back from the battlefield. He picked it up and turned it over. A name was engraved on it, along with a few letters and symbols.

"Clifford Unger, as you can see. I looked him up in our database. Found a match," Deadman stated. He fiddled with his cuff link and projected the 3D image of a man dressed in a combat uniform.

There was no mistaking it. It was him.

"He was US Army Special Forces. Fought in Kosovo, Iraq, Afghanistan."

Sam hadn't heard of any of those places, but he assumed they had all once been battlefields, too.

The hologram of the man looked tougher than the one Sam had met on the battlefield, and whose head contained only the most basic of thoughts. He was brimming with youthful brute strength. He seemed sure of himself. There was no sign of the sad expression he had shown on the battlefield.

But what did Lou have to do with any of this?

"Well, that's all I've managed to dig up so far," Deadman conceded.

Sam nodded back at Deadman and placed the dog tag in his pocket. It was an important clue linked to Clifford Unger, and the key to unraveling his connection with the BB.

Clifford's hologram disappeared and silence descended

upon the room. In the middle of it was the BB. Both Sam and Deadman stared at the pod, searching for something to say.

"Sam, I owe you an apology." The first to speak was Deadman. "Lou was the name you were going to give your own baby. If he'd have made it. I should have pieced it together sooner."

Sam sighed. It wasn't like it was a big secret or anything, but Sam never made a point of talking about it to anyone else. It was only natural for Deadman to find out about it if he was already looking into Bridge Babies and the origins of Bridges, as well as investigating Die-Hardman.

"I found some records from ten years ago. Something about the sudden death of a young woman in a small town on the outskirts of Central Knot. An ex-therapist by the name of Lucy. Nobody knew until it was too late. It caused a voidout. Her husband was a member of Bridges. He even had DOOMS. He tried, but he couldn't get to her in time. The whole town was wiped off the map… leaving nothing but a big crater. And him. Because he was a repatriate." Deadman looked at Sam as if he was gauging his reaction. "People wanted answers. Did the man hide his wife's body on purpose? The only survivor was the only suspect. He was easy to blame, and people did. And pretty soon they were blaming Bridges, too. The man felt responsible. So he left. Lucy had been pregnant, poor woman."

Sam watched Deadman take a deep breath at the end of

his sentence and responded with a sigh of his own.

"They were going to name their kid Lou," Deadman continued.

Sam bit his lip and said nothing.

"I didn't just fish that out of the database, though. Bridget told me. Once her condition deteriorated and she could sense the end was drawing near, she told me about all the things that were off the record."

In other words, stories that had been embellished based on Bridget's and Deadman's subjective whims. They weren't reality, and they weren't anything that Sam was interested in hearing.

"It wasn't you who Lucy met last before she committed suicide. It was someone else. I truly believe that. Bridget said the same thing. But on record, you're officially the last person she met. I don't know if Bridget was covering for you, or if you didn't tell her the whole truth about what happened. All I know is that she was sorry to see you go. She used to talk about how you didn't have to cut ties and walk away."

CENTRAL KNOT CITY OUTSKIRTS

Lucy had just concluded her first therapy session with Sam Strand. It was not held at the patient's request. Sam's adoptive mother, President Strand, had approached her in the hope she might help her son overcome his aphenphosmphobia.

Sam was an intriguing case. His reluctance notwith-standing, he recognized that his condition had and would continue to cause him much distress. Lucy suspected it was rooted in a childhood trauma, but unfortunately, she had only just scratched the surface, and couldn't even begin to speculate what it might be.

Like many of the Bridges core team members, Sam was a DOOMS sufferer. Unlike them, however, he was also a repatriate. Whether or not this was related to his aphenphosmphobia, Lucy couldn't say, but he would hardly be the first to manifest phobias as a result of his abilities.

As an infant, Sam lost both parents and was adopted by President Strand. Owing to her stress and time-consuming responsibilities, Lucy could only presume that she was unable to afford him sufficient attention, which is to say that a distant relationship with his adoptive mother may have been a contributing factor. Sam was still very reluctant to talk about himself, and as an intensely private person it would take time to build trust and convince him to open himself up to her.

Progress has been slow, but Sam finally started to open up about himself. However, his recollection of early childhood was confused and contradictory. He had difficulty distinguishing between genuine memories and reoccurring dreams. Sam even claimed to have met his stepsister Amelie on the Beach several times while quite young. An impossible claim, to say the least.

Lucy was only a little older than Sam, but she was born before the Death Stranding—a fact that tended to affect the way people thought about the Beach. In her professional opinion, the Beach was a figment of their collective imagination. A shared delusion. But people born later were more likely to take its existence as a given. She wondered if they found comfort in the belief because it helped to explain phenomena like BTs and repatriates like Sam?

Similarly, her theory was that Sam's manufactured childhood memories of the Beach were his way of coping with the fact that neither Amelie nor Bridget spent much time with him. She believed this to also be the reason he still clung to the dreamcatcher Amelie gave him even now, as an adult. You could call it his security blanket. It could also be the key to overcoming his aphenphosmphobia. If Sam were to emotionally distance himself from Amelie, it could reduce his resistance to physical intimacy. She decided to propose this approach to him in their next session.

It came as no surprise when Sam was unreceptive to Lucy's suggestion and rejected her assessment of his relationship with Amelie. He asserted that he was not dependent on her or Bridget, and even went so far as to question Lucy's credentials as a psychotherapist. His pronounced resistance to the idea only served as further evidence to Lucy of his dependency. Nevertheless, there was little she could do if Sam was unwilling to explore the possibility, other than continue to share her observations and hope that he eventually changed his mind. For the time being she decided to focus instead on Sam's feelings toward Bridges and his place within the organization. Given that it was founded to support and protect his adoptive mother, and that the other core members had DOOMS like he did, she thought there was something to be gained from the discussion. His growing responsibilities within Bridges due to their expanding mandate and his abilities as a repatriate surely put him under greater pressure, and she wondered if his enthusiasm for their mission was sincere.

Based on their time spent together so far, she believed he may have embraced his role because it helped him to cope with the feelings of isolation—that he pledged himself to an impossible endeavor because it was preferable to living and dying alone.

Lucy decided a different approach was required, and so she requested a meeting with the president. Discretion was vital, as any information which might suggest she was receiving mental health treatment could be exploited by her opponents. The meeting was listed as an interview in official records—though she was more than willing to offer her services, had they been requested.

She opened by asking about Sam's childhood, to which the president responded with an immediate and heartfelt apology. Her frankness shocked Lucy. Bridget expressed deep regret for her failure to engage with him, physically and emotionally, as she felt a mother should. At times it felt as though she was apologizing to her son by proxy. Her candor was as impressive to Lucy as it was appreciated.

The president told her that her daughter Amelie had mostly taken care of Sam in her absence. She glossed over the details, but she divulged that Amelie also had DOOMS, and claimed that she would often take Sam with her to play on the Beach.

President Strand loved her son. Lucy's meeting with her confirmed that beyond any doubt. The question was whether or not Sam perceived his mother's love. Both Sam and the president talked about the Beach as though it were a real, physical place, but Lucy remained convinced that it didn't exist—that it was a shared delusion, and that Sam and Amelie's so-called "visits" were mental constructs. Sam would not necessarily be convinced of this—especially if it had been "planted" in his mind… But such an explanation would fit with his claims that he had never been able to visit the Beach of his own volition.

What if, subconsciously, Sam had developed an attachment to or longing for the Beach—one that paralleled his feelings toward his sister and mother? Furthermore, what if they had all become, in essence, objects of veneration? Upon further consideration, it wasn't so hard to imagine. President Strand was an exceptional woman who exhibited panromantic qualities—as did her daughter, Amelie. This was surely one of the reasons why they had been able to commit themselves so completely to the cause of American reconstruction, their one true love. Sam, on the other hand, Lucy diagnosed as demisexual. His sexual desires were strictly limited to those with whom he had formed an emotional connection—excepting family members like Amelie, of course.

It was only natural to regard those more highly with whom he developed an intimate emotional connection. For children, this could lead to veneration. Yet there was also an inherent contradiction in this, for divinity is distant by nature, even as we yearn to grow closer to it. Lucy came to the conclusion that this contradiction was at the root of Sam's aphenphosmphobia.

"What the fuck?!" Sam exploded in rage when she told him her theory. "I'm a repatriate. A fuckup whose soul gets bounced back from the Seam every time I die in a horrible explosion!"

Lucy had decided to share with Sam her working theory

regarding his condition. She was prepared for some resistance, but the intensity of his anger was surprising. He glared at her as he reframed her assessment as wild speculation that he had been brainwashed by a cult. It was the first time Lucy had managed to coax such a powerful emotional response from him, and while she found it a little frightening, she did her best to remain professional, welcoming the breakthrough and the reduction in the distance between them. That was how she presented professionally, but a part of her was delighted by his aggressive response.

Emboldened, she pressed him further, until she finally told him to snap out of it. To renounce his fantasies about the other side.

For an instant, she thought he might explode in anger again, but instead he grew quiet, and after a long moment rose to his feet and left the room without saying another word. She feared she may have pushed him too hard...

Sam turned up for his next appointment, right on time. He looked calmer than usual, though that might have been wishful thinking on Lucy's part. He'd been thinking a lot about their last session, and how it had ended. He said he wished she was right, about the Beach, and what it meant to be a repatriate. That he appreciated the time they'd spent together—that Lucy had spent listening to his stories.

"It isn't all in my head, and I can prove it," Sam said as he pulled out a syringe. Sam was calm, but Lucy wasn't. Then he stuck the needle in his chest.

It all happened so fast. Lucy froze in her chair as Sam went into convulsions, eventually falling out of his seat. She ran to him, then, as he was laying on the floor, motionless, removed the syringe and performed chest compressions. But it was too late. Lucy sat there, next to him, for what felt like an eternity… And then he opened his eyes and sat up, still wearing that same calm expression. There was another handprint on his arm—a fresh one.

Sam was awake now and began to talk.

"I'm a repatriate," he said. "Every time I die, I get stuck in-between, and then come back." He was searching Lucy's eyes now, reaching for the words as much as they were struggling to come out. "That world won't have me, and neither will this one. I'm only free to come and go when I'm with her. With Amelie…"

There were tears in his eyes. He looked so lonely. Lucy started crying, too. She'd taken his hand in hers without realizing it, but he didn't pull away. Lucy squeezed, and he squeezed back.

He needed someone he could be close to, be intimate with. Someone outside his family. Someone who wasn't Bridget, or Amelie. Someone to whom he could reveal the whole of himself, someone who'd devote themself to him.

Her. Sam smiled and nodded and they held each other for a very long time.

A few days after the incident in her office, Lucy tendered her resignation. A classic case of countertransference—the therapist getting emotionally involved with their client—and there was no way her professional pride would permit her to continue working. She felt guilty, of course. There was a permanent shortage of therapists, and many of her clients would struggle to find help elsewhere. But after what happened with Sam, she didn't see any other option. She'd already come to terms with it. What she was doing for Sam more than made up for it. She'd never normally use this word, but she really did believe his aphenphosmphobia had been cured. He'd shown so much progress that, absent an extremely traumatic experience, she doubted his symptoms would ever return.

To Lucy's surprise, the president didn't have any problems with their relationship. If anything, she was pleased. It meant that she'd soon be joining the Strand family, together with this new life growing inside of her.

Their baby was doing well and they'd been told they were having a girl. Sam had already picked out a name for her—Louise. Lou, he liked to call her. He talked to her a lot, touching Lucy's stomach, telling Lou to grow big and strong.

Bridget was delighted when she found out, and suggested that they take a family photograph—Amelie was out of town, so it was just the three of them blushing and smiling. And that same blush, that same smile, when they received the printout, along with apologies for being old fashioned. There was a funny little message on it—"Be stranded with love"—handwritten and signed. "It's unique now. You can't digitize or copy it," Bridget told them.

Lucy was twenty-eight weeks gone. The doctor just checked them both out and said they were doing fine, but she wasn't so sure. Lately, she'd been having the same terrible dream every night.

When she opened her eyes, she would be all alone on the Beach. She was lonely and afraid, so she would start to wander around, looking for someone, anyone. She always spotted Sam and Amelie, standing at the water's edge, their backs to her. Relieved, she'd call out to them. Amelie's hair shimmered in the gray light, but when she turned it was Bridget's face, twisted with sadness and pain. She spoke.

—*I'll be waiting for you on the Beach.*

Lucy woke herself up with her own screams.

"What do they mean, Sam?" Lucy asked, but Sam never gave her an answer. She began to feel like she was trapped in a cage of questions with no answers.

Everything had gone wrong. She couldn't understand it. She was a therapist, a good one, but even she couldn't make sense of the nightmares, or what was happening to her...

Lucy grew more and more weary. That's when Bridget visited and saw Lucy's face.

"They're not nightmares," she stated matter-of-factly.

Lucy felt Lou stirring inside of her as Bridget continued.

"I'm sorry, I had no idea this would happen. Lou's special. Lou has Sam's blood, and through her you're bound to the Beach. You don't have to be afraid, though. You cured Sam—made him whole. You gave him a life to live for, to protect. Made him a part of this world. The world is a jumbled mess with life and death all mixed up, but Sam might be the one to make it whole again, like you made him whole. Without him, our fate is sealed; but with him, there's still hope for a future. The Beach exists within each of our minds, but that doesn't mean it's just a figment of our imagination. It has value, purpose, and in time... you will understand."

Bridget gently squeezed Lucy's hand.

She took Lucy's hand, like Lucy had taken his on that day a lifetime ago. She smiled and squeezed.

There Lucy was, on the Beach. Everything she had seen in her nightmares, she saw in that instant. Somewhere inside her, Lou was laughing. And then it all fell into place.

Sam's birth, his family, the Death Stranding. For the first time she saw how all the pieces fit into a terrible truth that she didn't want to believe, but couldn't deny. She saw her part in it, too, and little Lou's.

She remembered those funny little words on the picture. "Be stranded with love." And she was.

Lou's kicking woke her up. She was alone, still half-asleep, so everything around her looked askew. It was that all-too-familiar feeling of the waking and dreaming being tangled up. But Sam and Bridget and Amelie must have led even more muddled lives. A reality between life and death, between this world and the next. Because of all this chaos and confusion beyond imagination stranded on their shore…

"Help me, Sam," she begged internally.

She took the pills on the table next to her all at once. She tried to make sense of it, but this was never her world. She was born into an older one, one without a Beach, where the dead stayed buried and life moved on. She was shaking so hard. She didn't think the drugs were working. She had some syringes loaded with sedatives. She thrust one into her arm, one after another, until she ran out.

MOUNTAIN KNOT CITY // PRIVATE ROOM

"I'm sorry, Sam, I didn't mean to go digging up your past. I just wanted to understand. I just wanted to understand the connection between you and Lou," Deadman explained, lowering his head at Sam, who didn't know what to make of Deadman's frank apology. It made him feel like the dick in this situation for being so furious, and he wasn't sure how to deal with it. It was him who had attached the phantom of Lou to this BB and acted like he was atoning for the life he hadn't been able to save. He was irritated by Deadman's prying, but he couldn't blame him for it either.

"Seventy percent of my body is harvested from cadavers. I was a coroner before I became a member of Bridges. I know the dead, but I'll never be able to know the Beach." Deadman crouched down and looked into the pod at the BB, who had begun to sleep.

"Have you ever heard the tale of Frankenstein's Monster, Sam?" he asked.

Sam had heard of the story. In fact, it had been Lucy who told him it. (*Are you sure?*) She explained to him: "The reason that humans want to be makers is because we are ashamed of being mere creatures. Our creation myths were formed because we wanted to be more than that. We wanted to be special. The Beach is the same."

"I'm artificial," Deadman explained. "Grown from pluripotent stem cells. And when that vita spark didn't manifest in all my organs, they replaced the defective ones with those of the dead. People born the traditional way have Beaches. You have one. BB, too. But I have no such connections. No *ka*. I'm a dead man. No mother. No afterlife. No Beach. I never even had a birthday. I'm a soulless meat puppet."

As Sam looked up and met Deadman's gaze, he noticed that Deadman's eyes were full of tears. He couldn't believe it. This man had feelings. He was capable of independent thought. He was brimming with curiosity. He must have had a soul. (*Silly Sam. Consciousness and the soul are different.*)

"You see now why I'm so obsessed with it all? It was why I looked after the BBs, too. If this kid is just some piece of equipment, then what am I?" Deadman tried to touch the pod, but his hand slid right through it. "The battlefield, now that was an awful Beach. But strangely, I didn't hate it. Because I knew you were coming for me. I've never felt that before. Connected to someone. Anyone." Deadman turned his head as if to ask Sam for affirmation of that connection.

"Look, Sam. I sometimes think about this. If the Beach is linked to individual people, doesn't that in itself mean that the Beach doesn't actually exist? Doesn't it mean that the Chiral Network and that Beach of Fragile's that I use to jump from place to place is all just a delusion? That the only reason they form part of our reality is because we all share the same delusion inside our heads? That would make what we call connections extremely fragile. But it would also make things so much easier for me. It means that I wouldn't have to come up with these justifications about Frankenstein's Monster or cadaver organs."

Huh? Was that confession just before a big pile of bullshit? It all made Sam's head spin.

"You don't need to look so grim. I know that I don't have a Beach and that I can't even sense it. I don't have DOOMS. That's the one thing that makes me the same as other people. But I still couldn't stand it. I didn't feel like I was alive. I was jealous of you."

As far as Sam was concerned, if Deadman wanted his DOOMS, he could have it. It was because of those abilities that he had lost Lucy and Lou. An uncontrollable urge welled up inside him. If Deadman hadn't been a hologram, he would have hit him. (*Despite your aphenphosmphobia?*)

—*You didn't have to cut ties and walk away.*

Sam froze at Bridget's frail voice. He looked warily around the vicinity like a frightened hound.

But all he saw was the look of puzzlement on Deadman's face.

"That's what Bridget used to say," Deadman said. Had Sam misheard Deadman's voice? Or were they sharing the same delusion? "Bridget was right. I truly believe so."

"I didn't cut any ties. They were never there to begin with," Sam snapped back, afraid that he would hear Bridget's voice in his head again. The hoarseness made him feel even more strange. It had been ten years. After ten whole years without contact, as Bridget lay there dying and Amelie was trapped on the other side of the continent, she had begged him to help. But what her lot called "ties" were nothing but lies. He couldn't blame that frail woman for everything, though. He was here of his own accord. He was the one who hadn't been able to bury the past. He hadn't changed since the day he had been unable to protect Lucy or Lou.

But simply blaming himself like that was a distraction from what really mattered. He knew it. That's why he was afraid to look Deadman in the face. Deadman probably saw through everything.

Sam couldn't tell how Deadman was interpreting this long silence.

"I thought we had ties," Deadman muttered, severing the connection. The hologram disappeared. The space he had been occupying suddenly felt all the more empty. It was the same feeling Sam had back then. When all he could do was stand dumbfounded in the middle of the crater that had been gouged out of the earth. Where that city had once stood. When he remembered the ruins of the satellite city that Lucy and countless others had been snatched away from, he had the same feeling that he had when he thought back to Central Knot City, and how he couldn't save them either, despite taking Igor's BB. The actions of the invisible dead who were purging man from this earth kept Sam grounded and stuck in the past. Even if he stretched out his hand, begged them to give him sweet release, his prayers would never be answered. He would only ever be sent right back where he started.

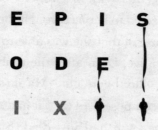

EPISODE IX

HEARTMAN

Sam brushed away the snow that was clinging to his goggles and checked his location on the map on his device. If he ascended the slope then he should be able to see Heartman's research facility.

It was seven days since Sam had departed Mountain Knot City. He had already surmounted two peaks, crossed a crevasse, and climbed and descended more slopes than he could count. The weather had been relatively stable, but the skies were beginning to turn a little more ominous now and it looked like a blizzard was on its way. Sam wanted to get to Heartman's place before it arrived. He couldn't risk losing cargo this precious. It was irreplaceable. It was something that Sam struggled to class as "cargo" at all. It was Mama's body wrapped tightly in a body bag.

After dying together with her unborn baby, Mama's *ka* had become connected to her *ha* through the *ka* of her child. It was likely because of that she was able to move her body as if she was still alive. Even after the umbilical cord that connected them had been cut, Mama's body neither necrotized nor decomposed. In fact, it had remained in the same state as when she had just died. Such an unusual phenomenon had piqued Heartman's interest and he had requested to examine the body. He thought it might provide a vital clue to understanding the relationship between the *ha* and the *ka*, and that between the worlds of the living and the dead that the Beach connected. If Sam was lucky, it might even offer some insights as to why Sam was the way he was, too. That's why it was so important to get Mama's body to Heartman. The long march to his lab felt like her funeral procession.

After circumventing the large rocks that began to protrude halfway up the slope, Sam's view suddenly expanded. He could see to the bottom of the basin and the frozen lake that lay there. It was hard to make out amid the snow flurries, but it seemed to be shaped like a heart. Like a simple heart that had been doodled by a child. Heartman resided alongside it.

As Sam reached the lab, the sensor scanned Sam and opened the entrance. The delivery terminal that was set up next to it automatically booted up, welcoming Sam to the facility. Sam was about to announce his arrival when he was greeted by a mechanical sound.

<Please proceed.>

The door opened and Sam proceeded into a long corridor that was flooded with light. In contrast to Mama's lab, Heartman's lab was immaculate. There wasn't so much as a speck of dust in sight, but no signs of life either. The hallway was almost silent. The sound of Sam's footsteps and breathing were the only noises echoing faintly between the walls, which felt kind of cushioned and springy, just like the floors.

<Please enter.>

Encouraged onward by the voice, Sam passed through the automatic doors. Suddenly, the hallway was cloaked in darkness. Sam couldn't make out what was in front of him, but luckily there was a handrail to grab onto nearby. Sam gripped it and waited for his eyes to become accustomed to the blackness. Music was playing faintly in the distance. It was a heavy and melancholic piano piece. It was Chopin's Funeral March. The moment Sam turned in the direction of the source of the music, something caught in his throat. Something that couldn't possibly be there was floating in front of him.

A BT.

Sam reflexively held his breath and stopped moving. Perhaps this was why he hadn't sensed any sign of human life in the lab. Maybe something had happened to turn this place into BT territory. But there was no response from the

Odradek. Deadman had assured Sam that the functionality of the reset BB had been restored, but maybe Sam had messed up when he was tuning the BB with himself. What if it was still too soon after the BB's memories had been wiped? On the way here from Mountain Knot City they hadn't had to go through any BT territory, so Sam hadn't noticed that the BB wasn't responsive. But now he realized that he hadn't been able to reconnect with Lou at all.

Deadman's face flashed before Sam's eyes. He could feel the anger billowing up as he imagined punching the liar square in the jaw.

Then, Lou let out a laugh.

As Sam peered down into the pod, Lou gazed back up. Lou seemed to be trying to tell him something. Sam looked back toward the BT. He could have kicked himself. It was a dummy.

Sam flicked it with his finger and carried on forward, led by the unending music.

Someone was lying face up on a padded lounge chair ahead in the darkness. The sleeping face beneath the glasses was that of Heartman, who Sam had talked to over codec a few times now.

"Heartman?" Sam whispered.

The man didn't look like he was sleeping. His chest wasn't rising or falling at all. He wasn't breathing. Sam had a bad feeling about this. This was why there had been no sign of life.

He supposed the piece of equipment beside the chair was there to monitor Heartman's vitals. It was similar to one of the machines in Bridget's room. It was most likely an EKG. The EKG reading should have depicted a wave, but it wasn't oscillating a jot. It was flatlining. Heartman's heart had stopped.

"Heartman?"

The music stopped. It felt like someone's funeral had just come to an end. Lou was staring at Heartman with a strange expression. The Odradek was still unresponsive. Then, a small device on the left side of Heartman's chest let out an electronic noise.

`<Administering shock. Stand clear.>`

Immediately afterward, the body shook. With an electronic beep, the EKG graph began to draw waves. Then the man drew a deep breath and sat up, and looked at Sam with the face of someone who was still slightly groggy, with tears in his eyes.

Sam still hadn't grasped what was going on when Heartman stood up and wiped the tears away. He adjusted his glasses then offered his hand to Sam. Seemingly unperturbed by an unresponsive Sam, the man began to speak.

"Well, you certainly caught me with my pants down. Glad you could make it, Sam. I'm sorry, I didn't mean to alarm you. But I am what I am."

Sam just stood there, not knowing what Heartman was talking about or how he should reply.

"Ah. Please lay her down there," Heartman instructed. He seemed to think that the reason Sam was so confused was because he didn't know what to do with Mama, and indicated toward a stretcher next to his lounge chair.

"Still no sign of them," Heartman muttered to himself, not paying Sam any mind as Sam laid the body bag down. Heartman was skillfully fiddling with his cuff link.

"You know your heart stops beating?" Sam said in an attempt to get Heartman to turn around.

"Don't worry about it," Heartman replied, pointing at the device on his chest. "It stops every twenty-one minutes. I spend three minutes on the Beach, and then return." His voice was as casual as if he was describing his day.

"Sixty deaths and sixty resurrections per day. Sixty opportunities to search the Beach for my departed family. This is how I live. This is my life," he explained.

Sam was becoming increasingly confused, but Heartman was paying no attention and continued to fiddle with his device. On a small table beside the chair stood a small hourglass, but for some reason, no sand was falling from the top compartment. Old books, images, and music neatly lined the ceiling-high bookshelves. Between the books and other objects stood a picture of a woman with a wide, innocent smile and a shy little girl. The ceiling was almost hidden from view by the hanging skeletal samples of whales and other creatures.

Somehow, the room appeared the way Sam had always

pictured a room belonging to Heartman would appear. The look of the man himself, still fiddling with his device, fit Sam's image to a tee, too.

The windows displayed on the monitor that monopolized one entire wall were closed one by one, until the monitor itself faded out. Then a large picture window appeared. The entire wall was a window. Heartman beckoned Sam, who was squinting in the bright light.

Outside the window, Sam could see the heart-shaped lake.

"That's my heart right there," Heartman said, pointing outside. "That crater was made by a voidout. I see myself in that crater. My wife and my child."

Sam was even more confused. Was that supposed to be some kind of metaphor?

"It's like looking at the shape of my heart," Heartman continued as the AED in Heartman's chest projected a hologram into the air. A 3D image of an animated heart was pulsating rhythmically. "The doctors called it myocardial cordiformia. Mine is an especially unusual case. It doesn't run in the family."

Heartman gestured toward the sofa and encouraged Sam to sit down. Heartman sat back down in his lounge chair.

"You know, I never came to terms with their loss. In the days that followed, I became obsessed with an idea: that the Beach is real, and they are on it. Some of my colleagues ridiculed me for it, they said that it was just a theory or the dogma of some groups who shared a particular paradigm, but I knew it was real. I would induce cardiac arrest—three minutes at a time—and search for them. Day after day after day…"

That meant that the two people in the photo on Heartman's bookshelf were his wife and child. Here was a man who Sam could somewhat relate to.

"All so you could say goodbye?" Sam asked.

"Quite the opposite. It is said that everyone's Beach is different. So what if everyone's afterlife is different, too? I find the thought terrifying. Spending eternity alone. Which is why I decided to find my family and make sure to move on with them."

"You mean die with them?"

Heartman smiled at Sam's question and raised his thumb.

"If death would see us reunited, then yes. But the repeated cardiac arrests took their toll on my heart. The muscle gradually deformed. And after a while they started calling me 'The Beach Scientist—Heartman.'" Heartman got up from his chair and held out his hand. "So, I'm Heartman. Nice to meet you."

Sam's expression remained blank as Heartman approached the stretcher. Mama's face slowly appeared as he pulled down the zipper. There was no paleness to her face, nor any hint of postmortem lividity or rigor mortis. It looked like she was sleeping peacefully.

Heartman let out a curious sigh.

"A body that doesn't necrotize. No sign of decomposition. It's as if she were still alive," Heartman commented.

Sam recognized that look. It was the same look that Deadman had given him when they had first met. The look of a scientist filled with pure curiosity.

"She's the perfect mummy. An impeccable corpse," Heartman continued, fiddling with the body. Behind his curiosity there didn't lie some great moral motivation to help mankind, but the innocent urge of child to disassemble a toy to see how it worked. Sam had to say something. He didn't like the way Heartman was tinkering with Mama's body so brazenly. It wasn't about respect for the dead, he just didn't want to see Mama's body violated like that when Mama's *ka* still lived on inside Lockne. Luckily, Heartman seemed to sense Sam's disapproval and looked up.

"Where's the other thing you were supposed to bring? Ah, found it. Behold."

Heartman showed Sam a small case that he had removed from the depths of the bag. From it, Heartman took out a transparent cylindrical container that Sam had never seen before. It seemed to be made of reinforced plastic and filled with some kind of liquid. Inside floated something that looked like a string. Were Bridges up to something again?

Sam remembered how Deadman and Die-Hardman had made him carry Lou all the way to the incinerator without telling him anything. Once again, he had found himself lugging cargo he was kept oblivious to. Back then it had been with Bridget's corpse, and this time it was with Mama's. He was furious at Bridges for once again using him as an unintentional errand boy. Sam's anger must have been showing on his face, because Heartman wiggled his index finger at him to placate him and indicated toward the container.

"It appears to be an umbilical cord, yes?"

Sam didn't even bother responding. He supposed that it did, but it also looked like the remains of some kind of weird creature. One that lived on a planet with an entirely different kind of ecosystem.

"Human, by the looks of it. I think?" Heartman remarked, showing Sam his cuff link and throwing him a meaningful look. Heartman was telling him to play along. Sam didn't know what Heartman was up to, but he could understood that much. The situation seemed awfully similar to when Deadman had raised his suspicions about the director.

"It doesn't look biological. I can't say for sure without looking into it further, but I don't think this was an ordinary conduit between fetus and placenta. It looks more like a BT's tether."

Heartman showed Sam the container up closer. Once he got a good look at it, Sam could see a substance like fine particles writhing around upon its surface. He had no idea that BT tethers that materialized like this could be harvested.

"And this was Mama's?" Heartman wondered aloud to himself.

Sam had been the one to sever it, but he had no recollection of picking it back up. Heartman gave another meaningful nod.

"Yes... A body that doesn't necrotize and an umbilical cord connected to the Beach... These are remarkable discoveries, Sam..." Heartman commented excitedly.

Sam began to back away, hoping to escape the hug that Heartman looked like he might give him at any moment. Heartman gave Sam an apologetic look, and placed the container with the umbilical cord in it back on the stretcher, before closing the body bag back up.

"Would you mind looking at this for a moment?" Heartman asked, turning to the monitor on the wall.

It showed a four-legged creature lying in a snow-covered field—a mammoth. Sam wondered if it had been dug up around here and continued to gaze at the monitor, unsure of Heartman's intentions.

"Look closely. Can you tell what it is?" Heartman asked.

He zoomed in on the mammoth's abdomen. The camera was picking up something strange. An umbilical cord was extending out from its belly.

"Do you see it? An umbilical cord is extending out of this mammoth's body. This record, made before the Death

Stranding, happened to get left behind. And look here."

Heartman switched to the next photo. This one showed an ammonite with a similar cord. It was dangling from the center of the ammonite's spiral-shaped shell.

"So far, I've only managed to dig up these two photographs, but I have been able to establish that neither of them are fakes. Now, the umbilical cord issue might be one thing, but what's stranger is that neither this mammoth nor this ammonite were found fossilized or preserved in ice as you might expect. Both of these species have been extinct for thousands of years, but, as you can see in the photographs, they look as though they only died yesterday. Just like Mama. And I'll bet that even more of these specimens are out there, waiting to be found. My colleagues are on the hunt as we speak. Once you activate the Chiral Network, I might even be able to retrieve some of the past records, too."

To Sam, it all seemed a bit out-there. Still, he couldn't tear his eyes away from the monitor. Had that cord dangling from the ammonite really connected it to the Beach? And what else did that imply?

<Five minutes to cardiac arrest.>

The AED's voice rang out across the room. Heartman shut down the monitor and the view outside the window reappeared.

The heart-shaped lake was right outside. If that lake which had been gouged into the earth by a voidout was the same as Heartman's heart, that made his heart itself a scar.

The fact that he had chosen to settle near it and looked down on it every single day as he went about his unusual routine told Sam that this man was living in the past as well. Mama and Deadman were the same. They may have adopted the name of Bridges, but they were attempting to build Bridges toward the past.

"Each person has their own Beach. Just as an umbilical cord attaches one fetus to one mother, we are attached to one Beach. That's the rule. But I'm the exception. My Beach is connected to others. As if it were the beneficiary of a coronary bypass. Maybe this twisted heart of mine made it possible. I just want to find them. I'll be back soon, hopefully from where my family are," Heartman said to Sam as he reclined in his chair.

"You probably think what I do is strange. That no matter how special my Beach is, that doesn't mean that my wife and daughter are still there waiting on it. And you're right. There's still so much that we don't even understand about this world, so how can we possibly expect to understand anything about the Beach? But I have a theory. When a *ka* departs its *ha*, it goes to the Beach, which forms a corridor between this life and the next. Under normal circumstances, a body is incinerated within forty-eight hours of its passing and before it can necrotize, so that the *ka* can pass over to the other side knowing that it has no *ha* to return to. Its attachment to this world disappears. But once a body necrotizes, the *ka* becomes bound to this world. But because it doesn't actually have a body to come back to, it becomes a BT.

"In any case, the *ka* doesn't spend a long time on the Beach. But there are exceptions. For example, those who didn't die a natural death. Those whose bodies were wiped out in an instant without necrotizing or being incinerated don't become BTs, but their attachment toward this world keeps their *ka* from leaving the Beach. You can laugh it away as the delusions of a mad man if you like, though, since no matter how many times I wander the Beach, I never find my wife and daughter."

<Four minutes to cardiac arrest.>

The AED announced how long Heartman had left.

"My body will never go back to the way it was now. I'm willing to bet on that. But it all has to have some kind of meaning. The battlefields—the endless wars you found yourself trapped in—they're from a time that actually existed. From a world war that took place over a hundred years ago. That war was a particularly nonsensical one. One in which weapons of mass destruction slaughtered people on a vast scale. The inherent meaning of each individual death was snatched away from those victims and they became nothing more than a number. They had no idea why they died. It's the same for those who die in a voidout.

"If that strong attachment to this world and the yearning

to stay connected to it created that battlefield, then that might support my theory about voidout victims becoming trapped on the Beach."

<Three minutes until cardiac arrest.>

"Deadman told me that man, Clifford Unger, was in the US Special Forces," Heartman went on. "He must have seen a lot of war in his time. His misery and hatred, combined with your BB acting as some sort of catalyst, may have brought these battlefields to our world. It's just a theory, but perhaps that man who can summon BTs also summoned Cliff's anger."

"You think Higgs is pulling his strings?" Sam asked.

Sam found himself unconsciously gripping Cliff's dog tag in his pocket. What if Higgs summoned Cliff and that battlefield to get in Sam's way, now that he could repel the BTs?

<Two minutes to cardiac arrest.>

"I don't know. But evidence does suggest that Higgs brought them here," Heartman mused.

The window on the wall went into shade mode and the lake outside disappeared. The interior of the room slowly grew darker.

"Oh, before I forget, I have a favor to ask," Heartman quickly interjected.

<One minute remaining. Please hold onto something secure.>

"Could you just... relax until I come back? Time stops on

the Beach, but not in the Seam. Rest assured, it'll only feel like three minutes to you," Heartman explained. Heartman closed his eyes and the gramophone placed at an angle to his lounge chair began to play music. It was Chopin's Funeral March again. "We'll continue this shortly."

The AED emitted a beep and the EKG flatlined.

As the Funeral March echoed quietly throughout the lab, Sam had no idea what to do. It was just him, Mama's corpse, Heartman's temporarily deceased body, and a gently snoozing BB. There wasn't a single person who was truly alive or truly dead in the entire room. Although it was unclear what really defined who was alive and who was dead in the first place.

All Sam could do was settle himself on the sofa and wait for Heartman to come back. He was still holding onto Cliff's dog tag. It was covered in scratches and listed his name, affiliation, and religion, but no matter how long Sam stared at it, he still didn't understand anything about Cliff. He didn't understand Cliff's relationship with Lou, nor anything about the man's life or death. If Higgs was harnessing Cliff's anger and summoning the battlefield to get in the way of Sam's mission, it seemed like a very roundabout method. There must have been other things that he could have done that would take less time and effort.

For someone who talked so big about bringing humanity's extinction, why didn't Higgs just use a nuke or voidouts or something to destroy all the cities and take out the Chiral Network knots? No matter how effective a repatriate's blood and other bodily fluids were against BTs, they were just still byproducts of one body. It wasn't like there was enough of Sam's blood to get rid of every single BT. They still posed a massive threat.

Higgs had once been a respectable porter. Fragile's comments and Bridges' data backed that up. In fact, when he first started working with Fragile, his main motive had been to help other people. But that had all changed when he jumped ship and began working with someone else.

That meant this new partner must hold the key to everything. But neither Bridges nor Fragile knew who it was. Higgs had made good use of Fragile's DOOMS and organization, so his partner must have offered him something even more powerful. Maybe Higgs's true intentions lay beyond extinction. His proud proclamations about how he was the particle of God and the arrogance that went with that claim seemed to imply as much.

<Administering shock. Stand clear!>

Sam suddenly snapped back to his senses. The Funeral March music was gradually winding down.

"No luck." Heartman sat up and wiped away his tears. He quickly tapped the hourglass on the table next to him and the still sand suddenly began to flow upwards.

Sam reflected on how this strange backward hourglass

represented Heartman's heart, which desired nothing more than to rewind the past.

"Oh, sorry. Where were we? I know it may seem like a nuisance, but I'm acclimated to it now. Most of life's basic functions fit rather easily into a twenty-one-minute time slot. Sleep is the tricky one," Heartman commented light-heartedly.

"I die for three minutes and live for twenty-one. The cycle of my life is much like yours, except for the fact that yours is split into twenty-four-hour periods, while mine is split into twenty-four minutes. But when I'm dead on the Beach, time seems to go on forever. Because time doesn't exist on the Beach. It's like how time passes when you're asleep. But this cycle is my reality. Consider the BTs that return from the past and the timefall that accelerates the degradation of everything it touches. How can our sense of time cope with such irrational phenomena?

"How do you think we got here? I believe that it was because of our awareness of time. We can imagine a future beyond ourselves. We know that even the Neanderthals buried their dead and laid flowers. We humans can see a tomorrow. We conceived concepts like eternity and an afterlife, helping our societies to outlast us as individuals. And in order for societies to outlast the lifespan of the individual, we conceived of an afterlife, and a future beyond ourselves...

"Alas, the Death Stranding threatens to undo all our

progress. Take me, for example. I want to find my family on the Beach and pass together with them into the world of the dead. This phenomenon has managed to produce a man as strange as me. Honestly, the twenty-one minutes I spend here—all downtime, nothing more. Time spent waiting to go back to the search. My body may be present, but my soul is on the Beach. I'm already dead…"

Sam thought that it was most likely a piece of fiction that Heartman had concocted for himself. It was to explain his truth and share it with others. If someone only talked about their own story to themselves, they'd go nuts. They'd withdraw into themselves, becoming the king of a kingdom they were the only inhabitant of. That's why we all need someone to share our story with. That's what making a connection is (*maybe Heartman, Mama, and Lockne and Deadman too were all struggling to try and create: a place for themselves in this world*). Maybe Bridget's plan to rebuild America was nothing more than a narrative, either. Immediately after the thought struck him, the cuff link on Sam's right wrist began to feel much heavier. He ended up blurting out anything to escape its weight.

"I know that feeling. Lost my family in an accident," he said, not really knowing what family he meant, in all honesty. Was he talking about Lucy? Bridget and Amelie? Or about the photograph he had lost. Perhaps he was even talking about the parents he had never even met.

"Well! I never expected you to open up to me," Heartman commented, inverting the hourglass. Through some sort of sorcery, the flow of the sand turned and began falling from the upper compartment to the lower one. The amount of sand sat in the top never lessened. Yet it still piled up below. "I'm the same as you."

MOUNTAIN KNOT CITY OUTSKIRTS // SATELLITE CITY

"Don't worry, it's alright. Trust me," a voice told Heartman.

Even if he closed his eyelids, the light raining down still managed to hurt his eyes. He was wearing a mask and vaguely aware that the anesthesia would make him drop off any moment now. The doctors had told him that the surgery would take the better part of a day, but when he next opened his eyes it would all already be over. Ten hours would pass in the blink of an eye. He experienced the exact same phenomenon whenever his consciousness switched to its Beach phase. But when he spoke of this phase to others, they always likened it to a near-death experience. The structure of his story and the motifs within were shared by many people. They always described looking down at themselves from above. That they heard their name called when they attempted to cross a river, only to find themselves alive again when they turned back. That they were going to meet the friends and family that had passed on before them. Or that they were passing through a tunnel with a light at the end. The records Heartman saw always mentioned the same details, over and over again. Then, after the Death Stranding, all of that was replaced with talk of the Beach. A beach and the ocean. All near-death experiences became the same.

Around the same time that the dead started to return from the Beach, some people began to be born with the ability to sense the world of the dead, and some people emerged with the transcendental ability to use the Beach to move through physical space. There were even those who were forced back to this world when they died—who, in effect, were immortal. They were called repatriates. A theory was even floated that suggested using the Beach to create a pathway for a network. The Beach evolved into a physical concept. It may not have existed in this dimension, but it existed in a state that could be utilized in the physical world.

"You'll be drifting off soon. Just a little longer." The surgeon's voice already sounded very far away.

Then Heartman was floating above his body, looking at it lying there with its chest clamped open. What was going on? Was he having a near-death experience? The EKG wasn't showing anything out of the ordinary. His other vital signs all read normal. Was he dreaming? Even though he had been anesthetized?

The doctors continued to move calmly and efficiently.

They looked like engineers fixing a soft biological machine.

It had been a few years since the problem with his heart was first detected. Since he found out that his heart had been stopping in his sleep. He had no idea. He was asleep! His wife suspected it was sleep apnea, but Heartman didn't really care. It wasn't like he was going to die, and besides, he didn't have time to be going and seeing doctors back then. He put aside his wife's concerns and threw himself into his work. He had been scouted by Bridges and he was busy grappling with all his data on mass extinctions.

It was around that time when he began to have the same dream over and over again. He knew what they were. They were dreams of extinction. Everyone with DOOMS had them. At the time, he had no idea that he had that condition. He knew he was a genius, but not this. He didn't even believe in the Beach. He had assumed Bridges was simply after his intelligence, but it seemed they had detected his DOOMS, too. Bridget even told him as much herself.

After the Death Stranding, people were rushing to figure out what had happened. It was completely unprecedented. They didn't even have a name for it.

Eventually, the annihilation events came to be known as voidouts. The monsters that came from the other side were named BTs, and they came from the world of the dead via "the Beach." The phenomenon itself was named the Death

Stranding. Naming all these elements was the first step toward objective study and discussion.

The first Death Stranding wasn't a voidout between the living and the dead, but a voidout between colliding matter and antimatter. Eventually, the theory mutated. It was us. Our dead became the BTs. It was the BTs that were responsible for the voidout. But why was it only humans that became BTs? Because the only ones who could perceive death and an afterlife were human beings. It was our astounding human consciousness that had detected the Beach and summoned the BTs forth. The tragedy of extinction was switched into the glory of being the chosen ones. It was elitism on a global scale. Only the ones who could overcome such a tragedy could go forth to the promised land. It was pure arrogance.

That's why Heartman hadn't believed in the Beach. Mankind was still intent on continuing to climb the stairs of evolution, when in fact we had already reached the landing long ago. New existences were already beginning to catch up with us from the other side. And if BTs were one of them, then we would just have to step down from that pedestal. Heartman hadn't accepted Bridges' invitation in order to save mankind or rebuild America. He just wanted to prove his theory.

He had immersed himself in data about mass extinctions to prove the universal truth of extinction. The whole reason that he joined Bridges was to discover the few records of extinction that still remained. He had come here together with his wife, who was also a member of Bridges, and his infant daughter. They were the only ones who had joined the expedition as a family. They were lavished with attention and admiration as a symbol of connections. But Heartman's dreams of extinction and his heart defect became more and more severe.

Heartman knew that the reason he had these dreams of extinction was because of his heart defect. They were just nightmares that reflected how unwell he was. That's why he underwent the surgery. To prove he was right. There weren't any operating theaters in the colony he was based at for his research, so he was transferred to an ICU in Mountain Knot City.

The surgery itself went well. For a few days after the surgery, he would have to rely on an artificial heart, but that was all part of the plan. His wife and daughter were relieved and asked if he would be home soon. He said yes.

Heartman and his family lived in a satellite city outside of Mountain Knot City. A place where a voidout-based terror attack would later snuff out the lives of his wife and daughter after they returned home.

Heartman understood what had happened in his core, it didn't matter whether people believed it or not. He had been asleep right up until the explosion. Then, as if still in a dream, two flashes of light burst before his eyes, one after the other. They were so intense that he couldn't perceive any other color in the world. He could feel the hospital room vibrating and the thunderous rumble of its foundations shaking. When color did eventually return, the hospital room lights were still out.

It must have been a blackout. Heartman was all alone in his room and there didn't seem to be a soul out in the hall, either. Heartman tried to call for help, but nothing came out. His chest was tight and he couldn't breathe. All he could feel was a sharp pain like a knife had been plunged into his heart. He tried frantically pressing the emergency button, but it was no use because the system was down.

The artificial heart had stopped working, and once more he found himself floating, looking down at a body close to death in the dark.

When he tried to sit up he found himself on the Beach.

It was a sandy beach. The waves were lapping at the shore. But it was also strewn with the stranded carcasses of whales, dolphins, and other sea-dwelling creatures that Heartman didn't recognize. It was just how the people who had near-death experiences described. It seemed so incredibly realistic. He couldn't believe that he could dream something so vividly. His stomach lurched. If he could see the Beach this vividly, then it couldn't be some subjective concept in his imagination, it must actually exist. But to accept that fact, Heartman would have to let go of everything he had always believed in.

He suddenly noticed several lines of footsteps leading toward the sea. Yet he still tried to write them off as manifestations of his own imagination. That was also why he saw people walking in the very same direction when he gazed in the direction in which the footsteps led. It had been his own head that produced these figures.

They were the *ka*s of the people who had died in the voidout. He didn't know any of them, he just saw hundreds of backs silently heading away from him toward the ocean. If he had known them, they would have been more than blank behinds. They would have been the backs of someone with a name.

Heartman stood up and looked across the crowd of people. Someone was stumbling toward the sea to the side of him. She was a small old lady. Heartman had never seen her before, he didn't know her name, nor did he know her face. The woman looked up at him, but her eyes were unfocused, and Heartman doubted whether she could even see him at all.

She simply stood there before raising a finger to her lips as if to shush him. Without acknowledging the confused Heartman himself, she prodded the AED on his chest. The pain went through him like an electric shock. That's when he saw them—his wife and daughter—and it dawned on him that they too had fallen victim to the voidout.

Heartman tried to shout out, but the pain in his chest wouldn't let him. Their backs were becoming more and more distant, like they were being washed away by a sea of people.

When Heartman stretched out his arm another jolt of pain shot through him. When he realized that the pain wasn't in his head and was proof that he was still alive, Heartman began to despair.

"Wait! Don't leave without me!"

He could finally speak. But they didn't hear. Another pain shot through Heartman's chest. The intervals between the shocks were getting shorter and shorter, and becoming more systematic. His heart was starting again. His body back in that hospital room was trying to call him home. He couldn't shout anymore and his legs wouldn't move. He wanted nothing more than to chase after his wife and daughter, but he couldn't get any closer to the sea.

None of these strangers were having a problem reaching the sea, so why did it feel like he was the only one stuck in the sand and unable to move? He didn't belong here. His place was still elsewhere.

Heartman would never forget the voice of the doctor proclaiming he had saved him. That same voice might as well have proclaimed that he would never see his family again.

It had been twenty-one minutes before the ward's backup generator finally kicked in. The artificial heart had started working again and an AED had been used to shock it back to life.

It was because of that heart that he had been ripped away from his family. Heartman had nowhere to direct his sadness, so instead he turned to anger because, at the very least, he had a target to be angry at. It wasn't even toward the terrorist attack that had caused the voidout in the first place. He was angry at his heart that had ripped his family apart, and the Beach itself. Everything had changed.

Once he knew that the Beach existed, he decided to focus all his anger into understanding how it worked. That anger transformed his heart. He became able to share the Beach of others. That's when this cycle of twenty-one minutes of life and three minutes of death began.

Heartman went to the Beach each time and searched for traces of his wife and daughter. Then, when he came back to this world, he continued his research into the Beach. He had managed to make a few discoveries. For one, he realized that when he was having dreams of extinction, his *ka* was already on the Beach. He had simply perceived it as a dream before because he had been unable to accept the very existence of the Beach. He came to believe that he had dreamed of the big five extinction events and lived these past extinctions vicariously in his nightmares. And that the accident in the hospital room hadn't been his first trip to the Beach. When he looked back in time, he calculated that he had been there an unfathomable number of times. His combined research into extinction and the Beach became his guiding light. And once he knew everything there was to know, he would finally be able to reunite with his family.

<Five minutes to cardiac arrest.>

The AED interrupted Heartman's long monologue as he shared his past with Sam.

Heartman sighed and wiped the tears from his eyes. Sam knew that this time they weren't just some reaction to chiral matter. If Heartman wasn't going to give up on finding his family, maybe Sam shouldn't have given up on searching for Lucy.

But he knew that he didn't have the tenacity of Heartman. (*Is that truly how you feel?*)

If Sam hadn't given up on Lucy and Lou, then maybe he could have asked for Amelie's help in searching the Beach for them or something. But Sam had missed his chance, and ran from Bridges. (*You didn't even think of that?*) It was inevitable that they would chase him once he started running.

"There's something I want to ask of you," Heartman said, fiddling with his cuff link. The huge display on the wall showed a map. It showed the location of a number of shelters that spread out like a spider's web from Mountain Knot City and Heartman's lab by the heart-shaped lake. One of the shelters belonged to the Geologist, who Sam had battled through the blizzard to visit. He remembered how the man had told him that he'd discovered a fossil from the Beach.

Everything looked fine and dandy until his focus fell on a black belt of terrain that lay to the east of Edge Knot City. It ran north to south, almost like it was partitioning the areas that had already been connected to the Chiral Network from Edge Knot.

"This is the only area known to contain fossils from the late-Cretaceous Period—when the dinosaurs died out. The assumption being that the last ones lived here, and here alone. You see, hiding in the earth, then, are memories of a major mass extinction. The fossil Beach that the Geologist found appears to be authentic, as well. Now that his shelter is connected to here by way of the Chiral Network, we've been able to share some more detailed data. HQ has even been able to restore data from the past, and the data of mine that was wiped out in the terrorist attack."

Sam thought he could see Heartman's face brighten. It didn't seem as heavy as when he was talking about his wife and daughter. His usual curious expression was back, too.

<Four minutes to cardiac arrest.>

Heartman muttered at the AED to shut up, and began to fiddle with it. The numbers counting down in the small window disappeared. Sam must have looked alarmed, because Heartman shot him a thumbs up of reassurance.

"Lots of us Bridges members used to be holed up in the shelters, excavating and researching the past, but thanks to the voidout terrorism and all the local destruction that number has dropped significantly. Luckily, we've been making a lot of noteworthy discoveries out here lately, but in an ironic turn, the more we discover, the more the tar seems to be eroding everything away." Heartman pointed to the black belt on the map. "We call it tar because that's the easiest thing to call it, but it differs from tar both in structure and in its properties."

Sam had seen it up close and personal when he had thrown the nuke into the lake. He couldn't forget how the tar absorbed the enormous energy of that blast.

"We set up some research shelters there before the tar started bubbling up, and even built a distribution center out there. Some relay equipment for the Chiral Network, too."

The map displayed what Heartman described in chronological order.

On the map, the tiny black specks on the map that had been small only one year prior suddenly expanded into an extensive belt shape. It showed that when Amelie and the rest of Bridges I had first arrived, it could probably still have been circumvented. It was just after she arrived in Edge Knot City when the tar began to well up and the scale of the erosion expanded. Something about it felt intentional. In fact, the timing probably matched up with when Amelie was first captured. The only person Sam could think of who could pull off such a stunt was Higgs.

"Then how the hell am I supposed to hook the west up to the network?" Sam asked.

It seemed like Heartman had been anticipating Sam's question, as he gave yet another thumbs up.

"I'm asking you for your help in building a new one. It won't be much, given the handful of equipment we've managed to scrape together. Nothing like the Knot Cities, that's for sure. But a knot is still a knot. Sam, I want you to use the Q-pid to put the scientists on the network, then go to Amelie. Afterward, we can get back to the important job of researching the Death—"

Heartman collapsed like the strings on a mannequin had been cut, and his body crumpled to the floor. Sam attempted to spring to Heartman's aid, but the floor reacted first. It expanded to absorb the shock of Heartman's fall and cushioned his landing. The AED on Heartman's chest began to count down until resuscitation. Exasperated by the fact that he would have to wait another three minutes, Sam went to sit himself down on the sofa. But before he made it, Sam's cuff link began to vibrate, indicating an incoming call.

It was from Die-Hardman, only this time Sam couldn't see him. Sam's cuff links had been set to sound only. Sam didn't remember doing that. Then he remembered the look

Heartman had given him when he took out the umbilical cord. When Sam checked the cuff link, he could see that the communications were going through the lab's firewall. That meant that Heartman didn't want Die-Hardman to see the cord. That could also explain why Sam had been made to bring it here in secret.

<Sam. You heard him. You can grab the order at a delivery terminal. We want you to activate the shelters where the Bridges staff are stationed, then we can get to work on replacing the lost waystation near the tar belt. Then you can head for Edge Knot. By connecting the shelters, we should be able to restore our research results and any past data that has been lost. That in itself is going to provide a huge boost to helping us understand the Death Stranding better. It'll also bring us one step closer to saving Amelie and rebuilding the UCA. Lugging the equipment for the replacement waystation is going to be heavy work, though. I know that it's a tough job, but you're all we've got. On the Higgs front, he hasn't pulled anything conspicuous for a while now, but I doubt that means he's just sat there doing nothing. Take care.>

Perhaps it was because Sam knew Heartman was hiding something from Die-Hardman, and because of what Deadman had told Sam during their own secret discussion, but the director's tone felt colder to Sam than before. It was a little late to consider now, but it seemed like Bridges had changed a lot since the Bridges he knew ten years ago. Deadman, Mama, and Heartman had all joined after Sam had left. And now that Bridget was dead, there weren't that many members left who even knew America as it once was. Die-Hardman was probably the only member remaining who was there when Bridges was first established. Sam had been born some years later, so even he wasn't sure how it was first formed.

Bridges wasn't one thick rope, but rather numerous fine threads bundled together, each with their own motivations. Sam was one of those strands, too.

Sam descended the outer stairs of the snow-covered lab and turned around. He didn't like leaving Heartman like that. It may have been routine for him, but to Sam, he was leaving behind a corpse that had gone into cardiac arrest. What if the AED didn't restart his heart properly? Wouldn't his body necrotize? Sam began to worry.

But Sam had his own routine to get back to now. Sam had to carry on doing his duty without letting on about his misgivings toward Bridges and Die-Hardman. As he began to climb a mountain, Sam activated the Active Skeleton that he had equipped in Heartman's lab. It was a piece of equipment that attached itself to both of Sam's legs, and improved his walking and stability. He felt so light! Once he had climbed the slope a little, the heart-shaped lake came into view.

Every time he took a step into the snow, the strap of his backpack dug painfully into his shoulder. Even though he was wading through sub-zero temperatures, he had to wipe the sweat from his face more than once. A whole day had passed since Sam had left Heartman's lab. It was only one more peak and then the rest of the journey would be smooth sailing. His legs may have had the help of the Active Skeleton, but it didn't do so much for his back. The weight of the cargo on it was making him want to admit defeat, but it was just a little farther. Once he had connected this area to the Chiral Network and made it to Edge Knot City, he'd be able to put this pack down once and for all. Then the UCA would be rebuilt, he could save Amelie, and he could free Lou. He would finally be able to confront his past self who had failed to save Lucy and Lou, and make peace with it. What's more, once the whole Chiral Network was up and running, Heartman could make even more discoveries about the Beach and extinction. And once they fully understood the Beach, then maybe, just maybe, Sam would be able to set Lou free from the Beach and himself free from the Seam. If he could untangle life and death in this world then they'd finally be free.

Sam caressed the pod, but Lou showed no reaction whatsoever. More than ten days had passed since Deadman had tinkered with the pod and they still weren't communicating as they had before. Lou spent most of the day asleep. But maybe that was to be expected. They hadn't approached any BT-occupied territory or experienced any spikes in chiral density lately. Babies were supposed to sleep a lot anyway. Besides, if regular babies needed so much sleep, then what about babies that hadn't even been born yet? It would have been selfish to wake Lou for no reason. Wait… wasn't he intending to reforge their relationship from the beginning after Lou's memories had been wiped? Calling this kid Lou was so self-centered of him. This kid could have been called by a different name when it was in its mother's womb. All Sam had done was project his past onto this poor baby. He was basically repeating what Bridget had done to him when she left America in his hands. He recalled her voice inside his head.

—*You're the one I wanted to send, Sam.*

No, America's finished! Bridget, you're the president of jack shit!

Sam thought back to the hospital room that had been transformed with holograms to turn it into a fake Oval Office. It felt like the weight of Bridget after she fell on him back then had been added onto his back. The children always carry the baggage that their parents leave behind. Whether it's debt or fortune, the parents force them to bear it whether they like it or not. Parents liked to preach that this was the baton of life and the succession of history. Their kids were even forced to grieve their deaths and usher their souls onward. (*Was that why you carried Bridget's corpse?*) But what were parents who outlived their children supposed to do?

A strong wind struck Sam straight on. It roared like an animal and blew past him. The snows thickened and all Sam could see was white. He got down on his knees to give his legs a rest and readjust his cargo. A pain shot through him and he let out a grunt. The wound he had sustained from a stray bullet on that battlefield still hadn't healed.

Sam heard a muffled cry from the pod. It seemed that Lou had reacted to Sam's pain. Maybe he was mistaken. Maybe he had arbitrarily determined that to be the case. Maybe he was being arrogant. It didn't matter. What did matter was that Sam felt the connection between him and Lou repairing itself. He stroked the pod. Then he let out a sigh and got back up. The wind had only blown strongly for a moment, but the snow was still falling and his surroundings had grown silent again. Everything was back to normal, except for one thing.

Something flashed in front of him.

Sam fell to his injured knee again, and then onto his ass. He pulled off the straps of his pack and set it on the ground. Then he removed the Odradek, thrust it into the snow, and switched it on. Sam's cargo was immediately blanketed in white and now resembled one of the many boulders strewn across the landscape. It was all thanks to his hologram projector. It was one of the new functions included in the upgrade the equipment underwent in Mountain Knot City.

Sam hid in its shadow. Unless he was mistaken, the light had bounced off something manmade.

Then the light flashed once again, adding weight to his theory. Now it was moving. Maybe it was some MULEs? The hologram should have blinded them to his presence, as well as invalidated any sensors. As long as he remained quiet, there was no threat.

But maybe Sam had been too optimistic, because the group had now plainly changed course and were heading this way.

Lou's fists were clenched tight in sympathy with Sam's nervousness. Sam could make out five people so far, each of them spreading out in a different direction. It seemed to Sam that they were trying to surround him and they were slowly but surely closing in. They were clad from head to toe in what looked like thick gray cloaks. Each one had a gun in their hand. These weren't MULEs. This was an armed group. If Sam had to guess, they were probably after the relay equipment he was carrying. But he had to wonder how they knew he would be delivering this equipment and how they had guessed the route he would take. Sam kept an eye on the five's movements as he quickly took out his bola gun from his backpack and assembled it. If his assailants had been MULEs, he probably could have distracted them with some spare cargo, but it didn't look like that tactic would do him any good here. They probably wanted to destroy the equipment. He also had to consider the possibility that these five were just the vanguard, and that Higgs was lurking around somewhere. A battle with the BTs could be imminent.

First and foremost, Sam had to protect his cargo. Putting his faith in the protection afforded by the hologram cloaking, Sam decided to try and draw the group's attention toward him. To his right was the slope he had just descended, and although his left was open, there were likely numerous crevasses lying ahead.

Sam dropped down and retreated. The group's reaction was swift. Every single one of them at once moved to Sam's left flank. They were trying to drive him toward the slope.

The guns they held were most likely loaded with normal lethal bullets, but all Sam had was his bola gun, which was intended to apprehend and immobilize and only fired binding bola wires from both ends. It wasn't deadly in the slightest. The enemy continued to close in. Sam flattened himself against the snow-covered rocks to use them as a shield, but the five enemies circled ever closer.

An uncomfortable feeling, like his organs were being squeezed hard, suddenly came over Sam. It was like someone had plunged their hand inside his abdomen and was churning his guts around inside. Sam felt like he was going to vomit. Lou was frightened.

There was no crying, but Lou was curled up as stiff as a dead body, eyes squeezed tightly shut. That's when Sam realized that it wasn't his fear that was being transmitted to Lou, but the other way around. Lou's fear was gnawing away at Sam. He hadn't had the same violent reaction when he was transported to Cliff's battlefield. He hadn't even felt this way before when he was crossing BT territory.

Lou's emotions were coursing into Sam like a raging river, and since Lou didn't know how to express them in words, they were doing a number on Sam's insides instead. BBs had no way to express themselves in words, which is why they needed to be connected to their host via an umbilical cord and use of the Odradek interface. It was actually because they didn't articulate the world in words that they could sense the world of the dead.

Sam closed his eyes and placed his hand on the pod. Lou was unusually afraid of these particular assailants. Shattering the silence, a bullet grazed past Sam's shoulder.

Now they were directly under attack. Sam peeked out from behind the rock to assess the situation. Several armed men were approaching his hiding spot to surround him. He counted five so far. At first glance they looked like ordinary MULEs, but they were obviously out for blood. Was this what Lou was so scared of?

Another gunshot rang out. This time the bullet scraped the rock shielding Sam. Then somebody raised their voice. Just like the MULEs, they spoke in a language that Sam didn't recognize, with short screams that seemed to make up a code that only their comrades could decipher. It seemed to be coming from nearby. Sam knew that it would all be over if he stayed where he was, so he readied his bola gun and sprung out from behind the rock.

The shooting continued, following him closely, but the Active Skeleton he was wearing helped him leap away. Sam threw some hematic grenades in an attempt to blind his attackers. He knew that showering terrorists in that precious blood of his was unlikely to do much, but the only weapons he really had at hand were supposed to be for the BTs, so they would have to do. At least if he left any corpses here, he would have the tools on hand to deal with them before they had the chance to turn.

As the splatter of Sam's blood blinded his pursuers, Sam ran at full speed for the snowfield.

The pain in his left knee had now completely disappeared as the Active Skeleton forced his legs to move whether they hurt or not.

An electromagnetic shot fired into the snow. MULEs used the same weaponry, so that meant these attackers must have been MULEs once. Having succumbed to their Porter Syndrome, they had transformed into Homo gestalts and were moving according to somebody else's will. Sam threw himself into the shadow of the first boulder he found and caught his breath, but his attackers were already scanning the field and were soon moving in. Sam heard another voice. It belonged to a man equipped with different weaponry— an Odradek on his shoulder and a BB pod on his chest. He must have been the leader. If Sam could take him out then he might be able to escape.

Sam felt another cramp in his gut. Lou was terrified. Clutching the pod close with one hand, Sam stared at the apparent leader. The umbilical cord connecting the man to his pod was emitting a heat like it was aflame. This was the man who Lou was so scared of.

Once it had all clicked in Sam's head, the man's Odradek immediately burst to life, spinning wildly. At the same time, Lou began to scream. The man's Odradek formed into a cross shape and pointed in Sam's direction. It was like Sam and Lou were the BTs for once. Lou was twisting and turning inside the pod and kicking at its walls. Was Lou what they were after? The BB pod on the man's chest began to emit a reddish-black light. It must have contained a BB. Did that mean that the BBs were resonating with one another?

The man screamed an indescribable sound once more and burst into a sprint. The four others followed behind, plowing their way through the snow. Sam forgot about Lou for the moment and fired his bola gun. The bindings, which were double-ended with counterweights, flew through the air and wrapped themselves around the legs of the man in front. As the man fell face-first into the snow, the electric shock emitted by the bola bindings should have knocked him out.

Sam set the output of his Active Skeleton legs to max and made another run for it. Jumping and dashing along the way, Sam aimed for the crevasse. It was like he wasn't in his own body. He had no feeling in his legs at all. What if something was broken? He couldn't stop now.

The Active Skeleton only had a little bit of power left, so Sam needed to put as much distance between himself and the men as possible before they gave out.

A belt of rocks came into view. The pinnacle-shaped boulders were around the same height as him and were huddled tightly together.

Sam's pursuers had called off the chase for the time being. Sam could still see where they were and they were no longer running. That being said, they were still closing in at a steady pace. They must have been homing in on Lou to detect the pair.

Sam tried to take a step forward, but the Active Skeleton made a warning sound. The battery was completely depleted. As Sam released the legs, he was reminded of his own body weight and tried his hardest not to succumb to the pain in his knee. It felt like he was standing on a different planet. One with gravity several times stronger than Earth.

Every step felt extraordinarily heavy compared to moments ago, and the distance he had tried so hard to put between him and Lou and their attackers was shrinking by the second. Sam dragged his heavy body, trying to convince himself with each passing inch not to panic.

As he got closer to the rocks, he saw that the boulders were shaped like spirals, almost as if they had been twisted out of the ground by giants. Or maybe they were more like trees that just looked boulder-like on the surface. In any case, it felt like he was entering a rock forest.

Sam felt a presence. Huddling behind a rock, he took a rope into his hand. It didn't matter that it was supposed to be for packing cargo. If an assailant approached, he wouldn't hesitate to use it on them, too. At least it would be more useful in close-quarter combat than any firearm would be.

Sam focused all his attention on the sounds around him and awaited the enemy. His and Lou's pursuers would have a hard time spotting him in here. He noticed as the approaching footsteps seemed to falter. Sam half-rose from behind the rock and sprung behind one of the men. Clutching each end of the rope, Sam slipped it around the man's neck, tightening the pressure on the man's carotid artery. Unable to fight back, the man slumped into unconsciousness.

It looked like Lou was still afraid, but had calmed down a little compared to before. This was still far from over, though, and Sam began to worry about the relay equipment that he had left in place. Their attackers might choose to destroy the equipment over killing Sam if the latter proved too difficult. Sam needed to prepare for that possibility.

Several meters away, the man with the Odradek who Sam considered their leader, along with the two other attackers, were advancing back-to-back. Sam jumped out from behind the rock, exposing himself to the danger, and without a moment's hesitation the men broke their battle formation and launched into an attack. As the bullets flew toward Sam, he shot back with his bola gun, sending bola bindings flying through the gaps between the rocks. He didn't manage to take any of the men down, but one did get hit by the weight on the end of the bola bindings right in the pit of the stomach.

Now there were two men left in front of him. Bullets were whizzing past Sam as he threw another hematic grenade toward a boulder. He wasn't throwing it for the effect of his blood but for the power of its blast. The boulder was tipped with a large, open red flower, and it was smashed into rubble by the explosion, showering the enemy with small pebbles mixed with Sam's blood. The two men let out bestial screams as the blood rained down on them, and began shooting wildly in every direction. Sam shot his bola gun in the shadow of the rocks, sweeping one of the men off his feet as planned.

Now there was just one left. The man with the Odradek

threw away his gun and charged. He had his electric spear in hand and was screaming inhuman screams. The tip of the spear gave off a white electrical charge. It was aimed straight for Sam. Sam hurled himself directly at the man's chest.

Their shoulders crashed into one another and a sharp, numbing pain rushed up Sam's neck. The attacker must have felt the same pain as he dropped his spear. But the man pulled back half a step and landed a kick right in Sam's knee. The pain made Sam gasp. He lost his balance and began to fall. He reached his hands out to stop himself, but unable to reach anything, Sam simply fell onto his back. The air in his lungs had been completely knocked out and he couldn't even groan in pain. The man kicked Sam in the side and sat on top of him. He squeezed down on Sam's neck with one hand and grabbed a knife with the other. Sam couldn't move a muscle and Lou began to shriek again.

The other man's BB pod was right in front of Sam's face.

The man was stronger than Sam had imagined. The man's knees were like vices digging into Sam's armpits. Sam's ribs were making worrying noises. It felt like they were going to buckle any second. The man continued to strengthen his grip around Sam's neck, until Sam could no longer breathe. He could feel the world becoming distant. He knew that if he couldn't break free then he would go into cardiopulmonary arrest. Or at the very least, his tibia was going to shatter. Lou continued to scream.

Sam snaked an arm around the man's back and managed to free one side of his cuffs. With his left hand, he tried to grab the wrist at his neck, but the man's arm didn't move a single inch. In fact, incensed by Sam's resistance, the man's grip seemed to tighten even more. Sam could feel himself beginning to pass out. He mustered the last of his strength, and in one last-ditch effort plunged the cutter from his cuff link into the man's back.

The grip around Sam's neck loosened right away. Sam continued to slash at the man's back. The man slumped forward. The stab shouldn't have been fatal. Sam pushed the man's body off himself and stood up. Then he simply tapped lightly on the pod and began to walk toward the shelter where the Evo-devo Biologist was waiting for him.

MIDWEST REGION // EVO-DEVO BIOLOGIST'S SHELTER

The likeness of the man destined to save this world flickered onto the monitor. It was an image of an unshaven porter with his hair tied at the back of his head. It was Sam Porter Bridges. The sole member of Bridges II. In this small, dim, and gloomy room that the Evo-devo Biologist both worked and lived in, the monitor seemed to glow all the more brightly with him.

She was excited because this man was about to come here and connect her lonely outpost to a vast new world.

It had been two days since Heartman had let her know that Sam was on his way, and when she estimated the distance between Heartman's lab and her own, she was sure that he would be arriving any time now. Her colleague had already sent her a message letting her know that Sam had dropped by. The Geologist had gone on and on about how wonderful it had been to use the Chiral Network to restore all the materials, data, and theories that had been previously lost. Every word of his message oozed excitement and hope.

He also reported that since he had been posted out here, he had been steadily investigating the local strata, and had discovered something that seemed to link past mass extinctions with the Death Stranding. A fossil Beach.

That alone would topple the prevailing Big Five theory. Once the Chiral Network covered the entire continent they could expect to make even greater discoveries. The Geologist ended his message with how much he hoped that Sam would reach her place soon, too.

Now, Sam was finally about to arrive. The Evo-devo Biologist had shared her hypothesis with Heartman and her other researcher colleagues, and now she wanted to verify it. She also had something she needed to ask Sam in particular. It was about a porter who had made deliveries here a few times in the past. She accepted it was unlikely that Sam would know him, but still, she wanted to know what had happened to the man.

"Did you hear about all that weird stuff that's been bubbling up out west lately?" The porter made a funny expression as he stored his cargo. "Would you happen to know anything about that, EV?"

EV was a nickname the porter had given the Evo-devo Biologist. Her real name was of Scandinavian origin and the porter, knowing he would never remember it, had opted to call her by her profession. EV was a shortened version of "evolutionary developmental biologist." Technically, she should have been called ED, but that was beside the point.

When she pointed out the mistake to the porter, he simply brushed it off with a "Don't sweat the tiny details. EV sounds like Eve."

This porter had been delivering cargo to EV ever since she had first come out here with Heartman and the others on Bridges I. Bridges had their own porters, but there had been a labor shortage, so they had enlisted the help of a voluntary porter organization. This man was a courier from Fragile Express.

A lot had happened since they first met. Her friend from Bridges I, Mama, had fallen victim to a terrorist attack, and

Middle Knot City had been wiped off the map in a nuclear blast. Terrorism was rife in this area, too. Ever since Bridges I had come here espousing about how they were going to rebuild America, they had met violent resistance from the separatists, who claimed that Bridges were "invaders" coming for their freedom. They were out there waiting, minds made up and guns in hand. But the porter still came regularly.

The strange substance the porter had asked her about was the tar that was bubbling up from under the ground. Although, to be more accurate, it was more tar-like. And just as the porter had guessed, it interested EV greatly. It was one of the inexplicable phenomena that had begun to occur after the Death Stranding. No one knew its structure, its properties, or where it originally came from, but EV had heard a theory that it welled up out of places connected to the Beach. And if she could investigate that, it might bring her one step closer to understanding the origin of the Death Stranding. The only thing standing in her way was the threat of terrorism if she went out west to investigate.

"Then I'll bring some back for you," the porter offered.

EV thought he was kidding. There was a possibility that this substance was connected to the Beach. It wasn't safe to go near without the proper expertise and equipment. Collecting something like that was the job of Bridges.

After EV saw the porter off she forgot about the porter's offer, brushing it off as a casual joke.

Then, three months later, the porter returned. Together with a case of the tar.

But even through the hologram, EV could tell that the man's vibe and appearance had dramatically changed. In the past, the porter had been a diligent young worker embarking on an apprenticeship, but now he seemed more like a shellshocked soldier. EV had never actually seen a soldier in real life, but the cylindrical device on his shoulder somehow also reminded her of them. There was a separate round container equipped to the left-hand side of his chest.

"This is a Bridge Baby. It can access the Beach," the man explained, caressing the pod attentively. "It was all thanks to this that I was able to get that for you."

The man pointed at the case of tar. His voice sounded hoarse and exhausted. The case contained five reinforced glass cylinders. Each one was filled with a black liquid.

"A scientist like you might make fun of me for saying this, but this world isn't what it seems to be. What we see with the naked eye is but one part. It's really made up of layer after layer after layer. When I use this Bridge Baby, I can see one of the layers that my eyes can't. When I went to collect this stuff, I got the shock of my life. There were holes everywhere. And I don't mean in the ground, I mean in the empty space around everything else. There's a hole there, too." The porter pointed at the space above her head and EV ducked.

"It's okay. It's so small that I barely even noticed it, but the holes the tar comes out from are much bigger. They're big enough for a human to pass through. I bet they lead back to the Beach."

EV imagined a cartoon of Swiss cheese in her head. She wondered if those holes were traces of a dimension that mankind's perception and thought didn't extend to. And this equipment could visualize them?

"I was able to get the tar using this Bridge Baby to avoid the holes," the porter continued. A smile spasmed across the porter's face for the first time since he'd arrived.

EV was trying to decide how to thank the man when he stopped her.

"I don't need your gratitude. Just tell me what you think this stuff is," he said.

Of course she would. EV's face broke into a smile, but the porter's expression remained deadly serious. It was starting to give her the creeps.

"This tar began to appear after the Death Stranding. You know that much, don't you?" EV asked. "Just like the timefall, the Beach, the cryptobiotes and the BTs. Chiral matter, too. Now, none of these things are good for humans. They all make it harder for us to survive. So, think back to when life first emerged on this planet, when the atmosphere was full of methane and carbon. It was completely different to how it is now. Then, one type of life called cyanobacteria emerged. It was an algae that fed on photosynthesis, and much like the algae of modern times, produced enormous quantities of oxygen. So much so that it filled the entire atmosphere with it. Unfortunately, much of the other life on this planet had evolved to rely on the carbon and methane. Oxygen was toxic to it. So, what couldn't adapt to this new environment went extinct.

"Tar and timefall are the defining features of the post-Stranding ecosystem. As you just heard, sudden environmental changes such as these invariably lead to the extinction of organisms that fail to adapt. Those that do adapt do so by virtue of 'enhancers'—the regions of DNA that grant successful organisms their advantages. These genetic factors are the key to evolution. But there are genes which have the opposite effect, those which disadvantage organisms. 'Extinction factors,' as they have been called. Some people say that the existence of these traits is proof that mankind is headed for extinction, but I don't think so. Sure, extinction factors are supposedly responsible for the extinction nightmares suffered by those with DOOMS. In fact, that's why they call it DOOMS—after ruin and the Last Judgment. But that doesn't mean that the existence of those with DOOMS has to usher in the extinction of mankind. On the contrary, perhaps those who can perceive extinction, can help us avoid it. Extinction factors are a broad concept that present across biology, psychology, and sociology. Their presence in these areas suggests that humans may already be adapting to this change in the environment.

"In the end, enhancers and extinction factors are the seeds of advancement and obsolescence. Such factors may lie dormant within us all, a choice waiting to be made. For every being since the advent of life itself.

"On the other hand, there's also a theory that hypothesizes the existence of something that blows past the millions of years that natural evolution and extinction takes—Extinction Entities. The Beach connects the worlds of the living and the dead, and the BTs came here via the Beach. Then, through contact with the living, they cause voidouts that turn everything back to nothing. In other words, BTs exist to drive humanity to extinction. Some people may disagree, but I believe that it is the BTs who are the Extinction Entities."

"Extinction Entities? Do those really exist?" the porter asked. After listening to EV quietly for a while, the color in the porter's face suddenly changed. "Then I guess extinction is a fate that we can't escape. But if it's already set in motion, why do we still struggle? Why do we crawl shamefully all over the earth delivering cargo, just to keep us here that little bit longer?"

The change in the porter's tone was so drastic, it was like he had suddenly switched personalities with someone. EV couldn't look at him any longer. It was like he was possessed.

"The same species can't remain dominant forever. Humanity can't be the only ones to survive extinction. Do you think the ammonites and the dinosaurs resisted extinction like we do? Of course not! They graciously accepted their destinies. They weren't just unintelligent enough to avoid it. Humanity goes around recording and sharing our past to help us predict our future, and because of that we just assume that we can change our destiny. That we can overcome something like the Death Stranding. But it's all lies. This world doesn't need us anymore. It's trying to evict us to make room for the next species. And the harder we try and the harder we struggle against it, the more we sully it. Being holed up in here, I bet you have no idea how beautiful the outside world is, do you? How harsh it is? The world didn't change into what it is now for mankind's sake. It's trying to change for the life that comes next."

The porter was talking so fervently he was foaming at the mouth. EV didn't have anything she could say back to him.

EV believed there was a way out of this situation. Wasn't that why she came here in the first place? Wasn't that why she continued this research all alone?

But, contrary to the porter's beliefs, EV knew the outside world. She had seen and experienced it through her fieldwork and when she first came here with Bridges I. That was why she couldn't refute him. She, herself, had been struck so many times by the virgin beauty of this world. And the ugliness of the cities that had been erected in its nooks and crannies.

"Why don't we just let ourselves go extinct? We don't have the right or the means to prevent it anyway. We should at least bow out gracefully. The ammonites and the dinosaurs managed it well enough. At least we'd be left with a little dignity. I heard about the Extinction Entities, too. Someone told me that an Extinction Entity is the one creating these BTs and connecting them with this world. And ever since I got this new equipment, I've come to believe that they really exist," the porter went on, showing EV the equipment on his chest. "This is a bridge that connects this world and that world. Our boss gave me this. He said that we are no longer just for transporting cargo. We're to bring 'extinction' over from that world and vacate our position on this one for the next generation of life."

EV had no answers for the man. She was afraid. The porter in front of her was no longer the porter she had once known. It was like he had been brainwashed by some cult. He was trapped in this extreme thinking that perceived extinction as being of primary importance. What if the equipment he had on his chest was what was feeding him these lies? But even if that thing attached to him wasn't brainwashing him, could the porter really be right in claiming that it wasn't the BTs that were the Extinction Entities, but something that existed on an even higher plane? There were certainly others who thought so, she couldn't refute him on that point either. Even if he had put the pieces of the puzzle together wrong, what could they do if the concepts they signified were real?

EV came back to her senses when the porter broke down crying like a child.

"What's happening to me?! Every night I have the same dream. It's always a dream of extinction. They frighten me," he sobbed. "I'm all alone on the Beach and even if I scream, no one answers. No matter how far I walk, the view never changes. Even though I know it's a dream, I feel like an infinite amount of time is passing and I can't breathe. I try to kill myself. Time and time again. But no matter what I do, it never works. Something comes toward me from beyond the sea instead. I try to see what it is, but I can't. I'm so petrified that I can't even run away. I'm so afraid that I try to kill myself before it can get to me, but that never works either. I'm so scared. Then it kills me."

The porter sniffled and looked up at EV. It looked like his expression was back to normal. The real him was back. At least, that was what EV wanted to believe.

"This thing, this equipment, it whispers to me. It tells me that I'm only afraid because I can't see what the thing I dream about is. It tells me that it'll show me what it looks like, that it'll tell me what extinction really looks like. Then I won't be afraid anymore. It tells me that I won't be afraid of dying or extinction anymore," the porter blabbered on.

EV nodded. She explained that the reason why the Death Stranding was such a terrifying phenomenon was because no one understood it. No one knew why the BTs, the Beach, the timefall, or the tar appeared, and that was why they feared it and walled themselves away in their cities. That was why people like EV had to keep on digging.

The porter feebly shook his head at her words. "But you've not been given the answers yet. And even if you spend years studying this tar I've brought you, we're all doomed to die before you ever understand anything." The porter stood up, followed by EV. "Promise me if you do find anything out about that tar, EV, that you'll tell me."

EV wanted him to wait. She understood what he was saying, but she wanted him to know that she was determined to find the clues that would help them sidestep extinction. But before she could open her mouth, the porter had disappeared. The hologram equipment that the pair used to converse had been switched off, but he should still have been physically present nearby. EV hurried up to the ground level entrance. As the doors to ground level opened, she was enveloped in the light pouring in from outside. She squinted in the brightness.

"Wait!" she screamed. But the porter had already left her shelter and was walking away. All she could see was his back. "Wait!" she shouted again. But the porter didn't do so much as even turn his head.

A few days later, reports of a terrorist attack came through from a colony outside of Mountain Knot City. A voidout had killed Heartman's wife and daughter, and left Heartman himself wandering the border between life and death.

EV carried on with her work. It had been two years since that conversation with the porter, but she still hadn't managed to fulfil her promise to him. Not because she hadn't seen him, but because she hadn't uncovered a single thing.

EV's job wasn't just to analyze the tar, but when she thought about it, that jet-black substance had been the only thing on her mind for some time now.

Now that Sam Porter had embarked on his quest to connect the Chiral Network, and the scientists in the east had been able to gradually restore some of the archives, EV had sent away for any data pertaining to Extinction Entities and the tar.

But since her area hadn't been connected yet, she had to rely upon the meagre telecommunications systems she was currently equipped with, and she was getting impatient. Forget movies, she couldn't even receive large images. All she could do was rely on a network of waystations to receive text data. But even when she received data in text format, she had lost count of the number of times it had arrived broken or with bits missing.

There was also the issue of the tar. The tar that had been bubbling up in the west had been more active recently, but she didn't know why. She hadn't even managed to find out where the tar was coming from in the first place, so there was nothing she could do.

Not only had the scattered bubbling springs of tar begun to increase in number, they were also getting larger and now formed a line that ran north to south. The points where the tar was bubbling forth had started to form a small river, and the area had become known as the tar belt. It continued to expand and had even swallowed up some nearby waystations that were supposed to be used for the Chiral Network. It was impossible to predict what the tar would do next, so they couldn't get too close.

To EV, Sam Porter was the messiah who would restore the waystation and finally connect her up to the Chiral Network. And he was due any day now.

Then the day finally arrived.

When she thought about it, it had indeed been quite a while since she had last received a visitor. It was because once EV found out that Fragile Express, the porter company that her porter friend had worked for, had effectively come under the control of Higgs, she had no choice but to rely on the few porters from Bridges or freelancers instead. When people did drop by it made her feel less nervous. But not this time. Sam was bringing the Q-pid and EV couldn't contain her excitement.

As soon as Sam entered the shelter, the delivery terminal activated and a hologram was projected into the air.

The projection showed the silhouette of a slender girl. She was a scientist named EV. He noticed her expression stiffen. Sam wasn't surprised, he hardly had the easiest face to look at. He hadn't looked in the mirror lately, but he assumed he was covered in blood, sweat, and mud like usual. Sam wasn't in the mood for greetings or explaining himself. The woman should have been notified that Sam was on his way, since even though this was a shelter, it was still under the control of Bridges. He was a visiting colleague, after all. Sam cleared security, but the woman's face was still stiff.

When Sam traced her gaze, he noticed that her attention was fixed on Lou.

"It is you, isn't it, Sam?" The woman's voice was trembling slightly. It looked like she was scared of the pod.

"I was instructed to come here by Heartman and Bridges. My name is Sam Porter Bridges. I'd like you to let me activate the Chiral Network here. Do you have a problem with that?"

The woman shook her head, but her expression didn't

change in the slightest and she continued staring at Lou. Not bothering to ask her why, Sam took out the Q-pid and held it up. That was when the woman's face finally relaxed.

"Go ahead, Sam, I've been waiting for you. Please connect me right away."

EV thanked Sam and he connected her shelter to the UCA.

"I'm sorry, Sam, but can I ask you something? That thing on your chest… what is it for?"

Sam faltered for a second at the abrupt question. Did she mean in the practical sense, or the theoretical sense? Sam supposed he could sum it up by explaining that the BB was used for sensing BT, but he knew the BB was more than just that. Still, did he need to explain so much to this scientist who was seeing a BB for the first time?

EV watched Sam try to come up with an answer and seemed to accept it when he couldn't. It was like she had guessed that there wasn't really an answer either way.

"I used to know a porter who carried one of those things," she told him.

Sam felt his own face stiffen this time, as he remembered the terrorist group he had encountered on his way here.

"He told me that when he used it, he could see all kinds of things. He said it had told him that humanity was destined for extinction. Does yours do the same, Sam?"

"No. This little one is my partner. Lou tells me when I'm in danger. If I didn't have this BB, I would never have made it all the way here alone," Sam answered.

If what the woman said was true, it meant that the thing attached to the porter's chest was no BB, it just happened to look like one. Then it struck him. The equipment that Higgs and the other terrorists had strapped to their chests might not have been BBs either. Or at the very least, they weren't the same as Lou. Maybe that was why Lou was so upset when they had encountered them.

"The porter I knew cried," EV recalled. "He said he was scared. He said that he was having dreams of extinction and had become unable to resist them any longer. He confessed that to me... then he never came back."

Lou gave a cry. It wasn't out of fear, but out of sadness. This had never happened before. Lou was looking up at Sam from inside the pod. Sam looked into Lou's eyes, but he couldn't tell where Lou's sadness was coming from.

When Sam looked back up, EV's hologram had disappeared. Perhaps she had finally given up on getting any answers at all out of him. Maybe she was just satisfied now she was hooked up to the Chiral Network. In any case, Sam's work here was done. It didn't matter how EV felt about things. Sam was worried about his crying BB and turned to leave. Something Sam couldn't put his finger on lingered in this place. Harsh noise echoed around the room. Sam turned back around to see the image of an unfamiliar man projected where EV's hologram had once stood. He was wearing a hood low over his eyes, so Sam couldn't really tell what the man looked like. He wasn't so tall, but Sam could tell that he was made from lean muscle. It was a body that looked like it had been honed through daily labor. The worn and faded suit the man was wearing bore the name "Fragile Express." On his left shoulder was an Odradek and on his chest was a BB. Both were slightly different to the ones that Sam used, but matched the ones the terrorists possessed. That meant that a terrorist was lurking in the basement. Was this a setup? Sam instinctively grabbed for the ID strand around his waist. It was the only thing he had to hand that could be used as a weapon.

"This is goodbye," the man began. "My body no longer belongs to me. I'm not afraid anymore."

The man's Odradek began to rotate, but Lou didn't react in the slightest. This was a recording. It was probably a message meant for EV. So, this was the porter she had been talking about?

"We cannot run away from our destiny and our destiny is extinction. Extinction will open the door to a brand-new world. That's why I have to take out that city."

What did he just say? Was he declaring an act of terrorism? Sam sensed someone's presence appear behind the hologram. The door that led to the basement floor opened. Standing there was EV. Her face was pale as she rushed up the steps toward Sam.

"EV, I believe that what you're doing is noble," the porter's hologram continued to speak. "You think that studying the past will lead to a better future. I used to think so too, back when I was a porter. You know, America was already gone by the time I was born. I don't really have any memories from when I was kid. Don't even remember what my parents looked like. All I remember is the face of Fragile's pop."

EV stood next to Sam, looking at the man.

"That man took me in and raised me. He told me all about how America used to be. He said America was so free before it all came crumbling down. He told me it had its problems that he wasn't proud of, but that the spirit of the ancestors who had founded the country still lived on. He told me we should look at the destruction of America as a fresh start. That we would build America again with our own hands. Even after the man died and Fragile took over the organization, that never changed." The porter fell silent. He was looking up, as though he was searching for something. Sam and EV watched attentively. "But we're never going to get America back. Bridges' Chiral Network is only going to build an invisible wall around it. That's not the real America. Or so Higgs says."

Sam's jaw stiffened at the mention of Higgs's name.

"No matter how much we struggle, while we're human we're never going to be able to build a perfect country on this earth. We can spout whatever grand ideas we like, any country we create will be nothing more than a sham. Higgs says that if we really want to make the perfect country, then we have to stop being human. That's why extinction is coming for us."

How ridiculous. Sam's inner voice of reason told him that this man was just rambling to justify his act of terrorism. But there was a part of Sam that couldn't deny what the madman was saying.

"See you, EV. I'm going to wipe out a colony near Mountain Knot City. It's okay, I promise you they won't suffer. The voidout will send them to the other side instantaneously. Then they'll travel to the land of the dead and finally be released from the curse of being human. It's all part of the Extinction Entity's plan."

The hologram froze like it was stuck in time. EV weakly shook her head and stared at Sam. She looked like she wanted Sam to comfort her, but there was nothing that Sam could do.

Lou cried out, breaking the silence. Lou's cries didn't sound as sad as before, but Sam could still feel so much emotion in them that they hurt. Lou's cries were so full of fear and anger that it was almost like they would shatter the pod. As if in response to Lou's cries, the image displayed by the hologram began to crumble, decomposing into fine particles.

But then the diffusing particles began to clump back together again. An invisible force was binding them together to create a different image entirely. Over its face was a hood, within it a dully glowing golden mask. There was an Odradek on the figure's shoulder and a pod on their chest.

It was Higgs. Sam couldn't see the eyes under the mask, but he just knew that the man's gaze was right on him. It was such an intense stare that it didn't seem like it could belong to a hologram. This didn't appear to be a recording. In fact, to Sam it seemed almost certainly to be some kind of interactively generated image.

"Thank you, Sam, for connecting up the Chiral Network for me." Higgs bowed his head dramatically.

"It's simply breathtaking. Now I understand why you were in such a hurry to finish it. I can restore the memories of the past. Color me surprised. I had no idea that was possible.

"The Chiral Network runs through the Beach, and the Beach connects to the realm of the dead and all the lost history found within it. That's a big deal. At best, I thought it would only be able to piece together and restore digital data."

It was clear that Higgs was trying to goad Sam with his overdramatic gestures and tone. Sam gritted his teeth and exerted as much self-control as possible. Lou seemed to pick up on his anger and drew into a tight ball.

"Keep it up, Sam. The idea of the UCA coming back doesn't exactly instill me with joy, but this… this is great. And if I have this, I won't have to make all that effort to jump through the Beach anymore just to find you, I can just give you another call."

Higgs reached straight out at Sam. Sam pulled back instinctively, but Higgs's arms stretched right through the BB pod, piercing through Lou, and into his chest. Sam was frozen stiff and couldn't move. Higgs broke into a cruel laugh.

"Don't be scared. I'm just a hologram. Just a virtual image. It's not like you're being touched by a person. Guess the Chiral Network is perfect for someone with your condition. Good luck."

Higgs withdrew his arms but something shone at his fingertips. Sam reasoned in his head that it had to be a trick of the hologram, but soon he couldn't keep his shaking at bay. Higgs hung the item that had flashed around his own neck. It was a golden accessory—Amelie's *quipu*.

Sam was in excruciating pain as he felt like his heart was being crushed in his chest, and he couldn't make a sound. His head spun and he fell to his knees.

"I'll be waiting for you on the Beach," Higgs said as he disappeared. Still on his knees, Sam looked up to see that there was nothing left where the man had just been standing. The pain in his chest had also vanished like it was never really there in the first place.

EV looked at Sam. Her face was drained of color.

"Are you okay?" she asked.

Sam nodded and got up.

"How about you? It seems like this place is connected to Higgs now."

"I'm fine," EV answered. "Just a little shaken up. I never expected something so terrifying to come through the Chiral Network. But at least that wasn't all it brought. Now I know that we can restore the past that wasn't recorded onto media." She was talking about the recording of the porter. "I had a feeling that he had gotten himself involved in terrorism, but it still hurt to hear it from the horse's mouth. To be honest with you, Sam, I can't deny the things that he said, even though I'm certain he was brainwashed by Higgs. But I suppose the important thing is not trying to disprove my friend's points, but to find a way to overcome them. And that includes all the things that Higgs said, too. We must keep expanding the Chiral Network and identify the EE to do that. I'm not afraid of what that means. Sure, this situation is frightening. But I don't have time to be scared."

Sam reassured EV that he understood. The theory of extinction that Higgs whispered into his followers' ears was a doctrine touted by the Extinction Entity. But Bridges' idea of America was nothing more than doctrine either. The only way to break free from them both was to give up on being human. Extinction and prolonging life were just opposite sides of the same coin.

"Sure, this situation is frightening. But I don't have time to be scared."

EV's words echoed around Sam's head, so Sam decided to get out of there while he could still hear them. Any excess noise now, and her determination and the confidence it gave him might just vanish. Sam put his pack back on and left the shelter without saying another word.

Three days had passed.

Sam had been worried about the rugged terrain and fickle mountain weather, but apart from that, it had been smooth sailing. Now he had connected all three shelters, all that was left for him to do was to reconstruct the waystation near the tar belt. EV had sent him a message while he had been walking.

She informed him that she had managed to restore several research reports into past mass extinctions. One report caught Sam's eye. It was data that suggested that extinct species other than ammonites and mammoths had been found with umbilical cord-like protrusions extending out of their bodies, including specimens of dinosaurs and trilobites. EV also mentioned the claims that these extinct animals were EEs themselves.

A little while after Sam received EV's message, he got a call from Heartman too, just as he was getting close to where the waystation was going to be.

<Sam! Do you read? You're about to hit the tar belt. Luckily, there doesn't seem to have been much

damage to the equipment, thanks to you. Now all
you need to do is take a look at the installation
point for us. Anyway, listen. We have less time
than I thought we would.>

Time before his heart gives out again, or time before extinction
comes for us?

<I mentioned this before, but the site we have
chosen was an original candidate for the waystation
we lost to the tar belt.>

Sam remembered. They had planned to use this site but
had ended up abandoning it.

<There were some concerns about safety. This
time, we're going to repair it and try operating
it as a knot. There are some places in this world
where it is easy to connect to the Beach. These
are places and objects of worship and holy grounds
and the like. People often refer to these places
as power spots. You could even say that megaliths,
like the Pyramids and Stonehenge, are traces of
where mankind attempted to make contact with the
Beach. Now, Beaches may vary from person to person,
but there are some places in particular that many
people find themselves drawn to, and the Beach is
inextricably connected to religious and spiritual
things. In other words, those places can be used
as knots on the Chiral Network. However, there is

also a danger of getting too close to the Beach. Bridges I took note of that and originally built the waystation somewhere else. That was the one that got swallowed up by the tar. But under the current circumstances, we now have no other option but to use the foundations of the original abandoned site. Luckily, the basic systems are still intact. Anyway, once you arrive, I want you to do something for me—check the status of your BB. It shouldn't be difficult. Just see if it's reacting to anything. It could laugh, cry, or even show fear. As long it shows some kind of reaction, it means that where you are is an access point to the Beach… Very perceptive, Sam! You just thought of the Knot Cities, didn't you?>

He hadn't. But Heartman kept on talking. Sam heard the <Five minutes to cardiac arrest> countdown begin in the background.

<The Knot Cities are built in places where the timefall doesn't fall. Theoretically, they're the places that are farthest away from the Beach. So why do we use those cities as large-scale communications bases? That's right, Sam! Places where many people gather are just like holy places and places of worship. Where there are as many Beaches as people. But at the same time, the cities are secular, with

no single unifying belief system. To solve this contradiction, Bridges I prepared a special system. It's top secret. Even I don't know much about it. In fact, I wasn't even briefed on it. I first heard about it from Deadman. He said he discovered it while he was investigating the BB experiments.>

<Two minutes to cardiac arrest> a robotic voice warned.

<Listen, Sam! I'm having this conversation with you through an old radio. It isn't being relayed back to HQ. It seems like HQ are hiding something about the BBs, about your Lou. It's highly likely that it's linked to the origins of the Chiral Network and the reconstruction of the UCA. Deadman was extremely scared that Die-Hardman was going to find out about our investigation.>

<One minute to cardiac arrest.>

<Anyway, if we don't get the network up and running then we'll never get anywhere. Trust me. Put your faith in this scholar of the Beach!>

The codec went silent and Heartman's three-minute death commenced.

TAR BELT SHORE

So, this is what the apocalypse looks like.

Sam was stood in a world that would usher in mankind's end. Or perhaps it was just the world's physical end. A sea of tar extended so far out westward that Sam had trouble believing that Edge Knot City lay beyond it all.

The shore was littered with masses of toppled jagged rocks and there wasn't a single sign of life to be found. No creeping moss. No microbes that inhabited the sandy soil. The sun was so thickly blocked out by the chiral clouds that covered the sky that Sam had no idea where it was. But it didn't feel like night. It wasn't even dark. A dim light filled the world. In Sam's mind, this was a world where nothing new began and nothing new was ever born.

A cross fit for a giant lay upon this shore of demise. It was made of a rough black iron. It was the apparatus of crucifixion.

But who was here to receive their punishment and atone for their sins? The crucifix lay forgotten on a shore where there was only sin and punishment, and no sign of sinner nor savior. It dawned on Sam that this was the abandoned Chiral Network knot. To him, it felt neither sublime nor ominous. The only distinct feeling he had toward it was the feeling that he didn't want to get any closer to it. Before he knew it, tears were spilling down his face. Sam didn't even need to check for Lou's reaction. He could feel this proximity to the Beach, throughout his entire body. It felt different to when he was in BT territory. Sam had never imagined that such a barren place could exist. Did it have something to do with the abrupt increased activity of the tar? Sam asked himself, looking out over the tar belt that stretched out beyond the crucifix.

If there was a perfect place for a communications knot, this would be it. Sam knew that much. Lou was getting worked up. Unless it was Sam's own uneasiness infecting the BB.

When Sam went to activate the Q-pid receptor, the power supply apparatus rose first, followed by the terminal itself. Sam unloaded the hefty cargo from his back and set it down according to the terminal's instructions. The units connected to the cross one by one and were stored inside. That was when Sam finally realized that the crucifix itself was the communications equipment. He followed the instructions in the message, which prompted him to activate the knot and help up his six metal shards.

An odor filled Sam's nostrils. His vision warped and he felt like he was floating. Tears flowed from the corners of his eyes. Now this area was covered by the Chiral Network. The problem now was what came afterward. Sam sighed in front of the tar belt. *How the hell am I supposed to make it to Edge Knot City?*

"Sam, I knew you could do it. Thanks to you, the relay is back online. So far there are no issues with strength or safety. Lockne's going to keep an eye on this area too, so there shouldn't be any need to worry."

It was Heartman. He was using the terminal's communications function to project his hologram.

"I just got back from the Beach. I've got twenty-one minutes until the next trip, so listen carefully," he continued.

The hologram suddenly disappeared. Maybe the connection was unstable. Or maybe this is what they got for such a hastily cobbled together piece of junk. Sam called Heartman's name out toward the terminal, but there was no reply.

Then, his cuff links activated. Heartman was calling again, requesting voice-only communications. Sam fiddled with his cuff link to pick up.

<I know that the Chiral Network is online now, but I want us to use this older system. I don't want anyone from HQ listening in.>

Sam detected what seemed to be a hint of nervousness in Heartman's voice among all the noise and static. Then, Heartman began to recount his incredible findings.

<I looked at the umbilical cord that you brought in with Mama's body. In reclaiming our past we've uncovered a number of vital clues, and using them I've come up with a theory. When you met with Mama, you experienced a strong antigen—antibody reaction, correct?>

Sam thought back to when he first visited Mama's lab. Heartman was right. Sam had the same feeling as when he approached BT territory. Lou reacted in the same way, too. But

Sam didn't think it was too unusual, given the situation there.

"There was a BT in the room," he explained.

`<There was. But something else may have been causing it. I've discovered large quantities of chiral matter in Mama as well. Not just the usual kind that collects on our skin or on our suits. It's in all her cells—cells that are no longer active.>`

Sam remembered how Mama's breath never showed white in her cold lab, and how she had unfastened her cuff link on one hand so that her vitals couldn't be detected. It was all evidence that pointed toward her being dead. It was only thanks to her connection with her BT daughter that she was able to move in the first place. Sam had surmised that much on his own, but now it looked like there was more.

`<The BT you encountered there was special. It was her child, but also her own soul. Somehow, her` *ka* `and` *ha* `failed to separate. They must have remained connected through the umbilical cord.>`

In other words, Mama was in a state of being both alive and dead. Did that mean that her *ha* and *ka* were both stuck between life and death?

Mama's daughter was like Lou. So if Sam was connected to Lou, did that make him just like Mama? Sam had so many questions, but he didn't feel like asking them out loud. Heartman carried on talking as if he took Sam's silence as an affirmation to continue.

<I have a message for you from Deadman. He says that he's sorry. That you deserved to know what you were carrying, but he couldn't risk Die-Hardman finding out about the case. So he had no choice but to keep it off the books. But thanks to you, Sam, the umbilical cord finally reached me all the way from Capital Knot City.>

"You mean that wasn't Mama's umbilical cord?" Sam asked.

<The umbilical cord was taken from Bridget Strand. Deadman removed it in secret at her request when she was still alive. The cord wasn't attached to a fetus. It was… "outside" her body. She asked him to take care of it. Said it was the key to unlocking the Death Stranding. Bridget's umbilical cord and Mama's body have a lot of things in common. They show no signs of decomposition or necrotization. It's almost like they're frozen in time. Like they've been released from the flow of time in this world. We also detected chiralium in the umbilical cord, just like what we detected in Mama. That means that the president's umbilical cord may have been connected to the Beach.>

Heartman's hypothesis was bold, but what was more shocking was the revelation that the umbilical cord was attached to Bridget. The fact that Amelie was born on the Beach must have been closely related to this umbilical cord.

<Life on Earth has been rocked by many extinctions, great and small, including the Big Five. And if you examine the Earth's strata—its history, if you will—you'll find chiralium deposits and Beach fossils that can be dated to each. What if the manifestation of Beaches and other associated phenomena correspond to extinction-level events? Our Death Stranding could just be the latest of many. The records and research you helped us to recover strongly suggest that we are in the middle of the Sixth Extinction.>

So, it was true. And this time humanity was up for the chopping block? There was no doubt about it now.

<Thanks to the Chiral Network, we've managed to piece together records of other extinct creatures being discovered with umbilical cords. Trilobites, ammonites, dinosaurs. The mammoth, the Iceman. All, without exception, found with umbilical cords. Which is to say that all may have been connected to the Beach. And this, when viewed in the context of the Extinction Entity (EE) Theory that EV is researching, leads me to surmise that organisms with strands are in fact Extinction Entities. You see, Sam, EEs are connected to the Beach via their strands, and it is through this connection that they somehow bring about a Death Stranding.>

Heartman had been speaking so fast that Sam had

barely managed to keep up.

"So you're saying Bridget was an Extinction Entity?"

<It's far too soon to say anything for certain. And since you burned her body, we may never know.>

Sam had a more pressing question on his mind, but wasn't sure how to put it into words. Higgs had referred to Amelie as an Extinction Entity.

<Sam, think. Assume that President Strand was an EE. Isn't it possible that her daughter is, too?> Heartman said, as if he had read Sam's mind.

"So, he kidnaps her for her EE powers or whatever to cause a mass extinction?" Sam mused.

<Perhaps, perhaps not. I doubt a single EE is powerful enough to cause a Death Stranding. Assuming Amelie, or indeed Bridget, is an EE. Although Higgs certainly seems to think she has what it takes.>

Sam knew that whatever Amelie was or was not, they still had to get her back from Higgs.

<One minute to cardiac arrest.>

Sam heard the countdown continue.

<I'm sorry, Sam. Time's up. In any case, we need you to go out west and save Amelie.>

Then the transmission cut out and Sam was left all alone again on the desolate shore. Edge Knot City lay out there somewhere way out west, but all Sam could see was the thick, black sea in front of him.

A fishy smell blew toward him from across the tar belt, the breeze it rode in on tickling Sam's cheeks. Sam may have been successful in activating the waystation's—that gigantic crucifix's—telecommunications terminal, but he had been stuck on the shore for quite a while now, unable to find a way across the tar.

He had walked all along the bank searching for a point to cross on foot, but it had so far all been in vain. Didn't Bridges know how bad it was out here?

Perhaps they had just been optimistic that if anyone could find a way across, Sam the repatriate would. But he couldn't. He couldn't think of a single solution. Even though he had reconnected the country this far, even though it was now just a final push until he reached Amelie, he was stuck.

—*London Bridge is falling down, falling down, falling down.*

Sam could hear the song that Amelie always sang for him on the Beach when he was a boy. He looked around but there was no one and nothing to be found. It was just Sam. The bridge had fallen and now there was nothing else he could do. He couldn't connect back to Amelie across the tar.

—*That's not true, Sam.*

It was as if he could hear her. The wind picked up. This time it brought another voice with it.

—*Do you still not get it? Or do you just not want to?*

The tar was swelling upwards, forming the shape of a human being. Higgs.

"Amelie is an Extinction Entity," Higgs began. "She may take the form of a woman, but she is connected to the realm of the dead. She connects all life to death. Heartman is right. All the past extinctions were caused by Extinction Entities like her. There's no denying it. It's the truth of this universe. This universe was created in an explosion. When stars explode their fragments produce new ones. The explosion of extinction gives way to new life. Listen here, Sam. We're not just going extinct, we're creating the next phase of existence."

It was all word play. Higgs was manipulating the language to affirm his path of extinction and affirm his desire to destroy. Sam's body burnt hot with anger. His clenched fists were trembling.

"That's the cross that humanity has to bear." Higgs pointed at the waystation and laughed. "It seems like there is someone working for Bridges with a sense of irony. I'll connect with Amelie, stick her on that thing and finally put extinction into motion."

"Higgs!" Sam shouted, rushing toward the belt of tar.

"Oh, still got some fighting spirit left in you, Sam? Then may the best man win," Higgs sneered, holding up a finger. Tar was sticking to both of Sam's legs. It seemed to be attempting to pull him down like it had a mind of its own. Before Sam knew it, the tar was already waist deep.

"Good luck, Sam," Higgs called. "I'll be waiting on the Beach."

Higgs disappeared. The tar surged into a wave, attacking Sam from above.

Sam couldn't see a thing. He couldn't hear, either. He was trapped in a sticky black torrent and being washed toward the depths of the earth. He was falling forever toward its center—

Sam was lost in a dark hallway.

All he could hear was his own breathing, the sound of sticky footsteps, and the beating of his own heart. They echoed all around him. The sounds he made shook his eardrums and reverberated inside his head. Infinitely looping, it was starting to drive Sam mad. He was walking around inside the guts of some gigantic creature. Never getting digested and never getting shat back out. He was just wandering with no idea where the exit was. Then he noticed that Lou wasn't with him. There was no Odradek on his shoulder. In fact, he wasn't wearing anything at all. Sam was naked and trapped in a place he didn't know.

He sank down to the floor and hung his head. He heard the sound of a heart. It was throbbing rhythmically without interruption. That's when he realized that he was hearing the beating from outside. The heart that should have been in his chest dropped like a stone, and elsewhere the other heart moved.

Then it clicked. This had to be the inside of his own body. He was lost and aimlessly wandering in a maze of his own guts. Unable to be at peace with himself, he had become lost inside himself. Sam wondered if destroying himself would release him from this shell. Or would he just die together with it?

"You're in the same state as the confused masses on this planet. They all believe that the world is here to accommodate them. It doesn't matter that it's all coincidental. It doesn't matter that if it's destroyed, they'll die too. In their heads, they're its kings and it'll do what they tell it to do."

Higgs's voice echoed around the internal maze, snapping Sam back to reality.

Sam had been brought back by Higgs. A dissonant sound echoed softly. When Sam woke up, the world looked twisted. Sam instantly felt nauseous, like his stomach was full of rocks. Unable to bear it, Sam got on all fours and vomited. He threw up an inexplicable amount of jet-black liquid that looked like mud. A stench that contained whiffs of blood and rotting flesh pierced Sam's nostrils. It felt like his body was rotting from the inside out.

Sam had no idea where he was. When he looked over his shoulder with as-of-yet unfocused eyes, all he could make out was the tar belt. Had he made it across?

"Welcome, Sam Bridges."

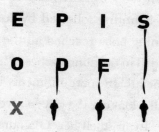

HIGGS

It was Higgs. He was hovering several inches above the tar.

Sam shouted his name and shot to his feet. Higgs responded with exaggerated surprise.

"Keep your voice down. You don't want to scare the poor girl away, do you? You came all this way to see her, didn't you? That's why I did you a favor and brought you over that tar belt. How about a little gratitude and respect?" Higgs said theatrically as if amused by Sam's loss for words, and pointing behind Sam with one hand. Sam turned around to find the silhouette of a city. It was Edge Knot City. It was his final stop. The place where he would find Amelie.

Higgs snapped his fingers. An upside-down rainbow appeared high in the skies above the city, which was subsequently drowned out by thick black clouds. There were several flashes of lightning followed by roars of thunder. Some of the lightning bolts reached all the way down into the city and exploded in dazzling flashes of light. The clouds began to rain timefall. In mere moments it turned into a torrential downfall, cloaking the city in a veil of rain.

"She's in there. I can smell her. Of course, I wouldn't've known for sure if it wasn't for you and your wonderful network."

Sam turned toward the voice, but there was no one there. Just a floating golden mask.

"Bless your heart," Higgs whispered in Sam's ear. Sam jumped away. Higgs's face had been just inches away from his own and his cockiness had snapped Sam back to his senses. Sam looked back, but Higgs was no longer there. Just his golden mask floating in midair.

"Thank you kindly," Higgs whispered, his words coming from the mask.

It was obvious Higgs was enjoying toying with Sam. Sam knew that he mustn't take the bait, but he could no longer control his rising anger. He stretched out his arm in an attempt to grab the golden mask and the gas mask behind it. But all his hand managed to grab was thin air. Higgs had disappeared again. With nothing to grab onto, Sam lost his balance and fell forward. His palms hit the ground, but when he tried to lift his hands back up, he couldn't move them. Tar was oozing from the rock below them. It covered the palms of Sam's hands like an amorphous creature, coiled around his wrists and bound him in place.

Higgs was approaching again. As Sam looked up at Higgs from the ground, with his hands tied, he looked like a criminal begging for forgiveness. His face began to burn with disgrace and humiliation. Higgs squatted down and brought his own face close. He grabbed Sam by the hair and with his free hand removed his golden mask.

His true face didn't look like the face of a destroyer. In fact, there was a delicateness to it. Like that of a philosopher. Or maybe it betrayed the truth-seeker in him that had eventually been caught up in this doctrine of extinction.

"Sam Bridges." A snake-like tongue poked out from between his captivating red lips and licked Sam's cheek. It was cold, like a kiss of the dead. But Sam's face was getting hotter and hotter in anger.

"I'm not the only one wearing a mask," Higgs said as his hand released Sam's hair and, with a wave, his golden mask appeared.

"There's your boss man, that woman... And... oh, let's not forget little ol' you." Before he had even finished speaking, Higgs was pressing the mask onto Sam's face. The mask immediately hugged Sam's facial contours as if it had been made for him. It was like he was wearing another layer of skin. One that had melted the real skin on Sam's face and fused with it. It covered his eyes, nose, and mouth. He couldn't breathe. His head felt like it would explode out of pain and anger. The inside of the mask that was stuck to Sam's skin was cold and clammy. Just like Higgs's tongue. Sam finally managed to free his hands, which had been stuck to the ground by the tar. He dug his nails into the mask in an attempt to tear it off, but its surface was hard as crystal. No matter how much he struggled, the mask wouldn't budge. In fact, it was Sam's nails that got ripped off instead, covering his hands in blood.

"It's okay. It's okay. I know it ain't easy wearing a mask all the time."

Maybe it was because the mask was covering Sam's eyes that it felt like Higgs was speaking right inside his head.

His body craved oxygen. It began to convulse.

"But now the mask can come off, right? Both yours and mine," Higgs sneered.

A burning pain blazed across Sam's face as if the mask had ripped the skin away with it. As it came off, Sam fell forward onto the ground. Higgs mercilessly grabbed Sam by the hair and held his face up. He thrust his free hand in front of it. In his fist was Amelie's *quipu*.

"I got this from Amelie," Higgs stated.

No. Sam shook his head. He had been the one who gave it to Amelie. Amelie would never give it to someone like Higgs.

"Mmm... poor sweet Amelie. She's holed up on a Beach nearby. Tell you what. What say we make it a race, hm?

Whoever wins gets to usher in the end of days. Nothing like the eve of extinction to bring focus to the mind. Makes folks honest. There'll be no need for masks soon," Higgs said, replacing his own. "But, I wonder—when you look death in her eye, will you blink? If you want to chicken out, now's the time to do it."

Higgs disappeared. A large clap of thunder boomed from the direction of Edge Knot City. Sam could see the timefall continue to pour down on the city, speeding up its demise.

Higgs may have gone, but black clouds still hung over Edge Knot City. The closer Sam got to it, the harder it rained. Sam had heard that this whole area was desert before the Death Stranding. The original coastline of the North American continent had been farther west than Edge Knot City was now, but that coastline had been significantly cut back because of the bigger explosions during the initial phase of the disaster. As a result, one of the manmade cities from the era of the United States of America, which used to be in the middle of the desert, found itself located right on the West Coast. It became the prototype for Edge Knot City. Its original name was Santa Maria.

The sandy soil was already saturated and, without anywhere to go, the water had begun to form into rivers. Sam had his hood all the way down over his face to protect himself from the timefall, but that solution only offered a temporary peace of mind. All he could do was cover Lou's pod with both hands and continue to walk. His soaked porter suit degraded more and more with every sheet of rain.

He was almost at the outer rim of the city. Edge Knot wasn't like the other knot cities. It had quite a complex structure.

—*It's the result of conflicting ideologies.*

Sam thought back to something Die-Hardman had said in a briefing. He wasn't even sure when it had taken place. Sam hadn't spoken to the director for a while now, and now that Deadman and Hardman had aired their suspicions about the man, he felt like talking to him even less.

Normal Knot Cities are surrounded by walls. Not only were these walls for protection, but they also formed a feature that clearly separated inside from outside. It was a way of visibly assuring the people who lived there of their autonomy, their independence, and their safety. That's why the Bridges distribution centers were always built alongside the outer walls of the cities and not inside the cities themselves.

But Edge Knot was different.

The people who lived here had inherited the West Coast spirit that had historically prized freedom and independence above all else, and that spirit had once again been demonstrated in how they coped with the aftermath of the Death Stranding.

It was the cities on the West Coast that were the source

of the secessionists. They had developed their own city revival plans, secured their own food and energy provisions, and had built their own distribution system. Edge Knot had its own delivery system and equipment. They didn't have a problem with Bridges borrowing from it. Had no problems with bringing in goods. It was the same as how trade worked in the old world, anyway. They wouldn't permit the building of a new Bridges center within the city. It was seen as equivalent to being occupied and colonized by America again.

Because of this there was no Bridges-owned equipment in the area. However, that didn't mean that Edge Knot City was made up entirely of secessionists. There were a fair number of people who supported the plan to rebuild America. There was also a fixed number of centrists who sat somewhere between the two extremes. In other words, the city was just like a miniature America of old. Its outer wall was made up of many twists, and in some places even two separate walls. It was like a manifestation of the immediate chaotic aftermath of the collapse of the United States.

Bridges had only been permitted to build a small facility on the eastern edge of the city, back when support for American reconstructionism had been stronger. Even the name Edge Knot City was one that only Bridges really used. Most people still called it Santa Maria.

This was the city that Amelie had left for all those years ago.

Originally, Amelie was a special envoy and was supposed to negotiate with the cities diplomatically, joining them to the UCA if both parties agreed. That was the procedure Bridges was supposed to follow. But Santa Maria had imprisoned her instead. And now Sam was going to have to force them onto the Chiral Network under the pretext of saving her. That was Bridges' plan now, but it didn't seem much different from an invasion to Sam.

Even if Santa Maria had already fallen, forcing it onto the Chiral Network would still be an act of aggression.

If Amelie's message was to be believed, the area should have been crawling with BTs. But even if that did turn out to be the case, Sam still wasn't comfortable with the task he had been given. Even if Higgs was after Amelie—Amelie the EE—and Sam had to confront the danger that he posed in his attempts to not only wipe out America, but all of mankind, that didn't mean he could accept what Bridges was up to either. But unless Sam kept on going, nothing would happen. Nothing would change.

They'd never be able to escape from here. Not from this continent. They'd never exist anywhere but here. There were no more promised lands for them like the ones their ancestors sought and fled to. Edge Knot City was as far as their ancestors from the east could take them. And now Sam was going all the way to that dead-end for Bridges. A different type of anger than when he faced Higgs began to bubble up in Sam's chest.

"This is bullshit," Sam found himself muttering out loud. It was a comment aimed at what man called destiny.

Sam had arrived near the entrance to the city, but the Bridges facility that he was looking for was nowhere to be seen. Perhaps it was because of the chiral clouds blocking out the sky, or the influence of the strange magnetic field of this area, but his compass wasn't working. Lou wasn't crying or anything, so he couldn't have been near BT territory.

Sam decided to enter a nearby building to get out of the rain.

As soon as he stepped inside he found himself in awe. Contrary to its rotting exterior, the inside of the building was expansive and magnificent. The walls and floors were clad in faux marble. Pterosaur skeletons hung from the high ceiling. The support that ran through the center of the elegantly curving spiral staircase read: "American Memorial Museum."

In the darkness of the entrance hall, Sam could make out rows of exhibition cases. As he stepped closer, he found most of the glass to be cracked and broken and the cases empty. Sam stopped. He thought he could hear voices coming from upstairs. He held his breath and strained his ears, but the noise had already gone.

Sam crept up the spiral staircase. The first thing he saw

at the top was something that looked like a long car. Farther away lay an overturned gramophone like the one Heartman had at his lab. Cameras, projectors, and what looked like circular canisters of film—relics of the old world—were piled up haphazardly.

Next to those were huge stacks of books. The exhibition cases that lined the walls were full of jumbled collections of bones, both big and small, and fur of animals that Sam couldn't identify. Farther along stood some bulky, deep-set monitors, along with a board that was captioned "Television Sets." And beside those was a strange-looking contraption that was made of a dial inscribed with the numbers 0 to 9 and connected by a cord to some sort of funnel-shaped device. Sam read the description card to find that it was an early telephone. He carried on down the hall.

Sam walked past an exhibit that depicted Native American life, before stumbling on a board that illustrated the concept of the Apollo program. Beside it was a case that was captioned "Moon Rock," but this also stood empty.

There was another exhibition about Columbus's discovery of America and the achievements of Amerigo Vespucci, from whom America took its name. The next exhibition area was a wall plastered with all sorts of images, including prints of red-and-white soup cans, a photograph of a cliff with the enormous faces of four presidents carved into the rock, a picture of a smiling family flashing the peace sign between two people zipped into a duck costume and a mouse costume, and print media that reported on a presidential assassination.

It was all that remained of the American dream. The American history that Bridget taught Sam about when he was young depicted an America that had already been torn to pieces and scattered to the wind. Would stitching America back together with a thread made from the remnants of the American dream really bring back the United States of America that Bridget dreamed of?

Sam didn't think so. If Edge Knot City was a miniature version of America after the Death Stranding, this museum was nothing but a metaphor for the America that had existed before.

Sam heard voices again. It sounded like they were whispering. They seemed to be coming from the next room. Sam exited the room he was stood in, walked down the hallway, and stepped into the room next door.

He was immediately confronted by a row of soldiers with their guns at the ready. Sam instinctively grabbed for his ID strand. But they were just life-sized replicas. Sam breathed a sigh of relief and scanned the room. It was full of life-sized mannequins. It was like a forest of people. When Sam inspected the models of the soldiers more closely, he found they all had different equipment and represented different soldiers throughout the ages. Among them was a soldier that looked just like Cliff.

And there weren't just soldiers. There were men in suits and cowboys wearing huge hats. There were even some models that looked just like the characters found in movies and comic books. On the chest of one mannequin that wore a red and blue body suit was a symbol of a spider, whereas the mannequin dressed in the black bodysuit had pointy ears. The face of the mannequin that had a star on its chest and a shield in hand was half-covered by a mask. Had the past heroes of the United States of America once worn masks?

Sam heard a voice from within the forest of people and made his way deeper, under the watch of America's heroes and cowboys.

—*Sam? Are you there?*

As Sam heard the voice, the mannequins all moved to the side, creating a path.

There was nothing between them now. Before Sam stood a woman clad in bright red.

—*Can you hear me? Sam?*

Amelie? Why? Sam thought he asked, but he couldn't hear the sound of his own voice. It felt like being trapped underwater. He couldn't hear a thing. Then his body became heavy.

—*I can see you, Sam. You came.*

Amelie said that she saw him, but it didn't look like her eyes were perceiving him. Her body and her eyes may have been turned his way, but she seemed vacant, like a mannequin without a soul.

—I'm on the Beach, Sam. Our Beach. The one where I was born. Higgs will never find me here. He can't. So, don't worry.

Contrary to what she was saying, Amelie seemed worried. Sam had no idea how she was accessing here from the Beach. Perhaps she was manipulating Sam's consciousness and speaking to him within a dream. But if what Amelie was saying was the truth, there was no need to be afraid of Higgs. Maybe this dream was just showing Sam what he desperately wanted to be true.

Wake up, he urged himself. *Dreaming about this won't fix anything.*

—Sam, I've kept things from you.

If this is a dream then wake up! Sam begged. The mannequins had formed a circle around Sam and Amelie. All of them were wearing the same mask—Higgs's golden mask.

—I've worn a mask for the longest time. Everything Higgs said about me is true.

All the masks on the mannequins tore away and fell to the floor.

—I could end it all. Us. Mankind. Extinction. That's what I am.

The faces of the mannequins were all flat. There were no eyes, no noses, no mouths. Even the heroes in their masks were the same. Their faces where the masks had been were gone. Even the faces of those heroes that had protected America had been snatched away.

—But it's not what I want to be. All I want is for you and me and everyone in this world... to be whole.

The mannequins collapsed to the floor, each one knocking down the next in a domino pattern.

—*Sam... Promise you'll stop me. Don't let me end it all.*

Amelie began to disappear from her feet up. She was disintegrating into fine particles, just like the BTs.

—*I'll be waiting for you on...*

She disappeared before she could finish her sentence. Sam was left all alone in this room among a pile of soulless mannequins. All alone in a museum that contained the last traces of America.

Sam's memories of leaving the museum were hazy. He had no idea how long he had stood in that empty room after Amelie disappeared. It was as if he had sleepwalked out of there. Before he knew it, he was back outside. The timefall was still falling.

Maybe this museum was the same kind of Beach as Cliff's battlefield. A fantasy museum born of an anonymous someone's lingering attachment toward America that connected to this world.

As if to support Sam's theory, the doors to the museum closed behind him and didn't allow him to enter again.

Sam hadn't realized when he first arrived, but the Bridges facility that he was looking for was right in front of the museum.

Sam's cuff link and ID strand were authenticated, and the door opened, greeting him with the smell of dust and rust. Sam was on alert as he entered, thinking how cave-like it seemed. There was no other sign of life in this manmade metal cavern. Bridges staff must have been stationed here once upon a time, but there was no trace of them left. Sam wondered if the staff here had been slaughtered along with the Bridges I members who had accompanied Amelie all the way to Edge Knot City. Sam fiddled with his cuff link and the delivery terminal rose out of the floor. He had been through this routine so many times now. The receptor that would receive the Q-pid was now ready, so all Sam had to do was hold the six shards of metal to it and activate the Chiral Network. The whole continent would finally be online. Sam would finally be able to put down the baggage he had been forced to carry ever since he had transported Bridget's body to the incinerator.

The America that she had dedicated her life to would be rebuilt. In this empty room, with no other witness, her dream would finally be realized. But there would be no jubilant applause nor shouts of happiness. Sam doubted whether anyone even wanted it to be rebuilt.

Sam removed the Q-pid from under his suit. The shards were floating slightly. It would be the last time Sam performed this rite, and he wanted to get it over and done with quickly. Sam held the Q-pid up to the panel. He was overcome by a severe allergic reaction to the chiralium as per usual.

Now, it's over. I kept my promise to you, Bridget. But as Sam thought those words, he froze. He couldn't believe what he was seeing. Maybe it was because there were so few people on the expedition, or because no sooner had they arrived here than Amelie had been taken. Perhaps the team that had been ordered to install the equipment at this facility had prioritized getting this place up and running first. They probably hadn't had time to make it look nice or think about security. The interior of the equipment that was usually covered in shielding lay exposed. And inside was the same piece of equipment that Sam had attached to his chest.

There was no mistaking it. It was a BB pod. The same kind of BB pod that had been attached to Sam's chest for almost a year now.

Why was it in there? What was inside the pod? Sam moved toward the delivery terminal to check, but it was already sinking back into the floor. As it was swallowed back into the earth, the east and west of the continent were finally reunited.

What have I done? The trembling in Sam's fingers wouldn't stop. It crept up through his arms to his shoulders, until his jaw quivered and his brain shook, and then back down his spine to his waist and his knees until his entire body was convulsing.

What was that? The feeling when he was confronted with something he couldn't comprehend, something his mind was unable to keep up with and a situation that he never could have imagined, was similar to fear. This thing that he didn't understand terrified him.

He sank down onto the floor. He felt helpless and his body wouldn't stop trembling. It felt like this building and the rest of the world were shaking, too.

But he couldn't just cower here. He had to lift this curse here and now. That pod he saw was just another curse to add to his collection. He had to sever every single strand of this chaotic bundle of cursed threads.

Despite his continued shaking, Sam got up. Then he opened the door and went outside.

The timefall was still falling. In the time since he had first arrived in the area, it had gotten worse and worse. The ground in front had been transformed into a sea—a black tar-like sea that seemed to drain the color from the world.

The Odradek activated and transformed into a cross shape. It was pointing forward and was firm in its target. Lou wasn't crying, but when Sam looked into the pod, Lou was curled up into a ball, fists clenched. This wasn't fear. It was hostility. Hostility toward the menace that was approaching. Lou wanted to fight.

Sam followed suit and glared out in front of him.

The timefall was acting as a heavy veil and obscured the looming threat that neared, but Sam could hear something steadily growing louder. The surface of the tar swelled and the remnants of the past were brought forth from the Beach.

An antique Buick and the bones of dinosaurs that had been on display in the museum bobbed up between the waves. The carcasses of the small whales and dolphins were mixed in with the waves of exhibits and became stranded on the shore.

Then Higgs appeared, tearing through the veil of the timefall.

"All preparations for extinction are complete," he proclaimed. His golden mask was slick with rain and was shining strangely like it was made out of the slippery skin of a reptile.

"Well done, Sam. Let me be the first to congratulate you on rebuilding America. You won't hear any gratitude or thanks from Bridget or Amelie. Not even from that director of yours. But you did struggle so. And it must have been so lonely to found a country like that. I'll give you that much."

Thunder roared. Every time Higgs gave the signal with his finger, the sky deafened Sam with claps of thunder like a salute of guns for completing his quest.

"You gave me everything I needed, Sam. A complete Chiral Network. Spread all across America, connecting all them precious little knots," Higgs declared, spreading his arms dramatically wide and looking up at the sky. A flash of lightning lit up the clouds. "I've got the whole world in the palm of my hand."

Higgs pointed up at the sky. Beyond his finger the clouds swirled, and in the center it looked like a red flower blooming. It was the shape of a person with their arms held straight out horizontally like a cross. He couldn't see her face very well because of the long blond hair that hung across it, but the crimson dress told him all he needed to know.

"Amelie?" Sam muttered.

Higgs put his finger to Sam's lips. He had teleported there in an instant.

His golden mask and gas mask were removed, showing his bare face beneath. Black tears were leaking out of both eyes.

"Don't panic. She isn't going anywhere," Higgs taunted, before he thrust one arm into the air and Amelie slowly descended. "Five. We've had five mass extinctions, each caused by an Extinction Entity. And now it's time for number six. I'm not talking 'bout the death of a few dozen species, no. This. This is the granddaddy of them all. BT antimatter voiding out all life as we know it."

Sam shook Higgs's finger off his lips. Sneering at Sam's rage, Higgs held up the golden mask in his hand. It was as if he was threatening to attach it to Sam's face again if he didn't do as he was told.

"And it wouldn't've been possible without a boy scout like you willing to 'make us whole again.' What do you say? Come on! Time to meet your ender," Higgs goaded.

"Amelie!" Sam shouted.

Amelie landed next to Higgs and slowly opened her eyes. She sensed Sam with unfocused eyes that had just woken up. Their gazes met. Some color returned to her face and the light switched on in her eyes. Those were the eyes that Sam knew so well. She was really here. Sam held his arms out for her, but Higgs quickly knocked them away.

With a sidewards glance at Sam, whose face was contorted in pain, Higgs embraced Amelie and placed the golden mask on her. Her face was completely covered.

"Listen, Sam. I'm knotted together with extinction. The great work is nearly complete. Every knot is joined. Soon I will merge them and all mankind's Beaches into a single shore. And then will come an extinction like no other."

The voice Sam could hear behind the mask sounded exactly like Amelie, but he couldn't tell if the words she was saying were her own.

"It will be a stranding more massive than any before it. It will wipe out mankind, along with the Earth itself. The Last Stranding. My reason for being. The first was nothing more than a prelude."

Did she and Bridget force me to bring the entire Chiral Network online knowing that?

Was it all to end the human race and the Earth along with us?

Was the plan to rebuild America just a cover?

Higgs was the one to respond to Sam's questions.

"Surely you've figured it out by now. DOOMS? People like us? She's the source of it all. The nightmares that haunt us? The visions of an inescapable future? Sound familiar? You can speed this up, or slow it down, but you cannot stop what we've started. Happy fucking DOOMS-day, Sam."

The clouds parted and several umbilical cords descended from the sky. Like the flailing tentacles of some huge beast, the cords ensnared Higgs and attempted to tie around Amelie. Sam removed one of his cuff links, filled the blade of the cutter with his blood, and tried to leap for the cords. But his legs wouldn't move. The tar had tangled itself around Sam's feet and wouldn't let him go. Higgs laughed at Sam as he struggled.

"Amelie!" Sam shouted again.

Higgs was being pulled up into the sky by the cord with Amelie in his arms.

"There's nothing you can do except grab a front row seat for the spectacle of extinction. If you want to do that, then come to the Beach. I'll be waiting on Amelie's Beach for the grand finale."

Higgs and Amelie disappeared as he fired one last vocal parting shot at Sam.

Sam knew that standing here staring at the clouds wouldn't achieve anything. He understood it so much that it hurt. He also knew that Higgs and Amelie weren't physically beyond those clouds anymore.

At Sam's level of DOOMS there was no way he could see or detect the Beach. Yet still he looked upward at the clouds, almost begging to be let in.

"Remember our promise?" Someone held an umbrella

open over Sam's head. A delicate-looking porter clad in a black uniform was suddenly by his side. It was Fragile.

"You were waiting for me, weren't you?" she asked. "I could see you looking up at the clouds. That's why I came. Like a regular Mary Poppins," Fragile said musically, twirling her umbrella. Sam didn't know what was happening. Only that right now, Fragile had appeared to him like a savior.

"You did it. You connected all the Knots. That's probably why the Beach feels so close now. That's why I could tell where you were," Fragile said, giving Sam a look that asked him to acknowledge her greatness.

"Take me to Amelie's Beach," Sam said with renewed strength.

Fragile's own expression became more serious.

"Okay. That's possible. You've been to her Beach plenty of times, right?" she asked.

It had already been years since he last went. He hadn't seen it since he was a boy. Ever since the incident with Lucy and his subsequent distancing from Bridges, Sam hadn't even seen Amelie, never mind gone to her Beach. If Bridget's death hadn't forced him into being a part of this mission, he probably would have never seen her again. In fact, he still wasn't sure they shared much of a bond even now.

"Make good on your promise and I'll help you get where you need to go. But bring him back alive. I'm the one who gets to finish him off," Fragile reminded him. That had always been Fragile's goal, and if her getting her revenge resulted in Sam being able to rescue Amelie, he saw no reason why he should deny her. Sam nodded and Fragile smiled in return. "Look, I can't send us both at once... But I'll be right behind you."

"Can't you go to her Beach, too?" Sam asked.

"I can't. I have no connection to her. But I can go to you by the ties that bind us together."

Fragile looked at Sam's wrist. Around it was his worn-out misanga bracelet. It was an ID that had been intertwined with biological information from Fragile's blood. It represented a part of her.

Sam had worn it since he departed Lake Knot City. It had traveled half a continent with him now, and was ingrained with the memories he had made along the way.

"And this will lead you to her," Fragile said, pointing out the dreamcatcher in Sam's hand. It was the one thing that connected him to her. "What are you going to do about the kid?" she added.

She was talking about Lou. Surely, Sam couldn't take Lou with him. He mustn't. There was no guarantee that Sam would come back and he wasn't even sure that he could beat Higgs in the first place. But who'd look after Lou if they both jumped?

Fragile seemed to share the same worry.

"I know a great babysitter," she suggested. "Goes by the

name of Deadman. Now that the Chiral Network's up, I can take Lou to him."

It wasn't like physical distance made that much of a difference, but Fragile would need to jump all the way to Capital Knot City. Sam worried that it would put a lot of strain on her body.

"Want one?" Fragile offered, holding out a cryptobiote as she munched on one herself. Sam gave a wry smile and took it.

"For this to work, I'll have to touch you," she explained.

As Fragile placed her hands on his arms with a smile, he thought he felt her hand tremble slightly. Fragile was probably just as scared as Sam was of Higgs's power. Pretending not to notice, Sam took her hand and placed it over his hand that was clutching the dreamcatcher.

"Close your eyes," Fragile told him. Sam placed his hands on Fragile's shoulders and his forehead to hers. "Now picture Amelie and her Beach."

Sam closed his eyes. For some reason, the image that appeared in his head was one of Amelie's back as she stood by the water's edge.

"You love her, right? You love her," Fragile whispered into his ear.

"Yeah," Sam said, his mouth almost moving of its own accord.

But before the words could reach Fragile's ears, Sam was already gone.

AMELIE'S BEACH

Everything was going to end here. Nothing would remain. The power of this Beach and the power of the Extinction Entity would bring mankind to an end. The vain struggle of humanity to keep on surviving and their resistance to their destiny would all be brought to a neat close here. They would have to say goodbye to the folly of their attempts to fix the Earth that had been so neglected by previous generations.

It would also bring an end to the days of the mask known as Higgs Monaghan. All that was left to do was to wait for Sam to get here. Then he would kill Sam and sever his connection with Amelie. Only then would Amelie be able to demonstrate her true strength as an EE.

Higgs wondered how long he had waited for this day to come. When he really thought about it, he felt like he had been waiting for this day since the first delivery he ever made.

When did that old prepper guy die? It was so long ago now that Higgs didn't know anymore.

The prepper had always been sickly, but this time Higgs hadn't been able to deliver his medicine on time. He could already see signs of necrosis, but there was no time to get him to the incinerator. That was why he carried the man's body all the way to BT territory. It was his second and only option and better than creating a new BT territory entirely, he deemed. Besides, the closest dwelling to here was his own shelter, so he would be able to keep harm to a minimum.

When he dumped the body just before it necrotized, he felt something—the presence of a BT reacting to the dead body.

Then the Beach appeared. But it wasn't the first time he had seen it.

Higgs had the same sensation long ago when he first disposed of a corpse in this way. It was a little stronger this time, though. *I'm being given the power to see them.* That's what he came to believe before he first obtained the mask, before he first started going by the name of Higgs. Back then he was still called Peter Englert.

Word of Peter's ability to sense BTs even reached a delivery organization on the West Coast.

They were an organization slightly smaller than Fragile Express and they had offered him a job. The organization operated in an area where Bridges didn't have a presence, and they wanted him to join them so that they could expand.

The reason Higgs had begun transporting cargo was to support himself as a prepper child, but his purpose for carrying out this delivery work gradually shifted away from keeping himself alive to helping other people. The preppers in his area now completely relied on him for their deliveries or they wouldn't be able to survive. *I'm needed*, he realized. After growing up all alone, he now had partners. They connected people. Peter wondered what his father would say if he could see him now. The father who had always said that the outside world was dangerous and all they could do was live and die in their shelter. Peter wondered what his old man would make of him.

Then his partner died. It was while they were crossing the mountains to make a delivery.

They were making the delivery in a team of two, but his partner had become lost in some fog. Just as Peter received a radio communication to ask for help, everything cut out. His partner was probably already in BT territory by then. Peter could see the light from the voidout from where he was. He wondered how many partners he had lost now. There were hardly any of them left anymore. There were barely any porters remaining who were yet to succumb to porter syndrome and become MULEs, and could still carry out their deliveries "sober" and in control of their own senses. His organization didn't have any porters who could sense BTs, or any decent equipment, either. And on top of all that, he could feel his own vital abilities waning. He had to do something. He needed more power. An even greater power than before. Peter craved it from the bottom of his heart.

Humans are made up of a *ha* and a *ka*. Once the two are separated, a person passes on from this world, but as long as a soul has a body to return to, it can come back. People used to use human-shaped caskets adorned with masks to preserve the body for all eternity

Peter had read all about it in an old book called *The Wisdom of Ancient Egypt*. The golden masks of the pharaohs were decorated with magical adornments to show the power and prestige they had possessed in their previous lives. Peter had no doubt that the appearance of the Beach proved the Egyptians were right about life and death.

Then I will turn myself into a living casket. I'll offer my soul to this world while I live. I'll adorn my own face with the mask of a pharaoh. Maybe that will transform this measly power of mine into that of a king. Starting today, I abandon my bare face. That's when the porter threw away the name Peter and became the man known as Higgs.

AMELIE'S BEACH

"Amelie!" Sam shouted.

Sam was heading this way. A shabby man desperately trying to survive. Higgs considered it uglier than anything else in the world. So much so that the very sight of him made him retch.

Higgs placed the mask in his hand over Amelie. She didn't resist.

"You ready to end this? Before the end of everything?"

Higgs asked before he thrust both arms into the sky, where Amelie hung in midair. Sam's grim face was fanning the flames of Higgs's belligerence. The debris and rocks scattered around the sandy beach ignored the law of gravity and flew into the air, surrounding Amelie in layer after layer of rubble. Everything was moving as he wished. Just as he had envisioned. Several umbilical cords stretched out from Amelie's abdomen, creating a spider's web. Amelie lay across the center, both like the prey caught in a trap and the predator lying there in wait. It was all just as Higgs wanted. "I'm just doing what I'm supposed to do," he said. "I'm keeping the Extinction Entity safe until the slate is wiped clean. Those of us with DOOMS. Her. We're all bound here for a reason."

Sam was shouting something back. But no matter what he said, Higgs was never going to hear. Even if Sam had reconnected the world, he was still just a laborer who moved things from one place to another. He hadn't accomplished anything great. Higgs decided to put him in his place by showing him what kind of place the Beach really was.

The sands swelled and several whales appeared. They cried as they breached the surface and slammed their massive bodies onto the shore. More followed suit, stranding themselves on the sands. The entire Beach was getting buried in the corpses of whales that neither came from the sea nor could return to it.

"We're all of us a part of the Death Stranding," Higgs declared.

It didn't seem to matter how Higgs explained it, but Sam never understood. As long as all he wanted was Amelie, he would never see the truth. Higgs had once been the same.

"And this place, this fucking 'Beach.' There's no repatriation here, no. One of us dies, that's it. He goes to the other side. Nice, huh? Lucky loser gets to put an end to this rinse-and-repeat bullshit once and for all. So... No BTs, no voidouts, no bullshit. Just a good old-fashioned boss fight. Stick versus rope. Gun versus strand. One more ending before the end... One last game over."

All Sam had was his ID strand. It didn't take a genius to figure out how this fight would end. Higgs aimed his assault rifle and pulled the trigger. *This gunshot will sound in the beginning of this rite of extinction.*

It wasn't long after Peter assumed the name of Higgs that he joined forces with Fragile Express. He may have professed himself to be the God particle and may have worn a mask to imitate the pharaohs, but he was still painfully aware of his own lack of power. The leader of the organization, Fragile, had DOOMS more powerful than Higgs had ever seen. Her organization was better than the one Higgs was a part of, too.

Now that Bridges I had finally departed on a mission to

rebuild America, terrorist attacks and assaults by Homo Demens were on the rise, and that, combined with the BTs and the MULEs, made it harder and harder for Higgs and the others to work. That's why it was better to join forces. The more porters they had, the easier it would be to cover the entire continent. Luckily, Fragile agreed with Higgs and they began working together.

Fragile's DOOMS was even more incredible than Higgs had first heard. Not only could she sense the Beach and the BTs, she could actually use the Beach. Compared to that, Higgs was nothing. All he had was the power he had received as the human corpses necrotized and became BTs. But now he didn't need it. He could use Fragile's abilities to make deliveries. Higgs didn't want to rebuild America as it once was, like Bridges. He wanted to create a new world on this continent, one that protected the freedom and liberty of every single person living within it. Higgs was practically drunk on that vision.

Yet he knew that it was a brittle and fragile dream.

AMELIE'S BEACH

Jeering at Sam, Higgs thrust the rifle at him. Out of bullets, it was now just a steel stick to beat Sam with. Even though he had a spare magazine, he no longer felt like using it. He wanted to fight Sam man-on-man.

Sam had already lost a lot of blood and was gasping for air, but he had lost none of his fighting spirit and continued to glare at Higgs. Unlike Sam, Higgs barely had a scratch on him.

"You just don't get it, do you. What do you think you're going to achieve by struggling like this? Fragile was the same. She gave up her time just to save a town that was gonna to get destroyed anyway. It's not like they've got long left here after all this. Now she's stuck livin' inside that shriveled body, just giving them hope for a fake future. Listen up, Sam. There is no future. If all there is to do is waste away waiting for tomorrow, isn't it better to graciously accept extinction? That's what the planet wants. So, you'd better start groveling before me. Then at least you might be remembered as a wise man. If you don't want to, then kill me," Higgs declared, waving a knife at Sam and slamming it into his windpipe. Sam managed to get away with a stagger, but Higgs simply tutted and closed in on him once more. As Higgs lunged, Sam's ID strand caught the arm that was flailing the knife. As he pulled on Higgs and Higgs braced his feet against the ground, their strength was evenly matched. The ID strand stretched longer and longer, looking like it might snap at any moment. Sam was breathing heavily with his shoulders, but it didn't feel like he would loosen his grip anytime soon.

Higgs could feel himself growing impatient. The situation

was overwhelmingly in his favor, yet their fight was not progressing as planned. *I need more power.* He sent his will to Amelie asleep in the spider's web, but she didn't wake up. *What does this mean?*

Sam's injury-riddled body suddenly seemed to look much more imposing than before.

Things between Higgs and Fragile Express went great at first. But Higgs soon had to face their limits. No matter how great Fragile's abilities were, they couldn't turn this world into one that he dreamed of for everyone. Even if they were able to make deliveries and keep people connected, people still couldn't go out into the outside world.

This world where the timefall fell, where BTs attacked, and layers of chiral cloud separated them from the rest of the universe would never change. It couldn't change.

Now that Bridges' plan to rebuild America had been put into motion there were more terrorist attacks than ever before. And with more terrorist attacks came more bodies and more BTs. Voidouts were happening everywhere. If they had just kept quiet and stayed put then this would never have happened. The Earth was crawling with different motives and purposes, each battling it out to reign supreme, but it felt to Higgs like he was the one choking on them all. These were the limits of humanity.

But then he met someone who surpassed those limits.

Her name was Samantha America Strand and Higgs knew from the moment he first spoke to her that she was the only one who could make his ideal world a reality. She told him that she would lend him the power to restore the world to its former glory.

The symbol of her power was a human-shaped BT sensor called a Bridge Baby. It wasn't a real baby. Instead, according to Amelie, it was a child who had been born on the Beach and who could connect the realms of the living and the dead. She explained that if Higgs used one, he could always stay connected to her. She told him that BBs were the new children born into a new age.

I'm no ordinary porter.

I'm the one who'll create a new world.

Higgs didn't need to borrow Fragile's abilities anymore. Now, he was able to dream again.

BBs were dolls who took the form of babies. But they weren't just any old dolls. They were neither living, nor dead. They were something in between human and doll, much like the mummies of Egypt with only their shriveled, dried-up hearts still in place in their chests.

Higgs believed the BBs were a symbol of humanity.

The Death Stranding was the sixth mass extinction event to strike life on this planet. Higgs saw it all in his visions. The visions that he was sure he was being shown because of his connection with the BB. In other words, the visions that were being shown to him by Amelie.

The voidouts that had suddenly occurred the world over one day, and the subsequent transformation of the dead into BTs that caused ever more, were all phenomena to speed human extinction along. It was already set in motion.

There was no meaning whatsoever in trying to rebuild America. No reason to sacrifice the lives of those already living for the chance of a tomorrow that would never come.

Higgs asked Amelie the true meaning of the Death Stranding. But she never answered him. Whether she knew it or not, she never told him anything. But Higgs somehow understood it all. So did Amelie. Extinction was a foregone conclusion.

Yet Amelie was still trying to rebuild America. Perhaps that was the final struggle. The final hesitation. Higgs couldn't understand what was going through Amelie's mind, but if she was hesitating, then he'd make the decision for her. He'd bring extinction to everyone on this planet. That's why he needed to get stronger. Detonating a nuclear bomb had been an expression of that urge. He wiped the whole of Middle Knot City off the map. Fragile had been the one to smuggle the bomb into the city. She didn't have the slightest idea that she was the one who delivered its destruction.

The city had blown up because of its connection to the outside. Connections brought ruin. It had been well documented for centuries. When people began to move between continents they brought new diseases with them, sometimes so bad that they wiped out over half the native population. The human race would die. Now even the delivery systems were being used to hasten the extinction. That must have been why Higgs had joined forces with Fragile. Why they had expanded the delivery network. Everything had been preordained from the start.

It was around that time when Higgs first heard about Sam Porter. He had DOOMS and the exceedingly rare ability to repatriate from the dead. When Higgs found out that he was Amelie's adoptive brother, the jealousy drove him insane. Sam had found meaning in survival by connecting people to people without connecting to them himself. Higgs felt like he was looking at a past version of Peter, and that only further fanned the flames of his envy.

After researching Sam, he realized something. Amelie was constrained by Sam's existence. She seemed to believe that if anyone could rebuild America, it was him. If Amelie was ever going to be able to demonstrate the true extent of her power as an Extinction Entity, Higgs needed to sever her bond with Sam.

After finding out that Sam was near Central Knot City, it was him who had formulated the plan to leave a dead body within it and cause a voidout. When he found out that the body had been discovered he summoned a BT to consume the men on the Corpse Disposal Team. Central Knot City was wiped out just as planned. Not only was it the self-proclaimed capital of America, it was also home to Bridges HQ and Bridges II. Higgs had wiped them all out. The plan to rebuild America had disappeared in a puff of smoke.

But Sam repatriated.

So even a voidout doesn't kill a repatriate? What a stubborn creature.

When Higgs found out that not only had Sam repatriated from the dead, but that he had now departed as the sole member of Bridges II, it only enraged him further. He decided to speed up the inevitable conclusion to this saga even more.

Your DOOMS abilities are worthless. I have SODOM. And with this power, I'll turn the Earth into my power's namesake and watch it burn in fire and brimstone.

AMELIE'S BEACH

"I am the bridge who brings the extinction!" Higgs screamed, letting go of Sam's ID strand and making Sam tumble back into a swamp of tar. Higgs took advantage of Sam's fall and charged. Connecting the Extinction Entity to this world and ushering in the extinction was his purpose. The tar grabbed at Sam's legs, making it more difficult to move as Higgs lunged at Sam's hips and took him down.

Sam was half-submerged in tar as Higgs grabbed his hair and punched him in the face. It no longer looked human, covered so thickly in blood and tar. He knew the truth of the Death Stranding. The meaning behind the Sixth Extinction that neither Sam nor even Amelie understood. Its horror. Higgs punched Sam again as he tried to shake Higgs's arm away. He gripped Sam's skull tight, wanting to crush it into dust, and plunged him deeper into the tar. It didn't matter that he was a repatriate. If he suffocated him here, Sam wouldn't be able to come back. It was time for Sam to die. "You can watch this world go up in flames from the realm of the dead. There's no way back for you this time. You'll just have to be satisfied with the show!" Higgs ranted wildly, strengthening his grip on Sam.

Then a jet-black hand grabbed Higgs's arm.

It was jutting out of the tar. It belonged to Sam. The tar's grip on him was slackening. Higgs's own grip on Sam loosened as the hand grabbed onto him with a newfound strength that made Higgs's bones creak.

Sam dragged Higgs down into the tar as well.

Higgs's vision was immediately plunged into darkness and a sticky tar-like substance mercilessly rushed into his mouth. The tar that he had always been able to manipulate freely was going against its master's will. How could this be? Higgs was backed into a corner.

Their positions switched and Sam was now straddling

Higgs. Sam had him by the chest and punched him in the face over and over. Higgs felt like he was blacking out each time.

The extinction is already set in stone. I'll deal with Sam first and then exercise Amelie's power. It's already decided. So, what's happening now is just some meaningless detour. Right, Amelie?!

But Amelie didn't answer.

The extinction can't be reversed. That's why you first appeared, right?

Instead of Amelie, Higgs was answered by Sam's fist.

As the taste of iron spread through his mouth and blood gushed into his throat, Higgs realized that his nose had been broken. Was he supposed to choke to death? Was that really the way he was to go out? Higgs was grabbed by the chest and shaken until he vomited out a mixture of blood and tar. He could breathe again. It was only afterward that Higgs realized how great a contradiction his feeling of relief was. How could he believe so fervently in extinction yet feel such relief when he was able to keep on living?

It was only then that Amelie finally answered.

"Sam!"

Why wouldn't she call out his name? Discouragement and doubt extinguished what was left of Higgs's fighting spirit. He saw that Amelie, wearing his golden mask, had broken free of the spider's web and was now standing on the Beach. It wasn't time yet. Amelie's appearance betrayed Higgs's vision.

"Well, congratulations. You won the game. Too bad you didn't stop shit. Well? Get on with it," Higgs said, staring up at the sky once Sam had hauled him out of the swamp of tar. Those words were half for Higgs's own benefit. If he abandoned his prayers, they would never come true. Even if he died, the path to extinction would never be blocked.

Sam looked down at him and shook his head.

Higgs could hear somebody approaching in the sand. They weren't Amelie's footsteps. Sam's face disappeared from his sight and was replaced by another.

"Fragile?"

Before he could ask her what she was doing here, she spoke: "Guess I left a lasting impression." His ex-partner's face drew near, a dreadful smile forming upon it. "I'm Fragile... but I'm not that fragile."

Those were the words she had recited back when Higgs made her dispose of the nuke.

"This time, you're the one who's going to break," she warned him.

"Is that right? I think you'll find our bond is made of stronger stuff," he sneered back.

Higgs knew it was all in vain. But he felt like he really would break if he didn't say anything at all and couldn't stop himself. He looked to Amelie again. She was stood there leaning on Sam, but it didn't look like she was fully conscious yet. She was still wearing his mask. In that case, he wasn't finished just yet.

"Give me power, dammit!" he screamed.

Amelie woke up, removed his mask, and simply discarded it onto the sand.

"Oh? What's this? You're already broken," Fragile remarked indifferently.

"What the fuck!? I'm Higgs!" he raged. "I'm the particle of God that permeates all existence. What are you? Honey, you ain't nothing but damaged goods!"

Fragile removed her glove and stroked Higgs's blood- and tar-stained face. It was a gentle gesture, like those she would make back when they were partners. But it was the first time he had felt it through her aged hand.

Fragile's smile filled Higgs's field of vision. Then came a thump and intense pain as her fist made contact with his face.

"You're damaged goods," she replied.

"Here you go. As promised."

Fragile grabbed Higgs's bound body along with his rifle and magazine of ammo. He looked so small now. The golden mask of his that lay nearby looked shabby and fake. Nobody needed it anymore.

"I've got a delivery for you, Sam," Fragile said as she stepped toward Sam and Amelie and presented Lou's pod. "Babysitting is hard work. Take your little one."

Sam took Lou's pod, but looked confused.

"I was going to ask Deadman to look after Lou, but he

couldn't make it. After I jumped you here, the Beach became unstable, so I had to keep the kid with me. I managed to bring it here by picturing it as 'equipment.'"

Inside the pod that Sam cradled, Lou laughed. Fragile returned the smile and opened her umbrella.

"The Beach is stable for now, so where should I send you?" Fragile asked.

"He doesn't need your help. He's got the Chiral Network. And he's got me. We can jump east together," Amelie interrupted.

"Lucky him." Fragile closed her umbrella.

"We appreciate everything you've done for us, we really do. But we're good for now. Besides, I'm sure they need you back at Fragile Express," Sam explained.

"Yeah. Who better to scoop up all the pieces and put them back together? Wouldn't want to settle for anything less than perfection. We're square. Nothing owed, nothing left to say. So long, Sam." Fragile turned her back on Sam and said her goodbyes, this time a rifle over her shoulder instead of an umbrella.

As she listened to Sam's and Amelie's voices grow more distant as they walked east along the shoreline, Fragile took a deep breath and gently lowered the rifle until the barrel pointed at Higgs.

The first memory Higgs had was of the gloomy ceiling of the shelter. He must have been crying, because right then a big hand appeared and blocked out his view. It was his father. He had come to shush the crying Peter and shouted something at him angrily, but Peter couldn't understand the meaning of his words.

The man wasn't Peter's real father. His real father had died while his mother was still pregnant. Then, just after he was born, his mother passed on too, of an infection. Baby Peter was entrusted to his mother's brother and moved from his parents' shelter into this one. His uncle was reluctant to become his foster father, and all Peter could remember from his childhood was abuse and violence. He had no memory of ever being loved. He was brought up to believe that the shelter was the entire world and that he and his foster father were its only inhabitants, but one day he dared ask the innocent question of where their food and resources came from. The only reply he ever received was a punch. But once it had taken root, that question never disappeared from Peter's mind. One day, he stole a glance at the monitor when his foster father wasn't looking, and it showed him the outside world for the very first time. When he asked his foster father about it, he was served with yet another fist to the face.

Peter's foster father eventually told him about the world that lay beyond their door. About how it was a dangerous world dominated by timefall and monsters, and one in which people must never venture outside. Peter's mother's death must have added to the man's paranoia. Never mind going outside, Peter was hysterically warned against even letting in the breeze. The man had to raise the baby he had been entrusted with by his sister to adulthood somehow.

The man's sense of duty and love manifested itself as the violence against Peter, but eventually that lost its original purpose and became nothing more than a daily habit. The man used to hit Peter just in case he ever even thought about venturing outside That was his way of showing love and protecting him. But Peter felt like he was dying, cramped up as he was. He may have seemed fine on the outside, but he felt like he was dying inside.

That's why he hatched a plan to escape the shelter. He prepared little by little, whenever his father wasn't looking. But he was discovered and his father launched into a rage and attacked him. Tables and shelves were overturned and the atmosphere inside the shelter reached breaking point.

Peter's foster father had held him down and shouted at him about how he could never understand the man's feelings. Peter's field of vision grew narrower. It became more and more difficult to take his next breath. The man was wringing his neck.

As Peter struggled frantically, he grabbed for a knife that had fallen to the floor and plunged it into his foster father's neck.

The strength faded out of the man's hands and his body slumped to the floor.

All Peter could see above him was the gloomy ceiling of the shelter once more.

Unable to process what he had done, Peter spent an entire night with that body in the shelter, but he had to get rid of it sometime.

Ever since he had first told Peter of the world outside their door, his father had also been careful to fully inform him of the terror of necrosis and the BTs. Peter knew that if he didn't get rid of the body, his father would come back and cause a voidout.

The body had already begun to give off a pungent odor. But there was no place or any way to burn it. All Peter could do was take it somewhere far away, so he dragged the body out of the shelter and got his first taste of the outside world.

What he saw was patches of jagged rocks and short grass as far as the eye could see. The mountaintops in the distance were hidden by chiral clouds. Peter was in awe of this spectacle he was seeing for the first time, but getting the body away from here had to take precedent.

But as he dragged the body away, he didn't notice the fog of black particles emanating from the corpse. It had already begun to necrotize. Time had run out. All Peter could do was dump the body and run. Then he had a vision. Both hands that had a hold of the body disintegrated into a mist.

Simultaneously, he felt the presence of a BT, attracted to the body from the other side. Ever since then Peter had been able to sense BTs, and that had given him the ability to work alone as a porter for so many years.

The necrotizing body had given him power, and whenever he had felt that power waning, he killed in secret. That was how he had managed to survive all alone.

AMELIE'S BEACH

Higgs raised his head and looked for Fragile, but she was long gone.

He was all alone. The golden mask, Amelie's *quipu*, and the human-shaped BB no longer belonged to him. He had lost everything. There was nothing left. There wasn't even anything left of his power he had intended to use to bring the extinction. He had believed that he was in control of everything, but he had been stupid. It had all been make believe.

He finally understood.

Now he was all alone on this Beach and there was no one to hear his mutterings.

I'm Higgs, the particle of God.

He was all alone, isolated without a person in the world to connect to.

This is how I'm supposed to be.

Peter Englert had been forsaken on this Beach with nothing else to do but continue to confess his endless sins.

HEARTMAN'S LAB

Heartman could hear the tune of the Funeral March. He had to get back to his body soon. The passage of time on the Beach was without end and as close to zero as you could get, but there was still a time limit. Humans perceive the passage of time not as the changing of events along a timeline, but as the switching of phases. Each individual event is not washed away by time to disappear, they remain intact as a perceived phase. That's what we call the past. The future is an as-of-yet unperceived event and humans, bound by time as they are, can only perceive one of a myriad of alternatives.

While Heartman's *ha* was bound by the laws of the world of the living, he was unable to search the Beach indefinitely. Choosing a song that mourned the dead as his signal to return to the realm of the living and wake up was Heartman's own little act of quiet resistance.

The Funeral March should have sounded the same as always, but this time it sounded different. It was hurting his ears. The sounds were overlapping. Perhaps, if he hadn't been listening so attentively, he would never even have noticed. It was the same tune, but there was a slight delay. It felt like listening to an optical illusion. Once one tune had seized all of Heartman's attention that was all he could hear, but when he disengaged his focus he could detect something very slightly out of synch. The realization affected his sight. The world around him that he perceived visually felt similarly layered, with a single layer slightly out of alignment. It was the first time he had felt anything like it.

Although, logically, infinite layers of parallel phases selectively unacknowledged had to exist.

Have I augmented my abilities? Heartman wondered, feeling a spark of excitement.

He looked out across the Beach as the limit of his stay approached. It looked different than before. The shoreline that stretched eternally into the distance was being followed by countless numbers of people. Each and every one of them was existing simultaneously within phases out of alignment with one another.

What's going on? His brain was on fire. It didn't matter that his heart had stopped, it was ringing like an alarm bell. Huge droplets of sweat merged with his tears, dampening his face. It was like the very limits of his consciousness were trying to break.

"Wait!" he shouted. For a split second, he thought he could see his wife and daughter's backs among the crowd.

"Wait! Don't go! Don't leave me by myself."

It was just like a repeat of what happened before. As the

realization first flashed across his mind, that old woman appeared and jabbed her finger into his chest. Multiple people grabbed at his legs. Heartman was being dragged down from the Beach.

When he awoke, the lab was empty. His image of the world was stable and clear, maintained in a single phase. Heartman turned toward the monitor to check his Beach logs. Now he understood. The entire Chiral Network had been connected. Sam had done it.

He had connected all the knots from east to west.

It was possible that this phenomenon that Heartman interpreted as phase misalignment was occurring on every Beach. He could perceive the potential phases from before choices were made and events were determined. It was like all cause and effect was being disassembled. Without the reintegration of this world using some kind of meta-level law, this world could become engulfed in a wave of potential worlds. It meant that while this world would exist, it would also disappear.

AMELIE'S BEACH

The sound of a gunshot echoed in the distance.

Perhaps Fragile had finally achieved her goal. Maybe she had finally got her revenge on Higgs. With any luck, maybe she had even managed to lay her past mistakes to rest alongside him.

"Come on, let's go. We still have work to do," Amelie said without the slightest hint of cheer in her voice. Sam should have had so many questions, but he couldn't put anything into words. He was fine with that, though. It was enough that he was able to see Amelie again—in the flesh, not as a hologram or in his dreams—and nothing else mattered. That said, seeing her again after all this time, all these decades, stirred up its own strong emotions within him. Amelie had to know what Sam was feeling, yet she silently began to walk away. All Sam could think of was to keep chasing after her.

"Do you still believe in me?" Amelie asked.

Wasn't it too late for that now? Surely it was more a question of whether he *could* believe in her. Whether he had no choice but to believe in her.

"It's true. I am extinction," Amelie admitted.

But that wasn't what Sam needed to know. He wanted to ask her if she was a living human being. The image that Sam couldn't get out of his head was her with an umbilical cord coming out of her body like those dinosaurs and ammonites in Heartman's lab, connecting her to the world of the dead.

"Did Bridget know?" Sam blurted out.

Had she known about all this when she had begun

involving people in her plan to rebuild America?

"I can end it all, just like that. But what I want—what I have always wanted—was to be a part of it. For us all to be one," she replied.

Sam didn't understand. America had been destroyed by the Death Stranding. And Bridget had dedicated her life to rebuilding it. But if Amelie was an Extinction Entity, then by giving birth to her, Bridget was responsible for why the world had collapsed in the first place.

It was like Ouroboros, the snake that ate its own tail.

"Maybe you don't believe me, but once we get back east, I'll tell you everything. If we don't let everyone in the Knot Cities and all of the preppers know that America is restored, then Bridget's plan will never come to fruition. At least let me see to that. I know you have questions, but let's save them for later."

Sam nodded silently.

"Let's go home." Amelie smiled for the first time and began to walk along the shoreline again. It seemed to stretch on forever. It looked like it stretched out even farther than the horizon. Sam wondered if this was the same Beach that he used to play on with Amelie. Or was this the Beach they had completed by connecting all the knots?

Amelie didn't look back toward Sam once, and simply continued to walk along the shoreline. All Sam could do was follow silently.

I don't want to go home.

Why had he cried so much when he was a kid?

Had he really wanted to stay on that Beach, where there was no one else but just the two of them? Like a baby crying and screaming in fear of being born?

Amelie suddenly stopped in her tracks.

A figure was standing next to the shoreline up ahead. They were too far away for Sam to make out any details, but he could tell that it was a well-built man. Amelie looked back toward Sam. She had a faint smile on her face but seemed nervous for some reason.

"Wait here. Okay?" she asked as she left, in the same tone she used to use when he was a kid.

A wave lapped at the shore. But it didn't pull back out. It remained in place. It had already engulfed Sam's foot and he soon found that he couldn't move. It was the same move that Higgs had pulled on him in the sea of tar.

Sam could see a delicate red silhouette next to the man.

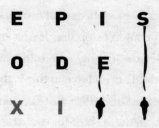

DIE-HARDMAN

"So you finally invited me to the Beach," Die-Hardman said, pointing his gun at the woman. "Remember this?"

Die-Hardman didn't think she would answer. All he could hear was the sound of the waves.

"It's that gun," the woman in red said, squinting as if bright light was coming out of its barrel.

"And now I'm using it to make things right," Die-Hardman spat. "You were supposed to make the world whole—not fuck it all up."

The barrel of the gun was trembling slightly. Die-Hardman was surprised at how pathetic he was being. Was he scared? He repositioned himself to try to hide the shaking from her. If he took one step closer the end of the gun would be digging into the woman's delicate chest.

The woman smiled and grabbed the barrel of the gun, pulling it toward her. Despite her small frame, she was so strong that Die-Hardman couldn't stop her. It was just like before.

"Okay then. Get on with it," she told him.

Die-Hardman didn't even have to think about it. He pulled the trigger and released his bullet. But she couldn't be killed.

"There is no atonement. Not for us," she explained. The bullet pierced Bridget Strand's chest without leaving a single mark.

How do you kill someone who's already dead? A heavy sense of defeat weighed down Die-Hardman's right hand, drawing the barrel of the gun toward the floor.

Die-Hardman couldn't tell if Bridget was smiling or crying, but he was sure he was making the same expression. If he was so determined to make Bridget pay for her sins, then he would have to face the same condemnation.

He had been the one to follow her and betray her, only to go and swear allegiance to her all over again afterward.

Bridget suddenly looked out to sea, her gaze landing on a swell on the ocean's surface.

Something was parting the water in two and emerging from underneath. If this was the Beach, that made that sea the domain of the past and the dead. But even if the past that Die-Hardman had cast away were to resurface, it made some kind of sense to him. It would be strange, but it wouldn't be inexplicable.

Four soldiers emerged, equipped with scratched-up helmets and clad in dripping wet army uniforms. They were soldiers from the US Army of a previous century. There was no flesh beneath those clothes. The skeletal soldiers were advancing, bones creaking and clacking together underneath their uniforms.

The sea breeze brought the stench of blood, mud, and gunpowder smoke. It was a smell that Die-Hardman knew well. Whenever he was surrounded by it there was only ever one thing on his mind.

I must survive.

He pointed his gun at the soldiers, but his finger lay paralyzed on the trigger. It looked like he wouldn't be able to kill what was already dead after all.

The four soldiers were a foreshadowing. Their presence indicated that the past was about to strand itself. An umbilical cord stretched out of each soldier's abdomen, sinking down behind them into the ocean depths below.

Those cords dredged up the past and beached it. The soldiers suddenly had skin, eyes, mouths, noses... Features that had been brought back to life with their malevolence and solemnity.

Die-Hardman knew that he mustn't look. He didn't want to see it. Yet he couldn't take his eyes off that past, either.

A man gently lifted his hands. As the umbilical cords attached to the soldiers detached, they spread out and surrounded him. His helmet burned away, exposing his real face.

As soon as Die-Hardman realized who it was, he dropped his weapon. Unable to support his own body weight, he fell to his knees.

The man came ashore. As Die-Hardman hung his head, all he could hear was the crunching of the sand beneath the man's feet. He felt a hand on his face. Like the hand of someone checking a dead body. His mask was removed.

Die-Hardman couldn't peel his eyes away from the man's face.

The man let out a sigh and a groan of what sounded like anguish. Die-Hardman couldn't tell what he was trying to say. The man was looking at Die-Hardman's exposed face with eyes that seemed unable to focus.

"You…" The man started to string a sentence together. The man seemed to be groping around desperately for information in the depths of his memory. Die-Hardman knew who he was, though. This was the man who had spirited Sam away to an eternal battlefield twice now.

"Yes, it's me. John. Remember?" Die-Hardman urged. He pieced the rest of the parts together for the man. "Your Die-Hardman."

There, he said it. Suddenly, he was gripped by a welling fear. He couldn't stop shaking. His throat felt dry and like a fish abandoned on land, he was desperately trying to fill his lungs with air. He was covered in sweat. Something cold and hard dug into the back of his head.

"I'm sorry. I'm so sorry," Die-Hardman pleaded.

The gun and his fear weighed down on him so much that he couldn't even lift his own face.

"BB," the man said. "Give me back my BB."

I'm sorry. I did the best I could. But I couldn't choose. Die-Hardman heard the safety switch come off. *I'm going to die here, all because I didn't choose.*

Die-Hardman closed his eyes tight. But no matter how long he waited, his retribution never came. The back of his head felt lighter.

"This isn't what we agreed on. Give me back my BB."

But the man's voice was no longer directed toward Die-Hardman. It was directed at someone else.

"You're looking in the wrong place," she said.

Die-Hardman heard her voice. It was an icy voice that cut like a blade with no hint of indecision or hesitation.

All Sam could do as he watched the scene unfold in front of him was stand there in silence.

To him, it was like a silent pantomime. There was the man in the mask, the five soldiers, and the woman in red. Sam could guess that the men were Die-Hardman and Cliff and his men. And the woman must have been Amelie. She had probably guessed that something was going on and had immobilized him here.

But even if he could tell who the actors were, he had no idea what the story might be about.

Why did Die-Hardman shoot Amelie? Had that really happened? Sam wasn't so sure anymore. Why was Die-Hardman kneeling in front of Cliff? And why was Cliff's gun pointed at Amelie instead? He didn't understand what they were doing. It was like he was watching a nonsensical play that didn't fit together.

Cliff was still pointing the gun at Amelie when his attention seemed to snap Sam's way. He couldn't see the expression on Cliff's face from such a distance. but he felt like it had pierced straight through him.

"BB!" Sam heard Cliff shout. Sam, who had just been spectating until this point, was suddenly drawn into the drama.

Cliff made one quick gesture at his lackeys and the four skeletal soldiers immediately began to run in Sam's direction.

Was this another eternal battlefield? If so, what battle happened here? What kind of atrocity took place on this Beach? How many died in vain?

The soldiers advanced at frightening speed. They weren't powered by logic or reason, but by some kind of emotion. He could tell they were coming here to kill him. But Sam couldn't move from the spot. The waves that had ensnared his legs had turned to tar.

"BB, I'll get you out of there!" Cliff shouted, black tears pouring from his eyes. But his eyes didn't show any sign of sadness. Instead, they were full of anger. Inside the pod, Lou's little body began to writhe and cry out in sympathy.

I'm sorry, Lou. I'm sorry I brought you to a place like this.

Protecting the pod with both arms, Sam had a sudden realization. What if Cliff's anger wasn't directed at other people? What if it was directed at himself? Maybe it was the same anger Sam felt when he couldn't protect Lou. Sam felt completely helpless. At this rate, it seemed like he would be engulfed by both Cliff's anger and his own. This was the end. If Sam's body was broken on the Beach, then even he wouldn't be able to repatriate. He would die here like anyone else. But maybe that was okay with him.

He felt at peace with that. Then—

Everything was red. It looked like fresh blood had taken up his entire vision. He was wrong.

Breaking through space and emerging in front of him was Amelie's red dress. She had transported herself here in an instant and now she was stood in front of him, ready to block the attack from Cliff. Sam screamed at her to get out of the way, but then he gasped. Beyond Amelie's shoulder, he could see Die-Hardman groveling. Next to him still stood the woman in red. Then who was this? And who was that?

As if to answer half of his question, the red-clad woman

covering Sam turned to face him. The golden *quipu* around
her neck swayed, reflecting the light. This one was Amelie.

"Stay back!" she commanded.

Sam could see his own face reflected in her eyes. It was
a blank face robbed of the ability to comprehend what was
going on. *What's happening here? What kind of plot twist is this?*
Amelie thrust out both of her arms and the tar released its
hold on Sam's feet. Sam's body flew up high. Yet he couldn't
tear his eyes away from Amelie's. He couldn't tear himself
apart from the Sam reflected back in them. He was falling
back toward them. Then those eyes as deep as the sea
swallowed him up and Sam disappeared.

The door would not open. Had there been a security breach
at the facility?

Sam broke the door lock with the grip of his handgun
and somehow managed to wrench open the heavy
reinforced-glass sliding door. There was no one else in
the hallway.

Had it already been dealt with? Had Lou been saved?

Sam proceeded down the dark, unlit hallway toward the
room he had been instructed to go to. Even if he couldn't
save the mother's body, he might be able to save the fetus.
That's what he had been told. But his time was limited.

The door to the room was unlocked. The lights were

turned off, just like in the hallway, and in its center stood a hospital bed.

Laying there, hooked up to all kinds of monitors measuring her vitals, was Lucy.

A man was looking down at her, but he wasn't a doctor.

Sam pointed the gun at the man. The stranger looked up and their eyes met. It was Cliff.

"Where is the BB?" Cliff asked.

Why was he here?

"I was told that I might be able to rescue the BB," Cliff said.

Sam shook his head, maintaining a firm grip on the gun. *The BB isn't here. The only ones here are a comatose Lucy and Lou. Your baby isn't here.*

The logical part of Sam's brain told him that he had been repelled from Amelie's Beach and was having a nightmare, but the anger emanating from Cliff still froze him in place. As Cliff approached with an anguished look on his face, Sam began to back away. But he backed into someone else entirely. When he turned around, he found Bridget.

It was the Bridget from before Sam left Bridges. The one who had been so happy about Lucy's pregnancy. Sam didn't even have the time to ask himself why she was here.

"Give me back my BB." Cliff grabbed Sam by the shoulders.

Caught between Bridget and Cliff, Sam was unable to move.

"I can't give it back to you yet," Bridget replied.

Sam had never heard her sound so cold before. Cliff's eyes

filled with sadness. Sam was reflected in them, now drowning in Cliff's eyes instead of Amelie's. Cliff's stare pierced him, controlled him. Once again Sam could no longer move.

"Give me back my BB," Cliff repeated, reaching out his arms. It was like they were trying to grab for Sam. They were extending like squirming tentacles. Even if Sam wanted to run, he couldn't. The palm of Cliff's hand pushed against Sam's chest and sank into him. Sam's skin burned, his flesh melted away, and once his ribs had crumbled to dust, Cliff grabbed Sam's heart. It began to jump and squirm like a fish trying to slip out of someone's hands.

SAFEHOUSE

Sam woke up in a private room somewhere.

His right hand had been clutching at his chest. Now it was numb and wouldn't move. Sam had to use his left hand to drag it away. When he looked under his undershirt, he could see a fresh handprint there.

Lou's pod was set in the incubator. Had everything since Fragile had transported him to the Beach been a bad dream? Sam certainly hoped so.

"Oh, you're awake." Deadman appeared. The outlines of his hologram were slightly blurred. "You're back east of the tar belt now, in the basement of a safehouse inside

Mountain Knot City. You just happened to appear here without any warning. Officially, anyway."

Deadman's body suddenly began to expand. His barrel-like abdomen inflated like it was about to explode, and both shoulders swelled to the point that they looked like they were going to engulf his entire face.

"The Beach is going crazy. Chiral spikes have become far more frequent," Deadman explained. The look of his hologram had returned to normal but now it was frozen in place instead. "I wanted to go there, too, and look after Lou, but… Heartman and Lockne think that the chaos might be a result of expanding the network nationwide. Too many Beaches sharing the same space. Wires get crossed and so forth. It might also have something to do with the newly connected consciousness of those who just joined the UCA still adapting to the system. Amelie said that it should stabilize in time."

"Amelie?" Sam asked.

"She's the one who brought you here. I wanted to be able to bring you all the way back to HQ, but she said that while the Beach was in such disarray that it wouldn't be possible."

So, Sam's experiences on the Beach hadn't been a nightmare. The gravity of the situation began to bear down on Sam again.

"Amelie could have probably jumped there by herself, but she didn't," Deadman went on. "After she left you there, she left us a message. She said that she was going to finish what Bridget started."

There seemed to be some anxiety and doubt mixed into Deadman's tone, as if he hadn't quite been able to process this chain of events either. Sam wasn't surprised, because nothing made any sense.

"The only record we have here is that you turned up suddenly, without warning. That you jumped there instantaneously from Edge Knot City. There are no other records. It's different from that time on the battlefield, there's nothing recorded on any of your devices. The only people who know what happened on the Beach are Fragile, Amelie, and you."

But they weren't the only ones.

"The director was there," Sam added.

"The director?" Deadman asked, his hologram suddenly springing back to life.

"And it wasn't just the director. Cliff and Bridget were there too."

"Sam, please. You yourself burned her body, remember? She wouldn't have remained on the Beach. Couldn't have. Not even if it was her daughter's Beach. The part about the director I can believe, though," Deadman said, looking up at the ceiling.

"I always suspected him. It was the way that he seemed to seek you out when Bridget was dying and put you in charge of Bridges II when the original expedition got wiped out. It all seemed a little coincidental. And then the BB experiments... he was the president's right hand. You can't tell me that he didn't know. And he never told a soul. They were definitely hiding something they were ashamed of there. And it was always him who so stubbornly insisted the BBs were to be treated as equipment. And him and the president who decided to scatter Mama, Lockne, and Heartman across the continent as part of Bridges I. If they had really wanted to understand and overcome the Death Stranding, then they would have kept them all together. They all have DOOMS. They're all experts in their fields. They should have kept them in one place and made them research countermeasures. They didn't need someone like me there. I'm just a coroner. I don't even have DOOMS. I suspected that the director and the president made the decision to split them all up so they didn't start looking too closely at the BBs and the Chiral Network. But now I'm starting to piece together a different narrative."

Deadman's expression was stiff. Sam didn't think that was the network's fault this time. Deadman may have suspected Die-Hardman, but he had probably wanted to believe in him more than anyone else. It was only a gut feeling that Sam had, but he felt like he could sympathize with Deadman. He knew Deadman's anguish of not knowing where he came from and doubting his own humanity all too well. Neither of them knew what it was like to have a parent who had brought them into this world, who was connected to them genetically or physically via the umbilical cord. There were plenty of unhappy kids throughout this world in the same boat, but what Deadman, who had no Beach, and Sam, a repatriate who was rejected by the Beach, had in common was their craving for the very existence of a biological parent. Deadman had probably seen a parental figure in Die-Hardman. And Sam… Sam felt a conflicting attitude toward Bridget, one of awe and dependence. It looked like Lucy's observations about the relationship between Sam and his adoptive mother had been true, after all.

"Something's been bothering me, you see…" Deadman's words snapped Sam back to his senses.

"We've been operating on the assumption that Higgs was controlling Cliff. But that can't possibly be correct. Because Higgs is gone and Cliff is still causing trouble."

Sam looked straight at Deadman.

"So Cliff is the mastermind?" Sam's question wasn't addressed to Deadman, it was addressed to himself. It seemed to make sense. Deadman gave a vague nod like he had guessed what Sam was thinking.

"It might sound crazy to you, but this is my theory. I don't think it's possible for Cliff to have been behind everything up to this point, but that's not to say he's had nothing to do with these events. What Higgs was so obsessed with was the idea of hastening extinction. Now, Bridget's plan was to bring all the cities back online so that we could rebuild America. The Chiral Network she envisioned could end up proving instrumental in helping humanity to overcome extinction, and with mankind reconnected and reunited and a connection to the wisdom of the past, that would give us a fighting chance of survival. But that gets in the way of Higgs's extinction ideology. So, he took Amelie, an Extinction Entity, to try and force extinction in one go. Now think, if Higgs really was Cliff's puppet, that would mean that Cliff also wants extinction, right? But Lou is the only thing Cliff has ever shown an interest in."

Sam didn't say anything, but nodded. It fitted so far.

"If Cliff is hoping for extinction, that would also mean that Lou is connected to extinction somehow. Maybe even all BBs." Deadman indicated toward the pod with his eyes.

Lou was sleeping with all four limbs crossed, connected to the womb of a mother lying far away in Capital Knot City. How could something like Lou be connected to extinction? Deadman said himself that his theory was crazy. Sam wanted to believe that it was.

"BBs are connected to the realm of the dead through their stillmother's womb and umbilical cord. Don't you think that's similar to the Extinction Entities that Heartman and Higgs described? Well, I don't, but we can't say that the

BBs created after the Death Stranding are in no way involved, can we? That's why I want to know how Lou and the others were born. I want to use the Chiral Network you connected back up for us to find out the truth."

Deadman's gaze was wandering all over. Maybe he was scared of Sam. Sam knew that the look on his own face couldn't have been friendly. Before he realized it, he was clenching both fists tightly, so tight they had gone white. Deadman looked away awkwardly. Then Sam said something almost in an effort to convince himself to do so.

"I'm going back to that Beach."

If Cliff was the mastermind, he would probably try to finish what Higgs had started. In which case, he might still be holding the director and Amelie there. And even if it wasn't, swapping theories and conjecture wasn't going to solve anything anyway.

"I see, I suppose that's all that can be done now," Deadman conceded. "But you won't be able to leave just yet."

"What do you mean? Is the Beach still chaotic?" Sam asked.

"Yes. Fragile is at HQ right now, but she won't be able to jump all the way to you. If you want her to get you back to Amelie's Beach, then you're going to have to make your own way here."

There was a large cracking sound, like the space Sam existed in was being torn in two. The electrical systems in the room all blacked out. Lou began to cry out in protest at being disturbed. Sam released the pod from the incubator in the darkness and placed it in his arms. "It's alright, Lou," Sam whispered quietly.

When Lou stopped crying the lights flickered back on.

Sam was once again greeted by Deadman's hologram. Only this time, Heartman stood next to him.

"Thanks, Sam. You did it. The continent is connected," Heartman said gratefully. "I'm at HQ at the moment, together with Lockne. Fragile brought us here."

"Can you ask her to take me there, too?" Sam asked.

"Sorry, but I don't think that will be possible," Heartman replied.

Heartman hung his head again and this time his hologram froze in place. Heartman kept talking.

"Deadman was right. The Beach is in disarray and it's far too dangerous to jump right now. Lockne and I were just lucky. Fragile transported us here after she returned from the Beach and before things became too jumbled. But now she's exhausted. She's been comatose since she got back. I'm afraid that if we don't let her rest, she could die. She said that she'd take you to the Beach once she had recovered, before she drifted off."

—*Wouldn't want to settle for anything less than perfection.*

Sam remembered the last words that Fragile had uttered on the Beach.

Sam hadn't meant for her to feel that way. She had

already sensed the danger when she tried to jump Deadman to the Beach. Yet she still transported Heartman and the others to HQ in case anything happened.

"It's too far. We know that, Sam. We know how much time it will take to get back to HQ from there. But there's no other way," Heartman implored as his frozen hologram began to disintegrate from the feet up, while Deadman's kept shrinking and ballooning. What was the point of the Chiral Network if it could only produce this sorry excuse for communications? Mama and Lockne pointed out the risk of interference on the Beach years ago. They even took steps to deal with it. Yet as soon as it was all connected, it still ended up like this.

What's the point of America if it can only produce crap like this? Was this why Sam had crossed an entire continent?

"Everything might be over already by the time I get there," Sam warned. "Cliff already has Amelie and he's going to make sure we go extinct. It's like Amelie said. Once all the knots are connected, all she has to do is connect the Beaches and then we're all done for."

"Do you think Amelie really wants to do that? All we can do is believe in her. We have to believe in the woman who went all the way out west despite knowing she was an Extinction Entity. It was the same for you. Nobody had any faith in a one-man expedition. But you still came through," Heartman replied.

—I can end it all, just like that. But what I want—what I have always wanted—is to be a part of it. For us all to be one.

That's what Amelie said. All Sam could do was believe in her.

"With all the Beaches so entangled, you should expect the mentalities of everyone living under the network to be in disarray, too. All the alternate worlds that have run in parallel with ours are interfering with each other. What we need now is a symbol to converge them in the same dimension so that we can unify them all. That is what America is for. It doesn't matter if there are a thousand interpretations of what a country means or what people want from America. It doesn't matter if people embrace it or reject it. Acceptance and rejection both require the existence of America as a concept. The important thing is that everyone's Beaches are reintegrated under the symbol of America. Only then will the Chiral Network be able to perform its intended function. That's why we need to hold an inauguration to appoint someone as the American President. That's why we need you to rescue Amelie, and that's not going to change even if she is an Extinction Entity. In fact, I think that Amelie's actions as an Extinction Entity will ride on what we choose to do now. Let's put our faith in that."

Heartman's and Deadman's holograms stabilized. Now they were clear, as if the two of them were standing in the room itself. What would Sam choose? Deadman and Heartman looked to be choosing life.

"The two of you share a very special connection. Your dreamcatcher... Her *quipu*... They are no mere trinkets. They are singular, irreplaceable totems—embodiments of your shared memories. They connect you two," Heartman explained.

Sam gripped the dreamcatcher hanging around his neck. Why had this thing never disappeared in all the years he had it since he was a kid? He was never without it. Even when he left Bridges. No matter what danger he faced. He never consciously took good care of it, but whenever it broke, it did seem to repair itself. It was like a part of his body now. As he grew up and his old cells were replaced by the new, it was the only thing that had remained constant. His oldest body part.

"Dreamcatchers are a product of Native American tradition—that of the Ojibwe people, to be precise. They were said to ward off nightmares, to alter one's dreams. If DOOMS is indeed Amelie's gift to us, her shared dream of our future, perhaps it's an invitation for us to change it. A test—challenging us to find hope amid the hopelessness."

Sam could almost feel the body heat radiating from Heartman. He was right. At the very least, Sam refused to get overwhelmed by this unjust world.

"I'll go back east. I'll go to find Amelie," he told them.

"While we await your return, I'll search the Beach for Amelie and the director. I doubt my ties to them are strong enough, but better that than sitting around doing nothing," Heartman said a little bashfully, lightly tapping the AED on his chest.

"I'll see if I can't find something in the records on the two of them, and Clifford Unger. Maybe they're more connected than we know." Deadman also seemed to have come to life in the room beside Sam as he mulled what might be coming in the future.

"Then we hereby enter into a contract with Sam Porter Bridges. We would like you to transport one repatriate all the way to HQ in Capital Knot City. We'll be here to receive you."

CAPITAL KNOT CITY // BRIDGES HQ

Are we doing the right thing? Deadman thought, sitting down and looking up at Heartman as the AED on his chest announced that he had one minute left until cardiac arrest. Heartman had been looking at a map of the continent on the monitor with a concerned look on his face. He headed over to the sofa and lay down.

The monitor was displaying chiral density in real-time. The different sizes and colors of the circles across it were fluctuating wildly. There was no pattern in the fluctuations at all. Uncontrollable energy was swirling around them. It made Deadman think of a newly formed primordial planet.

But it hadn't been this way until everything was connected.

Heartman explained it in this way: when each of the Knot Cities was connected it was like creating simple junctions between different galaxies, but once they were connected into a whole, they began to collide with one another.

The AED made a beep and Heartman went into cardiac arrest. Deadman stared at the monitor and sighed. Was Heartman accessing a Beach on that map somewhere?

There was no doubt that such huge spikes in chiral density would have a corresponding physical effect on the planet. Deadman imagined that regions that had never experienced timefall before were getting their first taste of its cruelty. That new BT territories were springing up all over.

We've gone and made a terrible bridge, Deadman thought to himself.

If they didn't change this world back using the meta-level laws that would integrate the Beaches, this would become the new normal. Deadman was trying his best to keep up with Heartman's hypotheses and explanations, but it was extremely difficult to wrap his head around. The Beach is just a concept in one phase, but real in others? Maybe Deadman was destined never to understand. He didn't have a Beach.

But Heartman was out there wandering the Beach at this very moment. Fragile had fallen into a coma from all her jumps through it. Deadman knew that he would never be able to think or feel about the Beach in the same way they did. He would never understand them and they would never get him. Not Mama, who had been connected to her BT daughter, nor the director, who people celebrated as the man who wouldn't die. It made Deadman feel lonely. So he exaggerated his differences. Broadcast them. Even though he wished for nothing more than for people to be able to understand him and for him to be able to understand others, he was different. That's why it was so impossible. He used that excuse as a shield. He told others that he was made of seventy percent cadavers. That he was grown from pluripotent stem cells. He wanted to connect with other people more than anything, but he used these tales as extreme cover stories to refuse the formation of those bonds in the first place.

For someone like Deadman, the BBs were special. He felt like they were something he could identify with, that they could be a means to understand himself. That they would help him to finally get closer to someone. In this case, Sam. Not being able to go to the Beach himself, he had seen something of a kindred spirit in Sam, who could only go as far as the Seam. It was like the BBs had become a bridge for Deadman to finally reach out.

Now that he felt like he finally understood someone, he had an epiphany. Perhaps the meta-level law that would integrate the Beaches was that kind of understanding. Maybe some kind of symbol that connected people.

Something that made it possible for people to understand each other or bestowed people with an identical delusion in which to share. It didn't actually matter what it was.

Once Deadman had his revelation, Heartman came back to life.

He looked at Deadman with a puzzled expression as he sat up and wiped the tears from his face.

Deadman realized that he had been crying, too. He began waffling on about his epiphany in a bid to explain his tears away.

Heartman listened to what Deadman had to say, showing him a smile at various points along the way. He was looking at Deadman with the pride of a teacher listening to a bright student, and watched as Deadman tried his best to explain his theory so animatedly that he broke out into a sweat.

"That's right." Heartman nodded in satisfaction and gave the thumbs up. "But let me elaborate a little. Both Neanderthals and Homo sapiens are believed to share a common ancestor in the form of Homo heidelbergensis, but there are clear differences between the two. Neanderthals were brutish and brawny, well-equipped to hunt larger animals and survive in colder climates, whereas Homo sapiens were slender-limbed, and only capable of hunting smaller prey. The Neanderthals even had larger brains than us. Normally one would think that would mean the Neanderthals would outlast us Homo sapiens. But they didn't.

"As millennia passed, Homo sapiens learned to create tools and hunt in packs. The Neanderthals also fashioned tools of their own, but these were crude in comparison, and developed little over 200,000 years—perhaps because these simple-minded beings favored small family units, so that even if a breakthrough occurred, it was unlikely to be shared with others. This isolation, more than any other factor, seems to have led to their decline.

"Homo sapiens, meanwhile, conceived religion, with which large numbers of individuals could be bound together in service to a common cause. Strength in numbers also made their communities more resistant to famine and other calamities. In other words, Homo sapiens grew stronger through interpersonal connections. By creating what came to be called 'society.' The meta-level law we talk about could be referred to as fiction. While each Beach belongs to an individual, what unifies them all is a common fiction."

After listening to Heartman's explanation intently, Deadman turned back toward the monitor showing the North American continent. The chiral density was still spiking wildly. What kind of fiction, what kind of story, would be needed to resolve this?

"There is something that we will never be able to influence, no matter how we apply ideology, principles, religion, myths, or disciplines like science. Homo sapiens are weak. If tossed out naked into a forest with no tools, we'd die extremely quickly. So we put distance between ourselves and our natural state to survive. But the price we paid was giving up a part of us that we'll never find our way back to. Despite its evident nature in all other living things, we became estranged from it. Yet we still struggle unconsciously against it. I suppose it's also why I keep dying for twenty-one minutes at a time, even though I know I'll never see my wife or daughter again," Heartman said, tapping his AED. "Philosophers named this part of us 'Id.' On a primitive level, Id thinks. Id determines. They recognized that this Id that humans can't control is what makes the world go around. That's why people make offerings. To try and appeal to that part of us that no one can reach. I'm sure you must know the song of London Bridge. There's a theory held by some that the My Fair Lady mentioned in its lyrics is a human sacrifice buried in the foundations of the bridge. The bridge was destroyed and rebuilt so many times that people started to bury others alive there, to appease whatever was causing such misfortune. Today we'd consider this illogical, irrational nonsense. But when everyone believes in something, it gives that thing meaning and a function in reality. This is another example of the meta-level law of fiction."

<Five minutes to cardiac arrest.>

An electronic voice put a stop to Heartman's long-winded speech. Heartman lay back down, wondering aloud if he had talked for too long.

"Id was what made this heart-shaped heart." Heartman pointed to the left side of his chest and winked.

"Maybe Id flows through the Beach and the Beach comes from our Id. Or maybe Id is the Beach itself. In any case, the Beach summoned the BTs here and acted as an intermediary for the Death Stranding. It's an unpleasant, frightening domain, yet we can still 'use' it. This is a new reality for us, a new dimension of fiction. That's why I believe that you have a Beach too, Deadman, even if it does differ from mine. Oh, looks like I've talked too much, it's almost time. I'm off."

The AED began to play the Funeral March and Heartman closed both eyes. All Deadman could do was look at the monitor now he had been left all on his own again. Heat was radiating from the center of his head. It was like his thoughts and emotions were swirling into a vortex. Just like those displayed all over the monitor.

SOUTH KNOT CITY OUTSKIRTS // SAFEHOUSE

Sam fiddled with his cuff link in the midst of a downpour and unlocked the door to the safehouse. He descended to the private room in the basement, connected Lou to the incubator, and had just sat down on the bed when he was finally overwhelmed by tiredness.

It had been more than ten days since Sam woke up after returning from Amelie's Beach. At least, that's what it felt like. Sam had already lost count.

The cuff link wasn't operating as it was supposed to. Both the vitals monitoring devices and the log system had stopped. Even the communications function was fickle. The map was still displaying properly, but it hadn't updated lately and still only showed the old data from Sam's outward journey. For all intents and purposes, it was broken. Or, to look at it in another light, Sam was now free from the shackles of all of Bridges' systems.

That might have made him quite happy once upon a time, but not right now. He had no idea about Amelie's movements or anything else that was going on around him and the stress was becoming unbearable. He had been repeatedly struck by a profound sense of isolation, like he and Lou were shut off in their own little world. His communications with HQ were limited to when he reached Knot Cities, Bridges facilities, and safehouses equipped with communications terminals.

Lockne deduced that the reason the cuff link was acting so strangely was due to all the chaos on the Beach. It was interfering with the flow of time and causing lags in communication. The system was completely incapable of handling its new load. Sam could communicate to a point using fixed communications equipment, but mobile devices were useless.

The timefall continued to pour. On his way here, Sam had seen the dense chiral clouds that blocked out the sky illuminated by bands of light. They were similar to the auroras that were observed at the poles, and looked like blood bleeding out of the heavens or enormous dragons crossing the cloudy sky.

The Chiral Network had warped and twisted this world—the time-space of this continent. And Sam knew he only had himself to blame. He felt shackled by the weight of his actions on his shoulders. He couldn't even excuse it by saying that he was asked to do it. Putting things right was the cargo he bore now.

Sam activated the communications equipment in the room. He established a link with HQ and connected with Deadman. The timeless, high-capacity Chiral Network was now just a network in name only and could only offer a voice-only connection.

They still hadn't found Amelie, Die-Hardman, or Cliff. Nor any clue about how to access Amelie's Beach. Deadman's investigation, however, had yielded some results.

<I've been looking into Clifford Unger and wanted to share my thoughts. To recap, Unger was a US Special Forces operative. His retirement roughly coincided with the Death Stranding. After he left the service, he somehow became involved in the early BB experiments. However, he died before they

ended. I'm beginning to suspect that these "battlefields" of his are at least partially sustained by his enduring emotional attachments. Anger, resentment, regret—I'm pretty sure it's got something to do with the BB experiments. That much seems clear given his repeated attempts to steal Lou. Cliff seems to be driven by a compulsion to "reclaim" our BB, as if that will make him whole again. A compulsion so powerful that he was not only able to drag himself from the depths of hell to do it, but bring a piece of that hell along with him.>

"That doesn't make sense. The first BB experiments took place long before Lou became a BB. That can't be the reason why Unger keeps going after Lou."

<That's a good point, but consider this. Cliff isn't after Lou, he just can't forgive the act of making a BB itself. The BB experiments were continued in secret on the orders of President Strand… supposedly with the primary objective of developing BT detectors and preventing voidouts. Any advancements that could be applied to the fields of chiral communications and Beach research were meant to be of purely secondary benefit. But it turns out that's just a cover story. The truth is, Sam… BBs were originally conceived as catalysts for the operation of the Chiral Network. They're

integrated into the infrastructure of Knot Cities
for that very reason—every single one you've
brought into the fold.>

Sam could still vividly remember what he saw when he
activated the communications terminal in that ramshackle
facility by the tar belt. How a BB pod was embedded in that
equipment that looked like a huge cross. So, he hadn't
imagined it after all. The thought made him feel sick.

<It was probably Amelie herself who installed
them as she moved west with the first expedition,
carrying out her mother's grand plan… making
sacrifice after sacrifice on the altar of progress.
On the surface, she was the president who cancelled
the BB experiments, but behind the scenes she was
still forging ahead with that inhumane plan. Just
because it was for the good of America, doesn't
mean that it can be forgiven.>

What were you up to, Bridget? What kind of America was
she trying so desperately to rebuild if she would go so far as
sacrificing unborn babies? What's the point of surviving
extinction if she was just going to throw away lives? Sam
wondered if the reason Higgs was so bent on having
humanity wipe themselves out was because he knew all of
this. Or was he just a vehicle for Cliff's intentions?

Had Fragile managed to get anything out of him on
Amelie's Beach? Sam needed to wake her up out of her

coma and get her to tell him everything she knew about Higgs. Yet another reason why he needed to get back east as soon as possible.

SOUTH KNOT CITY

Even after traversing back over the snowy mountains that had given him such a battering on his way west, passing by Mama's old lab where he had found her holed up with her BT baby, and finally arriving at South Knot City where Fragile's body had been ruined forever and sullied with the marks that caused her such shame, the skies hadn't changed at all. The timefall may have let up, but the clouds were still illuminated by beams of light that looked like bloodstained dragons.

Once he had arrived, Owen Southwick, a Bridges employee who was stationed in South Knot City, gave Sam the news that the Elder had passed.

—*I'm no prepper. I'm just a parasite.*

Sam remembered the Elder saying that as he gave his shelter over as a knot for the Chiral Network.

Ever since he had joined the UCA, America had gotten more and more involved with the Elder's life. The Elder used to refer to himself as a parasite, but now it was America's turn to exploit his shelter and feed off him. Maybe some people would call that coexistence or symbiosis, but while the Elder had died, America had lived. America had completed the Chiral Network and created this distorted world, all for the purpose of sustaining itself. The sole reason America disposed of the Elder's dead body was for its own preservation. It was like the Elder and all other people under the UCA were nothing more than resources. American reconstructionism was touted as a way to save mankind from extinction, yet all it had done so far was leave a trail of human sacrifices in its wake.

"The Elder seemed grateful to you guys," Owen told Sam. Even though the surface was even more dangerous than before, Owen Southwick insisted that meeting in hologram form would not do and he had come up specially to the cargo room on the upper floor.

"He told me to thank you and all the other couriers and porters. Fragile and her dad, too."

"Fragile and the others deserve gratitude, but not me," Sam commented.

Sam hadn't gone all the way to the Elder's shelter for the Elder's sake. It hadn't even been for something altruistic like saving mankind. The only reason he had taken part in this ridiculous plan was because he wanted to save Amelie and Lou. And underpinning all that was nothing but a selfish desire of wanting to prove his own self-worth as a repatriate. He just wanted to know why he had been born this way. In that sense, he was also a parasite, just one on America and this expedition.

"Come on, Sam. There's plenty to thank you for. It was you and Fragile who saved us for a second time, remember?" Owen said, reaching for Sam's arm. When Sam avoided his grasp, he looked a little dejected. Sam felt sorry when he saw Owen's expression. How could he possibly accept the gratitude of someone he wouldn't even let touch him?

"The Elder was amazed. He couldn't believe there were still people out there who were willing to put their lives on the line to save us. If that nuke had made it into South Knot City, he would have been caught up in the blast, too. But that's not all he wanted to say. Back when America was the United States, his uncle was drafted into war. America was getting involved in pretty much every conflict going—not that there was a shortage at that time."

The warzone that Cliff always brought with him was a senseless battleground from a war called the Second World War. It was a war fought with fighter planes, tanks, bombs, and other small arms—weapons that drowned out the voices and screams of their victims. Sam remembered the stench of blood, mud, and oil.

"The Elder talked about the nuclear bomb. He said it was a weapon that was created at the end of the Second World War. One that could slaughter thousands in one go. Made it impossible to tell who had died and in what way. He used to say that it was the symbol of mass-produced human suffering. Each and every human is precious. Every single one of us is irreplaceable. That's what we're all taught to believe, right? Well, a nuke extinguishes the sanctity of individual human life. When the Elder's uncle returned from the war, he fell ill with a heart condition and eventually went on to kill himself. But that wasn't a senseless death. That was a death that he chose. In his suicide note, he described it as 'dying with dignity.'

"If Higgs's plan back then had succeeded, he would have been yet another anonymous death. Another person killed en masse. If he hadn't joined the UCA he would have died all alone, necrotizing into a nameless monster and potentially a living nuke himself. And even if he didn't, no one would have even known that he'd died. Sure, all the UCA did was acknowledge his death and deal with his corpse, but there was a record of him. Someone knew. He was a part of someone's memory. And that was all down to the connection you made. And for that, the Elder was grateful." Owen removed a scrap of folded paper from his pocket and gave it to Sam. "The Elder gave me this before he died. He told me to give it to you if I ever saw you again."

All it said was, "Thank you, Sam." It was written in pen. The ink was blurry and the scrap smelled of tobacco smoke.

Along with the Elder's words of thanks was his name.

<Sam, I've made more progress in a certain investigation.>

Owen had probably notified HQ that Sam had arrived. As soon as he activated the communications terminal in his private room, he heard Deadman's voice.

<The security settings for these records were unusually strict. I couldn't access a lot of it, but I did glean a few scraps of information. It seems that Clifford Unger willingly put his own child in the care of the scientists conducting the BB experiments. It's been difficult to compare the records, but it seems like the reason that Cliff left the special forces was because he had fathered a baby. The timelines mostly match.

<It looks like it happened after the first Death Stranding, but I can't find a record of him getting married on the system, so I have no idea who the mother was. This is speculation, so take it with a pinch of salt, but I think he handed the BB over completely unaware of their true intentions. I'm certain that the number of people who knew what was really going on was extremely limited. It was probably only revealed to a handful of engineers and their superiors—which would have been Bridget

and those in her inner circle. I think when Cliff found out about their plans, he attempted to reclaim custody. And after he failed, the BB remained in the program's care.>

"Do you think it's his hate for the president and Bridges that's driving him?" Sam questioned, his voice sounding louder than he intended.

<Do you remember what Higgs told you in Port Knot City? He told you that Bridget Strand had died. But we made sure that fact never leaked out of Bridges. You even incinerated her in secret. But somehow, Higgs knew. I had suspected there was a traitor among us, but that doesn't appear to have been the case. I think that Cliff—being dead himself—sensed that she died. That's how Higgs found out. That would at least make some sense.

<Just because President Strand is dead, doesn't mean Cliff's hate died with her. No, I think he redirected it toward Bridges. Toward you and Amelie and anyone close to the director. Anyone who he sees as being involved with the BB experiments. And now that hate is driving him to set in motion the Last Stranding—to bring an end to the world as we know it.>

In a sense, the mass killings of the world wars and the mass extinction caused by the Death Stranding were one and the same. All those lives, each with a different face, a different name, different pasts and feelings, were mercilessly snuffed out by one horrific act of violence. Perhaps Deadman was right. Perhaps the hate and anger of losing his one and only child had pushed Cliff so far over the edge that he wanted to bring the extinction and violently trample all over the life and death that belonged by right to every other soul.

Lou didn't have a name—just the assigned number of BB-28—probably much like the other BBs installed in each of the Knot Cities. Bridges had stolen their personalities and names before they were even born. Neither Sam nor anyone else had any right to criticize Cliff's hatred. He could see why Cliff would want his revenge as he stubbornly called out for his "BB."

<I wonder if that's why he used Higgs to capture Amelie. He knew that she's an EE. When Amelie jumped away before, she left a message saying that she was going to finish what Bridget started. Now it's starting to make sense. Bridget originally took the BB from Cliff to turn it into a human sacrifice and avoid extinction. Now Amelie is going to go and try to prevent the Last Stranding that Cliff is trying to cause in retaliation. She must have gone back to the Beach to confront him. But no one has seen hide nor hair of Amelie or Die-Hardman since then. They both must have fallen

into Cliff's hands. Maybe that's why the world's so messed up right now. It might not just be because all the knots were brought online. We have even less time than I thought.>

Deadman's haggard appearance hung thickly in his voice. Sam couldn't see Deadman's face, but he could tell the man was physically and mentally exhausted. Sam was the same. All he could do was keep on inching his way back the way he came.

<Heartman and Lockne have barely gotten any sleep because they've been so busy looking for clues. Fragile is recovering nicely, by the way. She's not awake yet, but she's definitely out of the danger zone. Things are still touch-and-go, but at least things aren't getting worse. Look, where Die-Hardman is concerned, can you think of any strong connection that he might have with Amelie?>

Sam couldn't think of anything. All Sam knew was that Die-Hardman was always at Bridget's side. When Sam first joined Bridges, Bridget had been the director and Die-Hardman was her assistant. The impression Sam got was that Die-Hardman didn't decide anything. He was just Bridget's right-hand man, only there to loyally carry out her bidding. Sam couldn't even remember seeing him and Amelie together.

<There's no way he could've made the jump to

Amelie's Beach if they didn't share a strong
personal connection, right? Well I looked… and I
couldn't see one. The network should've contained
something, anything… but there was nothing
whatsoever. Lockne is trying to break through the
security on the archives, but it's airtight and
we're not making much headway. It keeps demanding
Bridget's or Die-Hardman's biometric information.
But Die-Hardman's entire life prior to his tenure
with Bridges has been redacted. His name, his past,
everything. There's no telling who he was. Which
led me to consider another possibility: that it
isn't the director and Amelie who have a connection,
but the director and Clifford Unger? And what if
that connection is what facilitated the director's
jump to Amelie's Beach? If it's those two who have
a personal history, then it might explain why Cliff
is holding the director hostage as well. But even
if that were the case, it doesn't answer the bigger
question… How the hell did Cliff and Die-Hardman
end up on Amelie's Beach? Heartman has this
hypothesis: 'If we want to fix the Beaches, we need
to do so using some meta-level law. A law that
governs human consciousness and brings a new
meaning to the world is required. Perhaps that is
Amelie's Beach.' I don't really understand it. The

Beach of everyone living on this planet can be compared to all of the individual capillaries that make up a living creature. In this case, the world.

<Each of them circulates blood without any of it crossing. So a higher plane of Beach that acts as a heart to govern this must also exist. That is a meta-level law. Until now, the life of this world has been in homeostasis. But now this new Chiral Network system is interfering with it, it's all collapsing. The only thing that can restabilize it is a Beach that exists on a higher plane. And what if the Beach in question were none other than Amelie's? Cliff may have summoned the director, but his true aim might have been to seize control of Amelie's Beach. To exploit its power over every other Beach... and trigger the Last Stranding. Amelie doesn't want extinction. She must have told you this? So, if we can eliminate Cliff, this world will be reborn as a new world that follows a new law. That's why we need you to go back to Amelie's Beach, Sam. That's the only way to stop the Last Stranding.>

The room was suddenly plunged into darkness. It went silent as if the communications had been cut.

All the systems were off. The only one left on and emitting light was the incubator containing Lou's pod. It seemed like Lou was trying to tell him something. Sam walked over to the pod. Lou was neither crying nor acting unsettled. Lou's eyes were staring at Sam, wide open.

Let's go outside. It felt like Lou was whispering to him.

The elevator arrived at the upper floor and the doors opened to wind blowing down the slope. The Odradek activated, but even without its help, Sam could sense that Cliff was approaching. Lou still didn't cry. Even though it didn't shed a single tear, Sam could tell his BB was frightened. He had the same feeling inside his own chest. But he wouldn't back down. Battling against the wind, Sam climbed up the slope.

Let's go. Lou was encouraging him somehow.

Cliff was here and he had brought a storm. Sam knew that Amelie and Die-Hardman must have been nearby, too. It was time to end it.

It was like the dragons in the sky had coiled into a vortex. An enormous funnel-shaped cloud, red like blood, let out a clap of thunder. It was like the roar of a raging dragon. It swooped down from the sky and swallowed Sam and Lou up in one gulp.

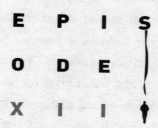

E P I S O D E X I I I

CLIFFORD UNGER

Night approached. The rain fell. There was no wind nor any sign of movement. The air felt like it was draped heavily around Sam's entire body and the stench of the dead hung in it.

As Sam attempted to get up, he put his hand out to steady himself, but instead of making contact with the ground, it made contact with something else. It was a dismembered human arm. Once Sam's eyes had adjusted to the darkness and he could finally survey his surroundings, he could see damaged shells scattered all around him. This wasn't Amelie's Beach. It was space-time that was full of death. Sam's immediate reaction was frustration. He had wanted to go back to Amelie's Beach. But then his mood changed. Just because this wasn't Amelie's Beach, didn't mean that Cliff wasn't here.

Sam took the rifle that the dead body was clutching.

Somewhere far off in the distance, Sam could hear explosions ripping the night air to pieces. The breeze picked up and the grass and plants swayed. The air that stroked Sam's face was damp and hot. This place was different from the battlefields of stone, earth, and cold, dry air that Sam had encountered before. It was overgrown with plants he had never seen before and the sludgy bogs beneath his feet made it hard to walk.

The only thing this battlefield had in common with the others was the thick stench of death that permeated throughout it.

The Odradek on Sam's shoulder rotated and stopped. It turned into a cross and glowed orange, showing the way to Cliff.

An explosion went off in front of Sam, as if showing him the way, and gracing the night with daylight for a split second. A green temple, filling Sam's vision from the floor to the sky, appeared before him. He looked around to find a cell assembled from what he assumed to be tree branches surrounded by piles of skewered bodies, one on top the other, all soldiers dressed in field uniform. Several men appeared from the grass. All of them were dressed and equipped lightly and spoke to each other in a language that wasn't English. Sam remained undetected as the men efficiently weaved their way among the intricately laid branches. Sam checked the direction that the Odradek was pointing and followed behind them.

The blades of a helicopter disturbed the night sky. Trees swayed wildly in the wind and the leaves that were torn off them danced through the air. The belly of the hovering helicopter opened and regurgitated its glowing, wet insides. Its long, tubular viscera that reminded Sam of intestines writhed its way down to the ground. Four soldiers nimbly descended. They were skeletal soldiers without skin, flesh, nor organs, but all clad in army gear. They didn't seem to have souls, but they did seem to have a purpose. One by one the soldiers arrived on the jungle floor, each guided by a purpose that had piled up on the battlefield like sediment and penetrated their minds through the backs of their skulls.

The end of the helicopter's guts was attached to Cliff's abdomen as he lorded over the world below from his helicopter. The organ wasn't like an intestine. This was an umbilical cord woven of all his negative emotions. It wasn't an organ to digest all his resentment and sadness and hatred, but an organ to transmit it.

Cliff wound the umbilical cord that hung all the way to the ground back into his abdomen. Then, he suddenly kicked off the deck and dived into the jungle below.

A flare went off, as if Cliff was challenging anyone who might have been lurking below. It pierced through the night and lit up the jungle like the midday sun.

As soon as Cliff landed, an extremely hot wind began to gust violently. Trunks of trees crashed into each other and the entire jungle began to creak.

The skeletal soldiers ran in the direction that Cliff instructed, as Cliff followed behind them.

Sam was running through the jungle, which blew fiercely with hot air. He could feel the resentment of the dead beneath his feet every time his feet made contact with the ground. He made sure to keep running so fast that they wouldn't catch him.

There was a burned-down village up ahead. The rice paddies around it were studded with holes caused by countless bombs. Dried-out fetuses were haphazardly thrown away. Sam saw one fetus wrapped around a gun that was the same size as itself. He passed a mountain of burnt and charred adult corpses. Sam kept on running, through a land where no one moved and no one breathed. The river was filled with the corpses of dogs and water buffalo and dead babies floated among the debris. The Odradek was pointing upstream. As Sam followed it, he could see flames and fires burning deep in the tropical jungle.

That must be where Cliff is.

Before he knew it, Sam had already entered a battlefield.

The ghosts of soldiers were fighting. It was the American soldiers who were clad in equipment that had been designed for killing. The weapons were engraved with the US insignia. Small-framed soldiers who didn't even have guns attacked the American soldiers. Even though at first glance it looked like the American soldiers had the overwhelming advantage, the other soldiers put up a hard fight, and despite the difference in firepower, continued to attack. Even when they were hit, they got right back up and continued to fight. As the war raged on, the same scene played out again and again in front of Sam.

The Odradek was unwavering as it showed Sam Cliff's location, but between them stood thick jungle. It was like a labyrinth and Sam couldn't see the other side. The smaller soldiers were using this situation to their advantage. If Sam didn't want to get caught up in their fight, all he could do was proceed cautiously straight ahead.

Sam walked out of the shadow of the trees and into a thicket, and then back into the shadow of the trees on the opposite side, holding his breath the entire time. He could sense something moving in front of him. He lay down on his belly and looked beyond the grass. Two of the skeletal soldiers were heading his way. It didn't seem like they had spotted him yet, though. If he stayed still they might just pass him by. The tension in Sam's body grew and grew, like a screw being tightened. If it surpassed his limits, he felt like his mind and body would both explode.

Once the soldiers were far enough away, Sam resumed his path. As he carried on forward, the jungle finally came to an end.

Now he was confronted with a swamp that was too wide to cross. He couldn't tell how deep it was. And there was no cover to be found.

He would have to go around.

He continued left, attempting to avoid the swamp, but soon found himself losing his sense of direction. He couldn't tell where the swamp was anymore. He could no longer hear the fighting. It was like both the ghostly soldiers and the sound of their weapons had disappeared. He was surrounded by the quiet of the jungle.

Sam climbed over the shrubs in the wild undergrowth that had grown undisturbed for thousands of years and the fallen trunks of giant trees, until he thought he could smell water. He started to suspect that he had gone in a circle and had arrived back at the swamp he was trying to avoid. Was this the way he came? Was he caught in a time loop and repeating the same thing over and over again? All he could do was rely on the Odradek and Lou. If he didn't, he would never be able to shrug off his doubts or escape the jungle itself. He would be doomed to wander it forever.

On the other side of the swamp, trees were burning. Cliff must be close. Sam was certain.

—*Give me back my BB.*

Cliff's voice echoed inside Sam's head. When he heard it for the first time, he had been terrified for some reason, but he didn't feel that way anymore. It may have been irrational and illogical, but Sam felt like he wanted to understand the man. Even if that only had its roots in Sam's motive of rescuing Amelie.

Gunshots rang out. Sam was hidden behind the trunk of a fallen tree, but the bullets showered down upon him mercilessly. He had no idea where the enemy was. Moreover, it seemed like he was getting shot by multiple enemies at once. A bullet grazed the bark of the tree.

Another penetrated the trunk. Each and every time, Sam felt like he could hear someone crying. Perhaps it was the sound of all of the memories accumulated by these fallen trees, that had seen so much war and death, as they burst open.

Something fell beside the tree trunk, but Sam didn't need to look to know what it was. It was a grenade. As Sam ran, the explosion chased him from behind. It threw him off his feet and headfirst into the ground. His world went dark. He couldn't hear anything anymore. He had fallen into pitch black, but the pain that seared throughout his entire body brought him back to reality.

He tried to stand up, but he couldn't feel anything below

his knees. He tried again, this time putting his hand on the tree trunk for support. Sam couldn't tell where his body ended. It felt like he had no definitive outline anymore. Like his consciousness was dissipating farther and farther out. Only the furious pounding of his heart told him that he was still connected to it.

Right beside his beating heart was Lou's pod. Sam could feel Lou's heartbeat, too. Their heartbeats became one, hitching Sam back to his body. Sam found his hands, feet, chest, stomach, and head, and pieced himself back together again.

"I won't let anyone take you away from me, Lou," Sam murmured, almost as if to spur himself on, and took off running.

On the other side of the thicket, Sam sensed something move again. The skeletal soldiers had returned. One had its back to him and was investigating its surroundings. Once again, it seemed not to have noticed him. Sam took aim at its back with his rifle. It was the only weapon he had and he had few bullets left. He couldn't miss. Knowing that he had to make this shot count, Sam's arms began to tremble with nerves. He couldn't control his muscles. The sound of the wind, which he had barely noticed until now, seemed strangely loud. At this rate, he would never be able to make his mark. He had to forget everything. He had to forget the background noise and imagine that he and his target were directly connected. He wasn't fumbling around for something in the distance, he was going to reach out and grab his target. He was going to hit it without the bullet wavering from its invisible. That's what he focused on. The trigger and his finger became one.

Seconds seemed to drag on for minutes, but Sam was sure he saw the bullet sink into the soldier's back. It smashed through the skeleton's spine, and ribs scattered across the floor. Sam had eliminated one of the obstacles that stood between himself and Cliff.

That single shot elevated Sam's senses onto another plane. Now, he could see the direction of the bloodlust that flowed through this jungle. He could sense where the rest of the skeletal soldiers were, where they were going and how they were going to get there. Even the seemingly chaotic jungle was formed of a kind of order that dictated the directions the trees grew in and the density of the underbrush. The creatures that lived in this forest were in tune with this order. The small-framed soldiers—who were beating their American counterparts despite their feeble-looking weaponry—probably knew how the jungle worked, too. They acted as though they were a part of it. The Americans were fighting against it instead, and losing.

The bullets in Sam's rifle weren't separate entities, they were a part of him.

Now that Sam had integrated into the order of the jungle and connected with his weapon, breaking through it no longer seemed so daunting. As Sam took aim it felt as natural as extending his own arm. It was like shooting bullets from his fingertips.

Sam had arrived where Cliff was waiting.

—*I'll get you out of here, BB.*

Sam could hear Cliff's voice again. He wasn't afraid of it anymore. All that was left to do was defeat him and take back Amelie. But Cliff was taking advantage of the jungle to knock the omnipotence-filled Sam down a peg.

The Odradek reacted violently. The sensor that had been pointing in the exact same direction until now began to rotate wildly. Lou had curled up into a ball and was laying in toward Sam. Lou seemed scared of the approaching terror.

—*BB... I'm gonna take you wherever you wanna go.*

Cliff's voice sounded even clearer than before. But Sam knew it was all in his head. Sam knew that he was around here somewhere, but he couldn't see him. Even though Sam now had a grip on the flow of the jungle, he still couldn't sense Cliff's presence.

—*Brought you an astronaut. Mankind can go anywhere. Even outer space.*

Sam screamed for it to stop, but Cliff had taken root in Sam's head and didn't seem intent on disappearing anytime soon.

Sam couldn't defeat what he couldn't see. He couldn't hit what he couldn't touch. He couldn't kill what was already dead. And he couldn't revive what hadn't been born.

A fire lit inside Sam's head. It burst into an inferno in a split second, engulfing Sam's entire body. In front of Sam stood Cliff, who was engulfed in the same flames.

—*Give me back my BB.*

Cliff extended a flaming hand and tried to grab Lou. Sam thrust it away instinctively. Cliff looked surprised and collapsed. But on his way down, he grabbed Sam's arm. Unable to keep his balance, Sam fell down to Cliff's level.

They were sinking intertwined into the swamp. Unable to even open his eyes, Sam blindly tried to shake away Cliff's entangling arms. Somehow, he managed to stand. Cliff had fallen forward and looked up. His entire body was covered from head to toe in a thick black liquid. Only the whites of his eyes gave off any light, boring two bright holes into the darkness. He looked like the primordial life that had one day crawled out of this swamp. Then he stood, too. Cliff managed to wrench himself away from the swamp and wiped the black liquid off his face. He had regained his features and was now glaring at Lou's pod. Sam could feel Lou's fear.

Even though Sam could stand, he was buried up to his waist in the swamp and couldn't move properly. Cliff grabbed him by the collar. Sam let out an angry groan, but

Cliff simply buried his fist in his stomach to shut him up.

Sam didn't feel pain, but rather heat. It felt like a mass of heat that had been driven into his guts. He convulsed as if his stomach had been turned inside out, and began to vomit blood and gastric juices. As Sam began to crumple up in agony, Cliff grabbed him by the nape of the neck and raised his head. Sam fell backward with the momentum and Cliff got on top of him. He began to try and unfasten the pod. Sam grabbed him by the arms.

—*BB, BB. Can you hear me?*

Cliff's mutterings echoed around Sam's head again and again. Sam was staring up at Cliff's lips, but they were tightly shut.

—*Can you hear me? It's Daddy.*

Sam began to hear multiple voices bickering, drowning Cliff out.

—*You saw wrong. Now check the other way.*

—*No, open it up. He's in there.*

The voices were muffled and Sam couldn't make them out clearly, but they sounded like they belonged to a man and a woman who weren't Cliff. Cliff's grip on the pod slackened.

Sam pushed Cliff off, and as he fell away, guns fell out of his uniform. Sam picked them up without a moment's hesitation.

Now the tables had turned. Cliff was now looking up at Sam thrusting a gun in his face. If Sam was going to shoot, now was his chance. But Sam's fingers didn't move. They felt like they belonged to someone else entirely. If he defeated Cliff now, he would be able to go back to his own world. Maybe Amelie would be released from Cliff's spell, too. Sam kept trying to convince himself to shoot, but he never pulled the trigger.

—*Shoot him!*

Sam could hear a commanding voice in the distance, but he couldn't tell who it belonged to. It was so muffled that Sam felt like he was hearing it through several layers of film.

Cliff reached out with one hand. Was he still after Lou? Sam tried to pull back.

But that wasn't the case. His hand was trying to cover the barrel of the gun. The palm of his hand was pressed right against its end.

—*Shoot him!*

Sam heard the voice again. He dropped the gun and Cliff dropped his arm. He was staring Sam right in the face. Then his gaze shifted to the pod.

But he wasn't looking at Lou. He was looking at the mascot that dangled from it.

—*Brought you an astronaut.*

Cliff's face twisted. Maybe he was trying to laugh. This figure had been attached to Lou's pod from the start. Cliff pushed himself up a little and reached out for the pod again.

"BB—Listen, I'll get you out of here," he muttered.

Sam threw his arms around the pod to protect Lou.

"Give me back my baby." Cliff's eyes were shedding tears. It was the unmistakable face of a father. Sam couldn't see it any other way.

"Are you Clifford Unger?" he asked.

A light switched on in Cliff's eyes. He blinked a few times. It was like he was looking at something far away.

"They told me your name was Sam Porter..." Cliff's mouth opened as he remembered his words. "But you're Sam Bridges. My bridge to the future," Cliff said, standing up. He removed the chain that was hanging around his neck. Dangling there was his dog tag.

"I was just like any other cliff. A dead end. No way forward. Nothing but an obstacle—looking on at the world that people like you were trying to build. Dividing people was the only thing I was ever any good at."

Cliff looked down at the dog tag and hung it on Sam.

"But not you, Sam. You bring people together. You're their bridge to the future... and mine."

Cliff laid his arm on Sam's shoulder. The astronaut hanging from the pod swayed. Sam could hear Lou laughing. Sam removed the pod and held it out to Cliff. But he didn't try to take it. He simply looked at Lou smiling and stroked the pod window with his hand. Something had been set free. Maybe it was the connection between Cliff and Lou, or perhaps it was what bound him to Sam. Maybe it was something else entirely. He didn't know what it was right now.

Cliff looked Sam in the eye and smiled. He stretched out his arms and drew Sam into a hug. Sam accepted. He could smell something nostalgic by Cliff's ear. It felt like Cliff whispered something to him.

But his words were drowned out by the sound of a gunshot in the distance.

PORT KNOT CITY

It was a faint voice. When Sam tried to reach out and grab it, it became even smaller. It was Cliff's voice.

He wanted to find the source of this memory and struggled desperately toward the ocean floor. He tried to sink all the way down to the dark depths, where no light could penetrate, but it was no good.

Sam was discovered near the outer wall of Port Knot City. He was curled up asleep in the fetal position, clutching his BB to his chest and covered in mud. It had been Viktor from Bridges who had found them and carried him back to a private room.

Although Sam had some external injuries, none of them appeared to be life-threatening. He may have been exhausted, but none of his vitals were showing any sign of danger. He had just been in a deep sleep.

Viktor laughed about how it had been difficult to prize the pod out of Sam's arms. Sam had been curled up around the pod extremely tightly. It was like he was protecting it so that no one else could take it away.

"You kept Igor's figure on there," Viktor commented, surprised but grateful that his little brother's treasure had remained intact. "Your pod didn't fare so well, though. There's a handprint on there that we just can't get off. We checked to see if it was yours, but…"

The handprint belonged to Cliff, but Viktor had no way of knowing that.

"Deadman asked me to pass this on to you," Viktor told him.

The monitor on the communications terminal activated and Viktor showed Sam a file that was protected by layers of strong security.

Sam opened the file once Viktor had left his private room. Then he decided to establish a line with Deadman. That was probably the procedure he was supposed to follow.

<Oh, you're awake.>

Sam flashed back to the day he woke up in Capital Knot City. When he had been unable to save Viktor's little brother, Igor, and the rest of the Corpse Disposal Team from a voidout, and repatriated from the Seam.

<It was the same as before. It looks like you

were caught in a supercell… And emerged an instant later on the other side of Ground Zero… Not far from Port Knot City. Where were you taken this time? Amelie's Beach? Or another battlefield?>

Deadman's voice was trembling slightly. He was probably recalling what happened that time he got caught up in the battlefield himself.

"Neither Amelie nor Die-Hardman were there. I was on Cliff's battlefield," Sam answered.

<So that means you still haven't managed to find Amelie either.>

"I don't think Cliff is our enemy. He's trying to tell us something. He described himself as a cliff. That's where his existence ends. And he can't cross over here from the cliff edge."

He was only half-dead—although Sam couldn't bring himself to say that. He could probably say the same thing about himself.

Right now, Sam couldn't bring himself to tell Deadman about Cliff's confession, either. He had heard it, but he didn't know whether what Cliff said was true or not.

Cliff seemed to be missing most of the memories of his life, and had come here through the power of emotion. Propelled by the regrets of the anonymous dead. If Cliff was a mixture of all those feelings—if he was an incarnation of that time of war and destruction—then Lou and Sam were following in the footsteps of Cliff and their other predecessors.

And they were destined to clean up the mess that their fathers had left behind. Maybe Cliff had come to apologize for that. Maybe both Lou and Sam symbolized that sentiment to him.

Sam tried to retain some balance in his heart by interpreting it that way.

—*Although that was something that you still weren't unaware of, either.*

<Sam, are you okay?>

Deadman brought Sam back down to earth after he fell silent.

<I've got something you should see. Found it in the archives while I was digging around. It's a prerecorded message from the director…>

The monitor went black. This time a hologram flashed up behind Sam.

It was Die-Hardman.

But the image didn't move an inch. This man in the mask and black suit resembled a statue of a knight—a devoted servant to his lord—heading out to war.

<It was labelled "If I Don't Come Back.">

Taking that as a signal to start, the image began to move. The message started silently with Die-Hardman looking back over his shoulder to check his surroundings. It wasn't the action of a knight, but the delicate action of a scout sent to infiltrate the enemy's lair. He looked weary.

—Alright. This message is insurance in case something happens to me. For Bridges' eyes only.

Die-Hardman began to speak.

—This was sent to me. It appeared suddenly and without warning. Its Chiralium density is off the chart, so it must have been sent via the Beach. Amelie said you might recognize it, Sam. She was the one who sent it. It's a Bridge Baby that the terrorists used. I've heard that they're on Cliff Unger's battlefield, too. As you can see, it's just a doll.

—If you were alive back in the old days, you'd recognize this thing in a second. There used to be these naked baby dolls that were made up to look like Cupid. They were popular everywhere. But this is different. It doesn't have the wings that an angel is supposed to have on its back.

—It can't reach the heavens, but it can become a bridge to the realm of the dead. Amelie said she'd take me to the Beach if I wanted. But I'd need this doll to show me the way. It's a trap. It has to be. But I've decided to play along—

The hologram froze for a second. Cradling the doll to his chest, Die-Hardman didn't look like a father protecting the dependent, but someone who didn't know what to do after being handed something strange.

—You've all been playing along too, haven't you? You know this mask hides more than just my face. Look. This is my real face. Do you see any burn marks? I put on the mask and fabricated a lie. But Amelie's a blank slate, too. No past. No record she ever existed. She's a ghost. And the thing about ghosts… I've never met Amelie in person. Have you? Ever seen her in the flesh? Shook her hand? Touched her? Felt her warmth?

—The original team we sent was divided into two groups. Amelie was with the first. Mama and Heartman were with the second. They had no direct contact with her. Have you ever seen her as anything other than a hologram—

The message froze again and Deadman interrupted over the codec.

<Yes… Amelie's group was wiped out in Edge Knot City. Everyone but her. Everyone who could say whether or not she exists.>

"Bullshit. They're not the only people who can prove that she's real. We've touched, alright. Plenty of times."

Sam could almost see Deadman flinching on the other end of the codec call. He fell silent for a few seconds. But then he replied with something that Sam didn't expect.

<Well, I've only ever interacted with her hologram.>

"I'm telling you, I've met her. In person. Lots of times when I was little."

<Yes, but on the Beach> Deadman said bluntly. Sam was blindsided. He searched his head for a rebuttal or something to disprove what Deadman said, but came up

empty. He couldn't remember a time when they weren't on the Beach. He was getting more and more flustered and couldn't find anything to say.

Die-Hardman's hologram began to speak again.

—Amelie was born on the Beach. Or rather, her physical body—her *ha*—was born into this world, while her spiritual essence—her *ka*—was born on the Beach. Medically speaking, they weren't sure what to call it. In the end, they settled on a diagnosis similar to what's known as "locked-in syndrome," a condition where the subject is mentally present, but physically unable to move their body—except for their eyes, sometimes.

—The president was able to communicate with Amelie's soul on the Beach, but her body remained in the hospital as it was when she was born. The president didn't even officially announce that she had a daughter, but, after around twenty years—thanks mainly to the president's efforts—a miracle happened and she began to show progress. Amelie's physical and spiritual selves gradually came together, and her body began to develop normally.

—It was right about then that they realized she was also a DOOMS sufferer and began to ascertain her incredible abilities. She can transport herself physically to her own Beach. Guess it makes sense—that world is more real to her than this one. She may have overcome her initial struggles, but she still spent most of her life on the other side. Eventually, the president came to feel that her daughter had been through enough. From that point onward, all communication with Amelie would be via hologram. I swore an oath to the president and to America. As far as I was concerned, her word was law. So when she said Amelie was her daughter and the best candidate to succeed her... I believed it.

—But when the archives were restored, I couldn't resist testing out my access privileges. I knew that I was going behind the president's back, but I just had to know. And that's how I found out Bridget was diagnosed with uterine cancer in her twenties, and couldn't have children. You see? Doesn't add up, does it? There's no way Amelie could be Bridget's biological daughter. So where'd she come from? Who is she? Is she even real? How can we be sure that Amelie is an Extinction Entity... when we don't even know if Amelie is Amelie? Hell, for all I know the EE theory might be bullshit. But if it's not—if she's the cause of the Death Stranding—then I have to accept her invitation. I've brought a special gun. It's special to her, to me, to him. To all of us. That's why I should be able to take it to the Beach. I'm gonna stop what she started... by stopping her—

Die-Hardman checked to see that the revolver in his hand was loaded and put it back down. Then he became silent and just stared at the gun. It looked like the message had frozen again, but Sam could see his lips trembling slightly.

—One last confession—

Die-Hardman looked up.

—I'm just a man. No powers. Nothing special. Don't have DOOMS. I can't repatriate like Sam either. Don't know the first thing about dying. I never tried it. Yeah, I've been to hell. Every single battlefield was hell. But no matter how terrible it got, I never died. Because all I ever did was run from death. Well! I gotta go. She's calling for me. Bridges, don't let me down—

The message ended.

<After he recorded this, the director jumped to the Beach. Or rather, Amelie summoned him there.>

Sam felt uneasy. It was like the frozen hologram of Die-Hardman was staring at him. It was hard to accept the man now his mask had been removed and he had an unfamiliar face.

"He shot Bridget when I saw him. She didn't die, but then Cliff showed up and got in the way," Sam said, trying to remember what happened on the Beach, in part to figure out his own confusion. "No," he continued, "I must have been mistaken about Bridget. Everything that happened on that Beach felt like an illusion. Even Cliff himself. I must have just holed myself up on my own Beach and imagined Amelie and Cliff."

Lucy used to say similar things to him in their therapy sessions before she became aware of the Beach and went there herself.

<Sam, no matter how you want to spin this, I

went to Cliff's battlefield too. Unless I, myself, am a fragment of your imagination, Cliff was there. I experienced that battlefield. And I have friends who have experienced Amelie's Beach. Right?>

<—Sam.> The voice on the other end changed.

"Fragile?" Sam asked. "Are you alright?"

Fragile said that she was, but a hint of exhaustion still lingered in her voice. At least she had woken up from her coma. That was reassuring.

<I had a little chat with Higgs back on the Beach. He said everything was part of her plan.>

What Fragile said didn't register at first. The sounds she made eventually formed into words and the words strung together to form a sentence. Everything was part of her plan? What was that supposed to mean?

<She was their leader. The terrorist voidouts at Central Knot, Middle Knot, South Knot, and Edge Knot, the whole extinction agenda—Amelie was behind it all.>

Fragile seemed to be finding this difficult, and it didn't seem like it was just because she was so worn out. Sam found it even harder. Sam felt like he was drowning all alone in his room. His lungs and brain were begging for oxygen. His fingers became so numb that he could no longer feel them. His arms turned pale like they belonged to a corpse.

<I know you don't want to believe it. Even I

wanted to believe that it was just Higgs trying to talk his way out of everything he's done, but it lines up with what Die-Hardman said.

   <Peter Englert used to be a porter. As a courier, he was absolutely obsessed with his deliveries. He was so serious that he used to tell me how transporting goods and connecting people was the one thing that kept him going. He had all the right attributes for the job. Talked to me about why he took on the name Higgs as an homage to the Higgs Field, that which gives mass to all particles within the universe. He said that the Higgs Field connected all particles, gave them substance and brought this world into existence. That's why I joined forces with him in the first place. I wanted to rejoin the fragments of this broken world. I let him use my power. I entrusted him with everything. But Higgs turned on me after he met Amelie. I never knew what it was that changed him. All he said was that her powers put mine to shame. He said that if he could rely on her power, then connecting the entire world would no longer be just a dream. He didn't need me anymore. Once he had Amelie and the Fragile Express system he had everything he needed. But he got so drunk on Amelie that he became her agent of extinction. He was no longer the Higgs who brought

mass to the world, but a Homo Demens who lived to bring chaos and destroy it. All of our abilities—the ability to summon BTs and the ability to jump through the Beach—they were all given to us by her. She was the one who stopped me making jumps. Everything was down to Amelie, down to the Extinction Entity. But Higgs soon forgot all about that and began to delude himself into thinking that he was the mastermind. Even though Amelie was the architect of it all, Higgs was made to believe that he was the writer and the hero of the story.>

Sam realized he was clutching his dreamcatcher and let go of it in a hurry. What had Amelie imbued into this charm that could supposedly turn nightmares into dreams? Was the dream that Higgs tried to have a nightmare?

<Higgs showed me inside his pod. And there was no BB in there. Instead, it was the same doll Die-Hardman had. This is their "bridge baby." They're different from our BBs. Their methods and yours are completely different. Your BB links you to the world of the dead. Their doll links them to Amelie—the Extinction Entity—and her Beach. There's this idea that the isolationists, separatists, and terrorists in the west brought back BB tech and Bridges was just following suit. It's garbage. But it is true that when Higgs started using the BB,

the separatists became more extreme, and that Bridges obtained BB technology as they prepared the first expedition. It seems like everything started from when we brought back BB tech. The two BBs may be different, but doesn't it feel like they're connecting something?>

<You know who else had dolls like this?> Deadman interjected. <Cliff. He was carrying them on the battlefields. Cliff, Higgs, the director—this doll may connect all three of them. Perhaps they were made to do the EE's bidding through it? But all of them acted so differently. So if Amelie is an EE, what is her true intention? Is it to wipe out all of humanity? Is it to get revenge on America? Or is to rebuild it? What does she want with our Lou? What about the possibility that Bridget was an EE with that umbilical cord of hers?>

<I know we're going round in circles here, Sam. But it's too much to take on alone. It's such a vast and complex picture that it's impossible to see from a single perspective. We can't see the whole thing without looking down from far above. But unless the timefall ever lets up or the chiral clouds clear, we're trapped down here. All we can do is rely on you. We need you to go back to Amelie's Beach and meet with her. Find out what an

Extinction Entity really is. And find out what it is
that she really plans on doing. At the very least,
Amelie presents as a human and speaks like a person.
I believe that she has feelings. I may not be
right, and she may have pulled the wool over my
eyes, but there has to be some meaning to the form
that she exists in. We might even be able to glean
some clues about how to stop the Last Stranding.
She's probably waiting for you as we speak.>

Amelie's intentions, huh? Sam thought back to Fragile's
earlier bombshell. Even if Amelie was an Extinction Entity—
even if she wasn't human—they could still talk to her. Sam
was going to go and find out what she was planning.

"I'll be back soon, Fragile. I'll leave it to you to get me there."

Sam heard a faint laugh on the other end of the line.
Sam could picture Fragile in his mind, forcing a smile.

<Alright, Sam. She's waiting for you on the
Beach, isn't she?>

CAPITAL KNOT CITY // BRIDGES HQ

—*John.*

He looked over his shoulder but there was no one to be
seen. Even though he knew he was hearing things, he still
couldn't help but search for the voice's owner. The voice was

only echoing in his own head, so the source had to be inside of him. Yet still he scanned the room around him in fear.

What if he wasn't just hearing things? What if that was just what he wanted to believe? Once John had heard the report of Sam being sucked into the battlefield, he knew that his time had come.

Clifford Unger had returned. He had returned to this world to exact his revenge. He hoped—prayed—that it was all just an illusion. But that was nothing more than wishful thinking.

—John.

It was probably just paranoia right now, but John knew that a time would come one day when Cliff would be whispering his name in his ear for real. That was why he had to go straight to the source and put an end to all of this right now. He had to confront the source of his fear. Die-Hardman could go back to being just John and finally die. It had always been on his mind. And now the time was here. Cliff was using Amelie to invite him to the Beach.

What happened on that day had always remained vivid in Die-Hardman's mind. He remembered it like it was yesterday. He was nervous as hell, but underneath that was a strange kind of euphoria. Not unlike the high he felt when he first went into combat years before—a nameless grunt stumbling around, surrounded by vets who'd seen it all before. Not that he'd stayed nameless for long. He turned out to be a born survivor, and before he knew it he'd earned himself a reputation and an audience with President Bridget Strand several months after her inauguration.

She'd looked him straight in the eye and told him that from that day one, he answered to her. That they were going to rebuild America together. It may have sounded daunting and intimidating, but he knew even then that wasn't her intent. She spoke like someone who'd lived a dozen lifetimes, who'd made the most of each and every one.

After she'd said her piece, she smiled and took a step closer to him. Her necklace, a simple Y-shaped thing, caught the light, and for an instant he saw something impossible. The necklace was glowing, radiant, spreading across her body, chest to abdomen. Like something was being drawn out of her *ha*, he thought at the time, though he couldn't say why. Every time he saw her with that necklace, he remembered the light.

"This child's special," Bridget proclaimed.

A life-support unit shaped like a pod was filled with artificial amniotic fluid, and the baby that had been safely removed from the womb of its brain-dead mother was curled up asleep inside. Bridget stared at the fetus from the other side of the glass.

This child was indeed a special child. If a mother suffered brain death at twenty-eight weeks, their fetus didn't usually survive.

The president loved that child deeply. She used to fret about his health and care for him like he was her own. She was both Gaia and Medea. That's why no matter how much love she had, she could still be so cruel.

John felt like he was going to get swallowed up by Bridget's big eyes as she stared at the baby and looked away. The baby's biological mother was being kept alive by life-support equipment and was laid on a bed beside the pod, still connected to the baby by an artificial umbilical cord, but he was already falling into the delusion that Bridget was the baby's real mother.

"This child will be the bridge that connects us all," Bridget told him. This baby, the prototype BB who would not only help rebuild America but might even save humanity one day, reacted to her voice and let out a tiny cry. Bridget caressed the pod and whispered, "It's okay. You're a special child."

He was already special to John. But John had only realized that a long time after the child had been removed from his mother's womb and the BB experiments had begun.

"You'll be out of there in no time." John heard a voice as he walked down the hallway. "And the second all this is over, I'm gonna take you wherever you wanna go."

Before John even had time to try to remember who the voice belonged to, his attention was snatched away by the open doors to the laboratory—which was dressed up to look like a hospital room from the outside. Someone had been sloppy. You had to pass through multiple layers of security to access this floor! Only a few people would have been able to enter the room, but if anything had happened to the BB, John would never be able to face Bridget again.

John held his breath and snuck over to the open doorway to check it out. He could see someone's back as they leaned over the pod. Even though his body was obscured by a shirt, John could tell the man was made of muscle.

"Look, BB. Brought you an astronaut."

Without warning, and without a sound, the man leaning over the pod turned around. Astonished by such a clearly drilled action, John couldn't take his eyes off the man's face. The man had the same reaction.

"Can I help you?" the man asked. The man's smile instantly jogged John's memory. Whenever John had escaped the jaws of death, that smile was always there to greet him.

"Holy shit, John, is that you?!"

"Captain?" John exclaimed in surprise. "What are you doing here?"

The two men embraced each other. Die-Hardman, the man who made it back from any situation, and Cliff, the man who always made it back from the verge of death, had met once again.

"My wife's checked in," Cliff explained, indicating toward the hospital bed by the wall. A woman appeared to be sleeping there surrounded by life-support equipment. She, herself, was brain-dead, and was "dreaming" of her unborn baby. John had no idea that she was Cliff's wife. He had no idea that the BB was Cliff's son. How much did the captain know?

"They don't want a repeat of last year." Cliff looked away from his wife and back toward John.

"Last year? The voidout in Manhattan?" John asked, careful to feign surprise. Cliff's wife and baby certainly seemed to fit the bill for the mother and child from Manhattan. This time they had managed to create a special child, a Bridge Baby, without causing another accident. But to think that this was Cliff's kid... Now the BB had a special meaning for John, too.

But the question of who the baby really belonged to began to spin around John's head. Did it belong to Cliff? Or did it belong to Bridget and America? It was Bridget and the American government who had saved the child from its mother's womb. He was expected to become the savior of America. He was supposed to become a child that belonged to all mankind, to be sacrificed. Just like Jesus who died on the cross atop the hill of Golgotha. Who had been Jesus' real father?

"This isn't what we agreed on. You said you'd do everything in your power to save BB."

Cliff hounded Bridget. It had been a few visits since Cliff and John had first reunited.

"We are. But we cannot release your son just yet," Bridget answered coolly. There was no hesitation in her cold voice. "Believe me when I tell you—it's for the best."

"Says some woman in a mask who's done nothing but lie to me," Cliff snapped back.

What Cliff was saying was right, but John couldn't take his side right now. It made him feel so frustrated and pathetic that he couldn't help his friend.

One discovery John had made in the time since he first saw Cliff again was that Cliff knew nothing about the Bridge Babies. All Cliff had been told was that his wife was brain-dead and the premature fetus had been rescued and moved to the NICU. His wife's corpse would have to be suitably disposed of due to similarities with the Manhattan case, but with the passage of time, they might be able to save the baby. To Cliff, the BB wasn't a Bridge Baby at all, but his actual child.

"I have a duty to protect our country. Lies are an unfortunate necessity." Bridget left the room, ignoring Cliff, who was about to say something back.

All John was able to do was scurry silently after her. He couldn't bear Cliff's stare.

"The president gave me the highest-level access privileges. I've used them to manipulate the security system," John looked up from the terminal and explained to Cliff a few days after the president brushed him off.

"We have five minutes before it resets, sir. Five minutes to talk… off the record."

After that day when John walked in on Cliff, Bridget had made a complaint about the defective autolock feature on the door. As a result, John's authorization had been upgraded to the highest level.

"They're moving your son to a new facility tomorrow. You'll never see him again. He'll serve as the foundation of a new communications network—a sacrifice for a nation that no longer exists," John hurriedly explained.

Cliff's face clouded over. It wasn't surprising. This was the first he'd heard about it.

"This child's special. Your baby is going to become a Bridge Baby for all of America."

John began to divulge all he knew about the BB experiments.

"It was a few months after the initial Death Stranding explosions. Some private hospital was doing a C-section. It was an unusual case. At seven months along the kid's mother had become brain-dead. They put her on life support for the baby's sake, but her blood pressure began to drop and the kid showed signs of bradycardia, so they had to perform an emergency Cesarean. The procedure went well and the plan was for the baby to be cared for in the NICU for a while. It was during the final stages of the operation when the voidout hit. The records show one of the doctors screaming 'I can see them!' At the time, medical procedures were broadcast on closed networks for medical interns. When the footage was analyzed, we realized the doctor shouted that at the exact moment he touched the umbilical cord to separate mother and child. That's when the voidout hit and the hospital became a crater. We didn't understand what it meant at the beginning, but as we researched the Death Stranding, we began to believe that the 'they' the doctor was referring to was the BTs. We began to think that maybe if we could find another mother and child, and use the umbilical cord that connected them to try to recreate the same conditions, we might be able to sense BTs and that might help us to finally understand the whole Death Stranding phenomenon. The president at the time went ahead with the project and experiments and testing commenced.

"It started back when we were still in the army. It was kept top secret. Anyone who wasn't directly involved didn't even know the project existed. At first, the experiments were performed in a government facility in Manhattan, but the documents and records from that time were so strictly controlled that even I'm not sure what really happened. What I do know is that the experiments ended in failure. In fact, the entirety of Manhattan Island was wiped clean off the map. It was a complete catastrophe. The president who oversaw the experiments was swept up in it all and killed, too. Then came Vice President Bridget Strand. She was next in line for the job, so she assumed the presidency. She ordered all the experiments to be canceled and the data to be destroyed. She was a strong leader and wanted to prioritize the quelling of all the chaos and social unrest left behind in the wake of the disaster. The official explanation was that something unexpected had made a brain-dead patient necrotize. The BB experiments remained a secret. That was why you ended up bringing your partner here."

John took a deep breath. His throat was awfully dry, but Cliff's expression compelled him to keep speaking.

"But the BB experiments weren't abandoned. Even though Bridget ordered them to be canceled, she took command. They continued, with even fewer people involved than before. Your baby was the subject of their experiments. At first, the president believed that we would be able to visualize BTs by using BBs, since one of the most dangerous aspects of the BTs is that they're invisible. Not being able to see them only made people more anxious and afraid. If we could see them, then the idea was that we could eliminate some of that fear and come up with some countermeasures against them. It was during the course of that research that we realized they could be used for another purpose. Not only could they be used to sense BTs, but we could also use them as a medium for a brand-new communications system that uses the Beach. It means that the BBs are no longer regarded as people, but as parts—as equipment. BBs are to become human sacrifices on the altar of American reconstructionism," John said, taking a scrap of paper from his pocket and passing it to Cliff. He was about to go over his five-minute limit. "Burn it when you're done. The rest is up to you, sir."

Cliff accepted it silently. But John wondered whether he would actually read it as he left the room.

A few days passed.

John heard a door open and close behind him, but he didn't turn back. It was time. He had done his part with security. The rest was up to Cliff now.

"You swore an oath to the president. Why are you helping me?" Cliff asked, drawing up beside him without making a single sound.

"Because you saved my life, sir. Again and again," John replied.

Neither man could look the other in the face. Both simply stared down at the BB's mother as she slept on life support.

"No matter what hellhole I got sent to, I always made it back. I was so successful that I was selected to serve by the president's side. Back then, I thought I was invincible. I thought I was some kind of action hero. But I'm not the hero. You are, sir. When you were no longer around, I had to face up to the fact that I wasn't the man I thought I was.

I can't live without something to dedicate myself to. At one time that used to be you, now it's America. You're the reason I'm still alive. And it's past time I paid that debt. Please let me help you this time."

John handed Cliff the gun he had concealed. Cliff's eyebrows twitched slightly. It was the gun he had once given to John.

"I can't terminate your wife's life support from inside her room. The system won't allow it. So this is the only other option. There's no reason to keep her trapped in this brain-dead state forever. She can't just keep dreaming of her baby forever. An alarm is set to go off if she flatlines. I've rigged the system to mimic her vitals... But you won't have long. Five minutes, tops. Don't hesitate, sir. This is the only chance you'll get."

John watched Cliff check the revolver's cylinder and silently left the room.

The first thing John saw was blood all over the floor.

Things hadn't gone as planned. As John's eyes followed the red trail back, he spotted Cliff at the end of it. Without a moment's hesitation, John sprang into action and ran to Cliff. He was slouched against the wall, his arms slick with blood. The pod containing the BB was covered in blood, too.

"Oh God! I'm sorry, Captain," John cried. He crouched

down beside Cliff, who looked up and smiled weakly. John could hear footsteps rushing down the hallway behind them and turned to find himself confronted with some heavily armed men. They were special forces. The security alarm had gone off.

"Hold your fire!" John stood up reflexively and opened his arms wide to stop them. All the guns were now pointed at his chest.

"Thanks for trying, John." John heard Cliff's voice behind him and felt the cold barrel of a gun dig into the back of his neck. He smelled the scent of blood. Cliff flung his other arm around him.

That's right, Captain. Use me as a shield.

With his arms still open, John began to back away with Cliff.

Then Cliff's grip loosened. John felt an almighty push from his back, and staggered and stumbled in front of the special forces operatives.

As the special forces operatives shouted among themselves, John took command of the room with an order that drowned out all the commotion.

"Stop! It's a dead end. He's trapped. Security will take it from here."

John may have been able to exert control over the special forces, but the situation still hadn't changed for the better. In fact, it was getting worse and worse. Cliff was going back on himself and now the only place left for Cliff to run to was back to the laboratory.

But by the time John reached the lab, there were already people outside. The other members of the security team were there, engine cutters in hand, trying to remove the doors. John didn't remember giving that order.

"This room is off limits. No one goes in!" John shouted, receiving looks of disapproval from the security team.

"But he's in there, sir. I saw him!" one teammate objected.

"You saw wrong. Now, check the other way. Go!" John barked back.

The men looked at each other. It was clear they were having trouble accepting an order that didn't make any sense. But John had to get them away from here. As he reached for his holster to pull out his gun, he heard a voice.

"No, open it up. He's in there."

It was Bridget. She was here with the special forces. There was nothing else that John could do.

The doors were prized open and special forces advanced on his old captain. John heard a gun go off and the special forces swarm around him.

Cliff was covered in blood and saying something to the pod.

Once all of Cliff's strength had left his body, the pod rolled to the floor. Special forces picked it up without a moment's delay and handed it to Bridget.

Bridget gasped. John was lost for words, too. Cliff smiled

sadly at the pair of them from the floor. He was holding the naked baby to his chest and smiling.

"Captain—" John muttered, dumbfounded.

The amniotic fluid was dripping from the pod onto the floor. There it mixed with Cliff's blood to form a vortex pattern.

Had Cliff already given up? Was he trying to die together with his baby?

John refused to believe that. Cliff had saved him time and time again. Cliff would be able to save his son.

Save him. Please save him.

"Shoot him, John."

A pain gripped John like someone was squeezing his heart tightly.

Why? Why his child? Why do I have to shoot the father of this child?

"Shoot him!" Bridget commanded again.

His trembling arms felt like they were acting on their own.

Cliff looked up at John. John couldn't believe that the pale face reflected back in Cliff's eyes was his own. His hand that gripped the gun and his finger on the trigger felt like they belonged to somebody else.

"I gave you an order! Shoot him! For America."

Two gunshots sounded. America had killed Cliff.

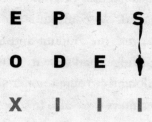

EPISODE XIII

BRIDGES

Sam had left Port Knot City and continued to head east. His destination was Capital Knot City. He was still making his way back to HQ—back to Deadman, Heartman, Lockne, and a comatose Fragile.

His movements were heavy, like each part of him had been placed in restraints. Even though he wasn't carrying any cargo, his back hurt and his hips groaned. Every single calorie he had ingested had been converted into energy for walking, and there was nothing else left. He had visibly lost weight and it felt like his body was shrinking in on itself.

He lost count of the number of times he had nightmares about his body wearing away to nothing as he continued to walk.

The one redeeming feature of his lonely march back was

that the number of safehouses he could take a rest at along the way had increased. As communications had become operational in this area, the amount and frequency of the cargo delivered by Bridges had grown. The safehouses had been constructed along this route to offer support for these deliveries. Chiral printers were also functioning reliably, so the east was reaping the benefits of being brought back online first. The only problem now was that communications were malfunctioning and no new bases could be established. It was like they had gone back to how things were before they had activated the network at all.

Unable to stomach the irony, Sam continued to drag his aching body toward its destination. When he finally found a safehouse for the first time in days, it was almost destroyed. While there were still stockpiles of food and medicine in the private basement room, the electricity supply was unstable and the communications terminal would not activate. He couldn't even use the incubator with communications in such a bad state. Sam was worried that he hadn't allowed Lou to rest enough on their way here. Lou was showing obvious changes. While Lou had been connected to Sam, the BB no longer dozed off as much anymore. Lou had become more curious about the outside world and was conveying much clearer emotions to Sam. It meant Lou was being pulled closer and closer to the world of the living. Lou should have been presenting with symptoms of autotoxemia by now, after spending so long away from the stillmother's womb, but there were no signs of it as yet. It was different from the last time Deadman had treated Lou. Sam worried about what this meant for Lou's future.

Sam held the disconnected pod to his chest and lay down. As he watched a dozing Lou, he fell into a deep sleep himself.

—*This child's special.*

Was this why he had to go through this? There were faces. Faces and faces. Countless faces were staring at him. They edged closer until they filled his entire view, before disappearing. Faces he had seen before, faces he might see in the future, faces he would never encounter and faces that died long ago; they all appeared before him and vanished. Pinned down like an insect under a microscope, he was unable to move. All he could do was let them examine him.

Which are you? A face he didn't know swam into view. *Am I connecting to you? Or are you connecting to me? Where are you? Are you in the past? Are you still alive? Are you in the land of the living? Or the land of the dead?*

Somewhere in the distance, a whale was singing. The sound of a mating call.

—*But is it? Couldn't it be crying out in sadness?*

One of the many staring faces, a woman, split from ear to ear, becoming one giant mouth. Small canine teeth crowded the mouth right to the back of its throat. It made a disturbing tearing sound as it gnawed through the invisible wall that protected him. The stench of rotting organs surrounded him. He watched a star explode, followed by a vision of a world full of the microscopic life that was first born to these lands. He slid down its throat, mingled with its gastric juices, before being pushed through its contracting and relaxing intestines. Finally, he was expelled from its anus.

A wave washed over the naked body, the *ha*, that was soiled with blood and excrement. As he was hit by the wave, he felt the world spin around him and he no longer knew where he was. He tried to stand, but fell back. He had neither hands nor feet. He was just a lump of flesh with eyes, a mouth, ears, and a nose carved out of it. The breaking waves were toying with him as they knocked him around the shoreline. An infinite number of sea creatures were stranded all around him.

A baby cried, but without his soul, Sam couldn't stand. All he could do was shuffle across the sand with his mouth as he looked for the child.

A gigantic wave carried Sam away, far from the shoreline. A sun more enormous than Sam had ever seen before appeared and broke the sky into two, mercilessly beating down on his back. All the water disappeared in an instant and Sam's skin began to wrinkle and dry out. Now he could only hear the waves. They no longer reached him. He could smell the scent of sea salt, but he couldn't get back to it. He dug his chin into the sand, and as pain engulfed his entire body, he struggled his way toward the baby's cries. His dried and hardened skin began to form spikes. Sam used them to try desperately to propel himself forward in the sand. His skin cracked and blood oozed out. Then the bloodied protuberances began to transform into long, thick limbs. Sam used his four limbs to keep on advancing. As he cursed his imperfect *ha*, he kept on moving forward. Soon, the sun began to sink toward the horizon and a frighteningly cold night set in. Both he and the sea froze over and all sound disappeared.

The sky was clear and countless stars glowed without a twinkle. This place was directly linked to the rest of the cosmos. It felt like if he looked up, he'd fall, so Sam closed his eyes tight. When he tried to draw his own body in tight to endure the cold, his arms and legs grew. Sam could finally stand. Guided by the baby's cries, he began to walk.

As he walked, his body grew. His thighs became more muscular, his hips became higher, and his spine stretched. Now he could look out far in front of him. Now he could move his arms at will and could grab objects with the palms of his hands.

Now he would be able to embrace the child.

As he grew more confident, the baby's cries seemed to grow louder.

When he called out Lou's name, he found a newborn

Lou crying at his feet. Sam kneeled and picked Lou up with both hands.

He held Lou to his chest. They were finally together. Lou's small hands grabbed the dreamcatcher around Sam's neck.

Lou. Sam called out Lou's name over and over. *Lou. I won't leave you anymore.*

—*This child's special.*

Sam's chest suddenly became light. The wind pierced it as though a hole had opened up within him. He wasn't holding anything anymore. There was nothing in his arms.

When he looked up, he was once again surrounded by countless faces. "Where are you?" he was asked as he began to feel his own body slip away.

Sam awoke to the sound of a steady tapping.

It was a quiet sound right next to his ear. For a moment, he didn't know where he was. He was curled around Lou's pod, asleep. Lou was fervently tapping on the window of the pod from the inside. Lou had brought him out of his nightmare. Sam's whole body felt stiff, but the ache gave him comfort in the knowledge that everything was real again.

Sam wiped the tears from his face, turned toward the pod, and stared at Lou. Had Lou been having the same dream? Sam felt anxious. He didn't want this child to be sullied with such a nightmare. He thought about the voice he had heard in his sleep.

This child's special.

"That's right. You are," Sam whispered to himself.

But there were no children who weren't special. Each and every child mattered. Had a right to exist.

Sam's eyes met Lou's. Lou was making a strange expression, and Sam realized just how angry the situation made him feel.

Once Sam left the safehouse, it was only a matter of time before he began to hurt again. He had begun to feel so numb that it was like he was walking in another person's body. He felt like he was putting someone else's foot on the ground with each subsequent step and was breathing through an invisible veil. He felt ungrounded, like he was still dozing in the tail-end of a dream. He slapped his cheeks a few times to try to wake himself up.

Although Deadman had denied it, what if Sam had been dreaming this whole time? He couldn't shake the idea from his mind. Maybe he was still inside his mother's womb, just tormented by the laws of this nonsensical dream. Not that there was any guarantee the outside world was any more sensible.

Was he dreaming? Was this real? The world all this was

taking place in was so convoluted. Numerous threads were entangled with one another and wove a complex and mysterious pattern. To escape from his dreams and to confront reality, Sam would have to head for their source.

Between the ridgelines to the north, Sam could see the faint shadow of a tower. It belonged to the incinerator where he had burned Bridget's body. Sam wondered what would have happened if he had just left her body in its hospital bed instead. Would her *ha*, with its umbilical cord that connected her to the Beach, have necrotized and turned her into a BT? Would she still have felt a strong attachment to America and tried to come back? Would she have betrayed her wish to see this world connected back up and caused a great extinction in its place? Questions kept running through Sam's head.

That incinerator was the first place where Sam connected with Lou. It was the place where he had sent Bridget off to the next world and begun his mission to save Lou. It seemed both so long ago and like something that had happened only yesterday.

When Sam finally approached Capital Knot City, all he could see was decay, like an old monument that had been slowly chipped away with the passage of the ages. Perhaps it was all in Sam's head. Maybe it had always been like this. Large cracks ran through the outer wall that surrounded the periphery of the city and the Bridges logo on it was dirty and faded. The air was heavy with the smell of rusted iron, to the point where Sam hesitated to breathe in. It looked nothing like the capital city of an America on the brink of being rebuilt. It was a city of death.

Nobody came to welcome Sam, so he took the elevator to the basement alone. It was the same route he had used when he brought Bridget her morphine. Even when the cage reached the elevator hall, Sam couldn't sense anyone around. Most of the lights were out. Sam proceeded through the gloomy hallways and opened the door to the president's old room.

"Sam!" Lockne burst forth. Sam instinctively moved out of her way. Sam grimaced at himself as he recoiled from his friend who had been waiting for him all this time. He could change the way the entire world worked, but he still couldn't change himself. Perhaps he just didn't want to.

"You're back! It must have been one hell of a journey, especially on your own." Deadman approached Sam, trying to gloss over the awkward atmosphere. "But now the whole team is together again," he continued, even though the only other person Sam saw was Heartman in cardiac arrest on the sofa. Deadman read Sam's puzzled expression and showed him to a bed against the wall. Lying there on the hospital bed was Fragile. She was hooked up to a respirator and a drip. Her vitals were being monitored by the surrounding equipment. Despite their earlier conversation, it still seemed like she had a way to go to recover. The sight of Fragile lying there like that reminded Sam of Bridget on her deathbed. He shook his head to try and get rid of the mental image.

"That's our fault. Too much traveling to and from the Beaches in such a short span. It's not just from transporting us. She's been looking for Amelie, too," Deadman explained. "Chiral matter contaminated her cells, effectively causing jet lag on a molecular level. Because of that, her homeostatic mechanisms were shaken. Don't worry—she's not in any danger. But she needs some rest."

Sam didn't understand all of Deadman's explanation, but he was relieved to see a bit of color in her face while she slept. When Sam heard the phrase, "jet lag on a molecular level," he had imagined an even more serious version of what she looked like from the neck down.

"The director—sorry, Die-Hardman—is back, too. He's being looked after in another room. Bridges personnel found him lying outside the isolation ward… Similar to when you came back from Cliff's Beach," Deadman added.

Then it seemed like the whole team was back together.

The AED kicked in and brought Heartman back to life. At first, he looked surprised to see Sam there, but his serious expression soon returned as he looked over to Fragile. He nodded as Deadman informed him that he had told Sam everything, and this time turned to Sam.

"This world is in a similar state to Fragile. Nothing is

integrated anymore. The cells that make up her body are all running on different time axes and egos. In Fragile's case, the solution is very simple. A single person is made up of a myriad of different components all intersecting and working together, but what connects all these components is a person's will. It's this will that will correct any misalignment for her. Now, in the context of this world, humans, and by extension our Beaches, play the same role as the cells in Fragile's body, and in much the same way, we also require a higher plane, an equivalent to her will, to retune everything so that we're all running on the same time axis again."

Sam thought he suddenly saw Fragile move from the corner of his eye, but she was still sleeping with the exact same expression as before. He had been tricked by a floating creature near her head. It was a cryptobiote.

"Traditionally, all of our Beaches have existed independently. We have connected to each other not through the idea of the Beach, but through talk of family and tribes, concepts of this world, the universe, and this planet. These concepts and connections formed the driving force behind the survival of Homo sapiens. But now we have this new concept called the Beach, which we have connected to our reality via the Chiral Network with the added component of the existence of an 'Extinction Entity.' Amelie's Beach exists on a higher plane that can control other Beaches. If each of our Beaches is a single capillary, Amelie's Beach is the heart that pumps blood to the rest of us. Capillaries are subordinate to the greater whole. A whole governed by the heart, which gives direction. Which dictates flow. You may be the only one able to travel against the flow and reach her."

Sam seized the cryptobiote as it floated by. When Fragile had first recommended one in that cave, he had been skeptical and turned it down, but he had found himself munching on one a few times now.

"But, having done so, if she does not wish to let you go, if she wishes to keep you, she can," Heartman finished.

"Fragile and Die-Hardman broke free from her Beach, didn't they?" Sam refuted, releasing the cryptobiote.

"I don't think it was any different from what happened to you. I didn't get out because I wanted to." It was Fragile's voice. She was sitting up in bed, chewing on a cryptobiote. "I was forced out. 'Repatriated,' if you will. By her."

Deadman looked like he couldn't believe his eyes and immediately checked her vital monitors. Heartman was looking at her fondly with a look of paternal concern.

"Welcome back, Sam. Guess you need me after all?" Fragile grimaced as she tried to get out of bed. Lockne immediately lent Fragile her shoulder.

"Thank you," Fragile whispered as she tried to grab another cryptobiote that was floating around the room. Sam plucked it out of the air and laughed.

"You want it?" he asked.

"There's no time to waste, right?" Fragile said, chewing on the cryptobiote and looking Sam straight in the eye. "Look, Sam. She wants you. Wants you to go to her. That's her final wish. Don't you think?" Fragile commented.

The words "final wish" rang in Sam's ears. How could Fragile be so sure?

"So that's it, huh. Amelie's the EE, and this is her endgame." That was the only way Sam could bring himself to ask. Fragile hung her head, but Sam couldn't tell if that was an answer or not. "Just so we're clear: if I want to stop the Last Stranding and come back in one piece... I need to go to her Beach and talk her out of it. That about right?"

"Correct. As clichéd as it sounds, you're our only hope," Heartman spoke up. "Though, quite frankly, I doubt even you can change her mind."

The room fell silent. Deadman was the one to break it.

"If you can't make her see reason... you'll have to kill her. And if you kill her..."

"You'll save the world, but you'll be stranded outside of it. Forever," Lockne finished Deadman's sentence, looking down at her feet and biting her lip.

Another bout of silence. This time nobody seemed to want to break it.

Sam gripped his dreamcatcher and raised his hand.

"Might as well make it official, then. You ready to

deliver the package?" he asked Fragile. She gave a sad smile and nodded.

"I'll talk to her. Maybe she'll listen. But with the shape the world's in, it'll only be delaying the inevitable. Still, if it buys us time to try and build something better. A new lease on life, at least for a little bit. Well, I can think of one woman who made the most of a chance like that. Nothing lasts forever. Not even the world. But we gotta keep it going as long as we can, right? Patch the holes, change the parts, all that."

Sam couldn't stop talking. And nobody else wanted to stop him, either. Deadman, Heartman, Lockne, and Fragile remained silent, hanging onto every word.

"Back when we met at the cave, the only thing I cared about was making it to the next sunrise. Sure as hell didn't care about America or 'the future.' I was living a lie, hung up on past regrets. I was broken. But somewhere along the way, I started changing. Started meeting people who made me think that maybe it wasn't all bad. People who put their faith in tomorrow and in me. That kept the lights on and waited for hope to arrive. So I gotta deliver, for their sake."

"Even if it means you never come back?" Deadman asked as if he wouldn't be able to bear it. All the others in the room had the same fear.

"Fucked if I do, fucked if I don't, right?" Sam shrugged.

There was no choice. As long as the hypothesis they shared stood true, there was no other option.

Sam disconnected his pod and passed Lou to Deadman. He couldn't take the kid to the Beach.

Fragile stood in front of Sam. Next to him, Deadman held Lou's pod in his arms, with a strange look on his face. Heartman and Lockne stood on either side of Sam. He looked at each of their faces in turn and then adjusted his grip on his dreamcatcher. Fragile gently placed her hand on it.

Sam followed her lead and closed his eyes.

"Okay, concentrate," she told him. Fragile wrapped her arm around Sam. He could feel her body heat. There was no aphenphosmphobic reaction. Sam accepted her. "Help me look for Amelie. Reach for her, Sam. Feel her."

Fragile tightened her grip and put her forehead to Sam's. Sam sighed. The pulse of another living being quietly came through. Amelie's warmth, her smell, her voice; Sam focused on all his memories of her. Even if he only ever had contact with her on the Beach, it didn't matter. Because those were the memories that were special to him.

"I know you love her. You love her!"

Normally those words would have flustered Sam, but now he could accept them.

—*Then you disappeared never to be seen again.*

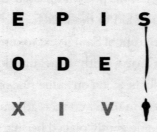

EPISODE XIV

SAM STRAND

Sam was lying on a sandy beach.

The first thing he saw when he opened his eyes was the color red. It was a shade that he had seen somewhere before, a color that lay in the depths of his memory. The color of blood that he first saw in his mother's womb.

Both the sky and the sea were red. Was this Amelie's Beach? He couldn't believe this was the same Beach she had brought him to so many times before. The planet floating in the sky made him feel even more uneasy. It looked a lot like Earth, but the landmasses were in a different shape. At the very least, it wasn't the same Earth that Bridget had taught him about when he was a boy. The land looked like it was in the shape of a curled-up fetus.

Sam brushed the sand off himself and stood up. He

looked this way and that, but there was no one else there with him. Maybe the jump had failed. Maybe now that the Beaches were in so much chaos, he had jumped to a different Beach from Amelie's.

"You're too late. What took you so long?" The sound of Amelie's voice erased Sam's worry. When he looked in its direction, he saw Amelie standing there.

"Amelie?" he called out as she stood there with her back to him, looking out over the ocean.

"You still don't know who I am, do you?" she asked.

The face of the woman looking over her shoulder at him was Amelie's. But the voice that belonged to it was Bridget's. "I've been waiting for you right here. You were supposed to stop me. Stop all of this."

"Bridget?" Sam gasped.

The woman smiled. "Yes. It's me, Sam," she replied.

Her voice sounded like it was coming from far away. Did that mean this wasn't Amelie's Beach?

"My daughter, Samantha America Strand, doesn't exist. At least, not in your world."

Bridget's riddles only made Sam even more confused. "I'm sorry, Sam. I've had to wear a mask for so long. Amelie and Bridget are both a part of me," Bridget admonished Sam with Amelie's face. Was she trying to confuse him even more?

"Do you understand, Sam? 'Amelie' and 'Bridget'—

those are just names. What I am is an Extinction Entity."

Bridget began to explain.

"This painting is a Da Vinci."

A man spoke. Bridget was looking at a painting of a woman holding a naked baby in her arms as it tried to wriggle its way out of them.

"It's called the *Madonna of the Yarnwinder*. The yarnwinder is the thing the baby is holding. The baby is drawn to the yarnwinder while its mother looks on worried. While her left arm is holding her baby, her right arm looks like it's about to pull the baby away, doesn't it?"

"With that horizontal stick, the yarnwinder looks a little like a cross."

As Bridget pointed out her observation, her father placed a large hand on her head. She may have pouted and resisted because she didn't want her father to mess up her hair, but in reality she loved receiving his praise. She looked up at the painting hanging next to her father, who smelled of cigars, that had been painted almost five hundred years ago.

"That's right. It's a cross. The baby is Jesus. The mother is the Virgin Mary. She was afraid that Jesus would be crucified on a cross in the future to sacrifice himself to save mankind."

"But how did the Virgin Mary know that was going to happen, Papa? Why didn't she stop it?" Bridget asked.

"Because we're only human," her father replied.

Bridget's father's face looked slightly cold. He seemed to smell of sweat. Bridget liked the smell of her father's cigars, they smelled like dried leaves, but she didn't like this smell.

"A holy sacrifice must be made so that humanity can keep on living."

Bridget didn't understand what those words meant at the time (*I was only five years old*). It took many years afterwards for her to finally comprehend them.

Bridget dreamt of the cross time and time again. For some reason, she always felt like she wasn't supposed to tell anyone about it, so she remained silent, taking her secret with her to the grave.

—*So now I can finally tell you.*

The shoreline stretched on for eternity. Bridget walked along it alone, looking out over the sea on her right side. Even if she carried on walking until her dying breath, she'd probably never reach the end. When Bridget realized that, it made her happy. It meant that this world would never end.

The calm ocean surface reflected the light of the sun. It was so gentle and beautiful. Bridget was a smart girl. She knew that all life on Earth came from the sea. The sand on the beach was white and felt good as it poured through her fingers. It was fun to mold the sand and make sandcastles and imaginary towns, too. She even built a breakwater so that her little town didn't get destroyed.

Bridget knew she was dreaming, but she always looked forward to these dreams so much.

But once she realized that the white sand was made from the corpses of coral and fragments of shell, she became afraid to dream. It became a beach of death.

Bridget didn't want to have that dream ever again, but she couldn't pick and choose. Eventually, she came to dream of that beach every night.

That eternal shoreline transformed into an eternal nightmare.

It was sometime afterward when she came to see the Beach littered with crosses. She saw them thrust into the sand, floating in the sea, and disappearing and reappearing on the horizon. Sometimes she even saw them in the sky.

Then, one day, she found a rotten, enormous cross discarded at the water's edge. It was so big, it looked like it could have crucified a whale or a giant. But all that was nailed to it was a doll of a baby angel that had its wings plucked away. She felt so sorry for it that she rescued it. She washed it with seawater and gently cradled it in her arms. She found it cute, how its eyes opened and closed when its head was tilted. Even after she woke up, the baby still slept within them.

After a while, other things began to appear on the beach. At first it was the carcasses of small fish and birds. They didn't appear to be wounded, nor did they rot, but they were cold and lifeless, so Bridget assumed they were dead. Those things had already died long ago in Bridget's world. They were animals that had gone extinct millennia ago. The corpses of extinct species, from ammonites and trilobites to mammoths and dinosaurs, increased and increased. The strangest part of it was how all the animals that washed ashore had umbilical cords.

Bridget was frightened by her dreams, but she couldn't tell anyone.

All she could do was hope and pray for the destruction of the Beach in her dreams. And it was granted. Although it wasn't quite destroyed in the way that Bridget hoped for.

When she fell asleep and awoke on the Beach, both the sky and the sea were stained blood red. For some reason, the old Earth that she had only ever seen in picture books floated above the horizon. The world was full of sadness. This time she didn't feel scared like she usually did, but like she wanted to cry. From beyond the sea, the source of her sadness approached. It was the "things" that had disappeared the moment that this world, and this universe, had been born.

The second those "things" met this world, the sea boiled and the sky fell down. A wave higher than any skyscraper washed ashore, stranding all the extinct creatures. Corpses piled up on top of the white sand made out of more corpses. A young Bridget could only cling tightly to her doll and watch. Nothing lived on that beach.

—Those were the dreams of extinction I had. Even as I grew older, they wouldn't set me free. In my dreams I watched the world end. So many times. Countless past extinctions that decimated life on this planet again and again and again. I even dreamt of the destruction to come. Human corpses used to wash up on my Beach. They all seemed to look like me somehow. All of them had the same umbilical cord.

That strong and intelligent girl learned to live with her nightmares of extinction. She could never escape from them, but she didn't let them overwhelm her, either. They never drove her to suicide or madness. Her dreams of extinction made as much sense as living in this world did. That's how Bridget came to accept them in the end.

Senseless people did things for senseless reasons. They started wars, they hurt each other, killed each other. It was the same as the Beach. Bridget decided that she needed to understand why.

Ever since she had tried to destroy her dream, the Beach had turned into an even more frightening world. She needed to understand why that happened, too.

Bridget devoured knowledge. She learned about life and the universe. She learned about people. About the world.

She learned about everything. She strived to understand this world in a human way. Her entry into politics was an extension of that learning.

—It wasn't quite the right answer for me, but it wasn't a mistake, either. Then I faced my first hurdle.

"It's stage three," the doctor explained, showing Bridget an X-ray. Bridget felt numb. It felt like this was happening to someone else. The doctor cast his eyes downward and cleared his throat. "I'm afraid it's going to require removal."

It was just after Bridget turned twenty when the cancer was discovered in her uterus. She'd be lying if she said she wasn't shocked, but she had no choice in the matter. Bridget obediently accepted the surgery.

As soon as she lay down on the bed and breathed in the anesthetic, she lost consciousness.

"Don't worry. It'll all be over when you wake up. You won't even know. You won't even dream. It'll feel like it only took a few seconds," the doctor explained before the surgery.

"Like Rip Van Winkle," Bridget smiled back.

What the doctor said was right. But it was also wrong.

Bridget was on the Beach.

The surgery was over in a second. As she came around, Bridget felt a dull pain and the faces of her doctor and parents swam into view. She was in a hospital room. It felt like she had only just been knocked out.

But Bridget was still on the Beach. She couldn't tell if she was dreaming or awake. She couldn't tell which side time was passing on.

—*I was split across two worlds. My* ha *in one, and my* ka *in the other.*

They existed simultaneously, but that existence was a contradiction. So Bridget came up with a story and gave the other Bridget on the Beach a name. "Amelie." *Ame* was French for soul. A soul that's a lie.

As a human of this world, Bridget had to abide by its laws. Bridget had to give birth to Amelie. Then she saw it. A human corpse had washed up on the Beach. One that looked just like her. If that was Amelie, then Bridget had to revive her somehow. She felt like if she didn't, then humanity would go extinct.

Bridget had consciousness and a body, but no soul.

Amelie had consciousness and a soul, but no body.

—*But Amelie wasn't restricted to the Beach, she could appear in this world, too. Just as I could visit the Beach in my dreams, Amelie dreamed and came to this world. Just like how a BT comes here, too. You can see dreams, but you can't touch them. That's why it's not incorrect to say that no one has ever met Amelie.*

Amelie on the Beach was Bridget. That's why she looked just like her (*even though I didn't have a* ha). That was fine at first. But in this world, Bridget's body followed this world's laws and began to age, while Amelie remained twenty years old on the Beach.

It was just after the first Death Stranding when Bridget realized she had to explain that gap somehow. America had collapsed and Bridget sensed the dream of the Beach she had been having since she was a child sliding into reality. The crosses, the corpses with their umbilical cords, the dolls, and the things from across the sea she had seen so many times. And Amelie's birth. She had to weave them all together to create one strand. She had to use it all to unravel the truth behind her extinction dreams and the situation that the world found itself confronted with.

The first lie that Bridget told was that she had a daughter named Amelie.

She confessed to her young but skilled ex-special-forces aid, John Blake McClane, that Amelie had been born before the Death Stranding and suffered from locked-in syndrome. That she didn't know why at first, but after she heard the theory that the Beach linked life and death, it all made sense. Her daughter's soul had deviated toward the Beach, but after the Death Stranding, the Beach connected to this world and her daughter's soul—Amelie's soul—finally linked back to her body.

His sympathetic disposition was a blessing. He could understand and attract others. His disposition was similar to Higgs, whom Amelie would go on to meet later. Despite the fact that he knew all too well how the world worked, he never exploited anything for his own ends. He was the kind of person who pushed forward without question, as long as it was for someone or something else's sake.

Bridget told him that Amelie had finally been born into this world. That her soul had converged with her body and she could move. Now, she could go back and forth between this world and the Beach. Maybe she could use such an ability to overcome this unprecedented disaster.

John believed in Bridget and swore to dedicate himself to American reconstructionism.

They formed Bridges and dedicated it to building a system that would restore America.

That system was the Chiral Network.

The Beach was connected to the world of the dead. Which meant that it was also connected to the past. Light and electromagnetic waves never disappear, they just continue to diffuse. They continue to the ends of the universe without disappearing. The electromagnetic waves given off by someone's brain, the memories of events recorded by the light… they never disappear. We humans perceive that world as the world of the dead. Which meant that if humanity could piece those fragments back together, then maybe we could find a way to avoid another Big Five-level extinction. It was a revelation to Bridget.

In exchange, an umbilical cord grew from Bridget's abdomen. It wasn't an umbilical cord that connected mother to child, but an umbilical cord that connected her to Amelie on the Beach. She tried to cut it again and again, but it always came back. It was just like the umbilical cord that she saw on all those extinct creatures on the Beach.

—*That's right. My umbilical cord was just like the one I saw on all those animals. I was the existence that you deemed the Extinction Entity. But why me? Why did humanity have to go extinct? That was another reason why I activated the Chiral Network. I wanted to know more about the past. Know more about the path the world had taken through extinction and rebirth. I founded Bridges for that reason, too. But events were keeping pace with me. The voidouts began to happen more frequently. People were born with DOOMS. The BBs were born. But the longer I fought my war against the inevitable, the weaker I became. My* ha *had cancer. The Beach's punishment, maybe, for not playing along like a good little EE. And then, just like that, my* ha *was gone. I couldn't finish what I'd started. So I asked you to do it for me… and you did.*

Amelie and Bridget were at the place where everything started. Once, there was an explosion… a Big Bang that gave birth to time and space. But it was more like a big fluke. All that matter and antimatter should have canceled itself out, leaving nothing. But somehow, somehow a tiny speck of matter survived—just enough. Enough to make this world and everything in it.

—It's like the universe is trying to return us to the nothing we came from. A world that should have gone extinct is a world in precarious balance. Maybe the Big Five were its best attempts to finish us off. But somehow, life always managed to survive—just enough. Enough to thumb its nose at the will of the cosmos. You know, I'm starting to think that extinction might be the key to overcoming total annihilation. It forces life to fight to survive. To endure. To exist. That's why the Big Five ultimately rekindled life instead of extinguishing it. From the ashes of the dead rise the living—stronger and wiser. Inheritors of the legacy of existence itself. They defy the universe and refuse to surrender. Extinction is an opportunity.

That was the truth Amelie discovered once the Chiral Network connected the entire country. It gave her hope and finally tied her existence to the existence of this world.

But much like Bridget and Amelie were two sides of the same coin, this truth also hid another side. A crueler side. The gap between knowing and action was too large to cross.

Even if mankind avoided total annihilation, they would still go extinct. Mankind was the species to be sacrificed on the altar of survival.

Amelie had spent countless nights on this Beach alone, despairing in solitude. Then she realized something.

Her dreams of extinction were collected memories that resisted the truth of the universe—that it sought to return us to nothingness—and brought her the revelation that could reweave Bridges into something new.

What Bridget did was discover a third alternate side to extinction.

—*It was me who made you a repatriate. It was me who tried to sacrifice you—as a Bridge Baby, as the savior of this world, as a human offering. And it was me who killed you.*

The phase of this world had begun to shift ever since Clifford Unger's wife had attempted suicide and been rushed to hospital. But for her it was already over. Once she was pronounced brain-dead, the doctors tried to resuscitate her, but it was impossible. There was an argument over whether life support should be continued, but in the end, she was taken down a different path. A direct order came in from a source close to the president.

Cliff wasn't informed of the details. He was fobbed off with lies about how his wife closely resembled a case from the Manhattan voidout one year earlier, so she'd need to be transferred to a government facility for the appropriate care. The woman was seven months pregnant.

Once her fetus was extracted, he became the subject of the Bridge Baby experiments.

Cliff believed that both mother and child were being cared for at first, but once he learned the truth, he tried to retake his son. He failed. Both Cliff and his baby died. According to the records, the one who killed them was the president's aide, John Blake McClane.

—*But it was me who pulled the trigger. I killed you and Cliff. I didn't mean to. How could I? How could I wish to kill our savior? (I wanted to save Sam instead of saving the world from extinction— Wasn't that what I wished for? To save Sam so that we could watch the extinction together from this Beach?)*

Bridget wandered around the Beach looking for Sam's soul. Just like in the real world, his abdomen had been torn in a cross by the piercing bullet. He had been left on the Beach, all alone. When she found him, she picked Sam up, restored his soul, and repatriated him back to the world of the living.

Bridget had trampled over the very laws of this world.

Bridget had killed a fetus. A fetus that may have been extracted from its mother's womb, but was kept artificially alive in a pod and hadn't even been born yet. Then she brought it back to life. Sam's body wasn't one that could be returned to. Amelie had restored his soul and now his body had to adapt. It was an action that flew in the face of the entire flow of time. She had forcefully applied the laws of that world to this one. It made the world scream.

—But in doing so, I upset the fundamental balance between life and death. I just wanted to save you. I am an Extinction Entity. It's my fate to lead our species to extinction. But that moment, you became part of that fate. You became a "repatriate." And DOOMS started spreading my nightmares to others throughout the world. It was I that got you and everyone with DOOMS into this. Not long after, the Death Stranding occurred. The dead clung to our world. Until then, voidouts affected all creatures. This world made everything disappear.

But after that it was only humans who necrotized, only humans who became BTs, and only humans who caused voidouts. I had pulled the trigger on the "Sixth Extinction."

I may have been able to avoid the complete annihilation of the universe, but the extinction of humans was set in stone.

Sam couldn't look Amelie in the face, but wherever he looked he was reminded of her story. A strangely shaped Earth hung in the red sky, now so big that it looked like it might fall down at any minute. The sea was calm, but silently reflected the blood-colored sky.

The shoreline went on forever. Just like Amelie's confession seemed to eternally go around in Sam's head.

"The Last Stranding has already begun. A Seam has formed from my Beach and the Beaches of every soul in America. And soon, it will be inundated by a vast surge of antimatter, starting here. Stay here with me and bear witness to the very end."

Amelie sat down on the sand. Her golden hair swayed slightly. Sam could smell her scent. It was the same Amelie he had played with since he was a boy. He still didn't understand what it was that connected her to extinction.

"You mean just watch it burn?" Sam asked.

"Together, with me, until the last flame winks out. Doesn't sound so bad, does it?" Amelie asked sweetly. Sam had no words in response to her casual tone. "The gates to the other side are already open. You can't stop what's coming. But… if you cut me and my Beach loose, perhaps you can stop it from spreading. You might just prevent the Last Stranding. And mankind will live to die another day."

"Then it doesn't have to end here?" Sam asked.

"But it does," she replied. "This Beach is doomed no matter what. One look ought to tell you that. Which is why we must sever our connection. But you can't stop the inevitable. The Sixth Extinction will happen, either today or tomorrow."

Amelie handed Sam a gun.

"You can either end it with dignity, quick, clean, and in a flash… or you can struggle in vain, knowing full well what's waiting come the finish. Those are your choices."

Sam couldn't tear his eyes away from the gun as it dully reflected the light. Until he arrived at the Beach, he was certain that he would take out the Extinction Entity. He tried to make himself believe that the person calling itself Amelie was a sham. An evil being that brought calamity.

To "close the gate" all Sam had to do was take the gun and blow her away. But that wouldn't change the course toward extinction that humanity was already on. Knowing that now, what would be the point of taking that gun? Having just heard Amelie's confession, she wasn't the only Extinction Entity. Repatriates, those with DOOMS, and even Bridge Babies—if they had been born to resist extinction, then he also had to acknowledge that they were

used to arrive at extinction. Sam gingerly reached forward
and gripped the gun.

He had to choose. Had to decide. Had to make a move
one way or the other. If he didn't, nothing would ever change.

He adjusted the weight of the gun in his hand. It felt
heavier than any other cargo he had ever had to carry, and
much more fragile.

The wind blew and the dreamcatcher hanging by his
chest swayed in the breeze. It felt like the wind was blowing
right through him, freeing him from all the weight. The gun
dropped out of his hand and fell into the sand. These human
hands that had forged so many tools over the ages to keep
enemies away now held nothing.

Instead, Sam reached out both arms like a newborn baby
grasping out for anything it could get its hands on.

He embraced Amelie.

He felt her warmth, smelled her scent, and felt her
heartbeat through her chest.

"We're always connected, no matter what. You taught
me that."

Amelie hugged Sam back tightly. Sam responded. Their
physical barriers dissolved and their *kas* connected.

—*Here. It's a dreamcatcher.*

Sam was a young boy when Amelie had given him the
dreamcatcher on the Beach.

—*Wear it when you sleep, and I'll keep the nightmares away. I'll always be with you. When you're all grown up, you'll need it to make us whole again. And when the time comes… you'll have to stop me. You're the only one who can. Promise you'll remember, Sam… I'll be waiting for you on the Beach.*

The fragments of his dream reconnected into one. The dreamcatcher turned bad dreams into good. But dreams are just dreams. Once you wake up, the same reality from before you closed your eyes is still waiting for you. But sometimes, the power of dreams that you had in the past can show you a different side to reality in the future. That was what Amelie had wanted to say back then. But Sam had been young and hadn't been able to appreciate the value of what he had been given. Now he did.

"You knew. You always knew," Sam said.

" I did and I didn't. I had so many dreams of the future. I didn't know which ones to trust. Which is why I decided to share them with you and the others. But, to connect the dots, to make sense of everything, you need perspective. You need time. Time has no meaning to me. I am not a line, I am a single point. Which is why all I could do was just show you all the choices, and let you decide."

"Our nightmares are your dreams?" he asked.

"You found the common thread—the strand that links them together. And you did that the only way possible. By living life one day at a time."

Amelie lifted her face from where it had been buried in

Sam's chest, and the outline of the pair that had fused into one returned to normal.

Amelie thanked Sam and looked at the gun at his feet.

"A gun won't help you here. But it still has a role to play. It was the bonds between people that brought the world together. And if that is what matters most to you, then I will stay here on this Beach. Once the Last Stranding starts, it can't be stopped. I can't go with you. All I can do is try to spare you the worst."

"Why do you have to stay on the Beach?" Sam asked.

"I am the Beach. And I must stay here and ensure that the extinction happens. Even if it takes tens or hundreds of thousands of years. That's what an EE does. If I stay here to pay the price—to be the sacrifice—then you should be able to have some more time. It's just that…"

As Amelie looked at Sam, she smiled a human smile.

"I couldn't take it anymore. I got so tired of waiting. And I figured that no one would blame me if I just got it all over with, so that's what I did. I don't remember when or where, but that's how I felt."

Maybe that was the little girl talking who was yet to arrive at the truth. Maybe it was the old lady whose entire body was afflicted with cancer cells. Maybe it was even the woman who had the epiphany about rebuilding América. She had a dream and she couldn't talk to anyone else about it.

"But you and the others came together—connected. And

you may be living on borrowed time… but you still have hope. Before each of the Big Five, life rebelled. They fought back. Evolved in order to survive. The extinction isn't just an ending. It's an opportunity. And if I have to pay the price for that, then so be it. Even if we aren't together, we will always be connected."

Amelie pulled Sam into another tight hug.

"Thank you, Sam."

Those were her last words. The strength in her arms suddenly slackened and the sandy beach had been swallowed up by a sea of blood. They were held afloat in a bottomless ocean. But only Sam was dragged back down. Amelie's voice echoed in his ears and her warmth remained in his chest as he sunk to the bottom.

EPILOGUE

"For too long have we lived as strangers to one another, divided by walls built to keep us safe. But now we have a new world."

Sam had his back to the wall by the window and was listening to that voice. There was nothing outside of the window frame, but the backdrop of Capital Knot City was plugged into it. In the president's Oval Office, where Bridget had breathed her last breath and where everything had begun, Sam was listening to the inaugural speech of a new president.

He hadn't spoken about what had happened on the Beach to anyone. He couldn't quite explain everything himself, so he didn't feel like filling in any of the others.

Humans lived by interpreting the world based on their own experiences. That was part of the reason why the Beach belonged to each individual person.

There was no need for every person to see exactly the same thing from the same perspective and place.

People had been calling for the ceremony. "A new country needs a new leader," they said. That's why this room had been decorated by hologram.

"And with the completion of the Chiral Network, we may at last move forward as a people united. Today, we come together to celebrate the birth of a new nation. A new nation for a new world—the United Cities of America."

That network now broadcast the president's message across the entire country. To the citizens of this new nation it was like their new president was speaking in front of their very faces.

"I once took an oath to support... and defend the Constitution of the United States. And so, as your president, I hereby swear once again to support and defend you, the people of the UCA. To share your destiny as a new me."

There was a slight commotion. Sam looked up.

"Let there be a new America. An America where we can face one another—where we can speak our minds and open our hearts. The old ways die hard. But I believe, my fellow Americans, that we have the strength and the courage to rise above our past and embrace our future."

Die-Hardman stood there, maskless. But even though the new leader had removed his mask, that didn't mean that every veil and embellishment had disappeared. It was like there was an entirely new layer. Sam looked down at the worn-out photo and sighed. It had returned with him from the Beach. The picture showed Lucy, Sam, and her. It was different from what was in Sam's memory.

"The Death Stranding is a part of that past. An enduring shadow. A constant reminder of what could have been. That we stand here today is testament not to the greatness of any one individual, but to our capacity to come together. To the bonds between us. To our collective greatness. All things must come to an end, ourselves included. But as long as we savor each moment, find joy in the promise of tomorrow, embrace hope and reject despair, we will endure. President Bridget Strand and her daughter, Samantha America Strand, sacrificed everything in their pursuit of hope—that we, the people, might be whole again. That they are not here today to see the fruits of their labor fills us all with a profound sadness…"

Bridget's and Amelie's portraits were projected behind Die-Hardman. Nothing was said about their true self, but they were instead allowed to be remembered how they depicted themselves.

"But we find comfort in the knowledge that their memories will live on in the Chiral Network… and in our hearts. We will always remain connected. There are other heroes in this story."

Sam put the photo away and began to walk.

"You whose achievements seem destined to go unrecognized. America still needs that hero. Those without whom we would not be here. The name is unimportant. You know who I mean. And for those unsung heroes, I have a message… It was you who brought us together, you who made us whole again. And while you and I will eventually pass on… we will be survived by our legacies—our lives and our memories preserved for future generations. Maybe a day will come in due course when we can stop the Death Stranding with our own strength. For that we must work as one. We must never stand alone again."

Sam pushed open the Oval Office door and stepped out into the empty hallway. He could still faintly hear Die-Hardman's speech. Sam wasn't upset or disappointed that Die-Hardman didn't mention him in his speech. Now that he had thrown his old mask away, Die-Hardman had to don the new one that came with being president. Sam also had to live with his secrets.

She had embraced him. Then they separated and Sam fell to his own Beach. Sam was a repatriate. It was the first time he had visited his own Beach. He couldn't tell it apart from the one that Amelie had taken him to. There was no red sky. No red sea. No BTs. Just a quiet and calm Beach. The only thing that remained the same was the shoreline that stretched on and on for eternity.

The baby doll that Amelie had spoken of was cleansed by the waves. Its head was dark and there were marks all over its arms, legs, and chest. It looked sad and worn out, like a kid had finally gotten tired of playing with it. Sam scooped it up, when a slip of paper fell from inside it. Sam tensed up. It was the photo he thought he had lost. The photo of him, Lucy, and the smiling Bridget stood between them. It was the photo she had gone out of her way to print out and write a message on. Bridget had said that it would make it a one-of-a-kind that could never be replaced. After the word "Strand" came the word "Again."

When Sam placed the photo in his chest pocket, the doll caught his eye. Now it was clean, with no marks. Now it looked just like a newborn baby. An accessory sparkled gold around its neck. It was Amelie's *quipu*. The *quipu* that Sam had given her all those years ago was now in the baby's hands.

I add a knot when I make a friend, child Sam had told her the day he gave it to her.

Even though he shouldn't have been able to increase the number of knots on an empty Beach, he did. He wandered around and around, looking for an exit, eventually tiring and falling asleep. Every time he woke up, he added another knot. The *quipu* was keeping track of the amount of time Sam had spent there. Once the *quipu* was full of knots, they disappeared and it all started over again. Had Amelie counted her time here in the same way? When Sam thought about how damaging that must have been, his naivety as a child frustrated him.

Once he had cycled through the *quipu* knots yet again, he began to think that he was trapped in an infinitely looping hell. Just like Cliff's battlefield and the Beach Amelie spent her life as an Extinction Entity on. If Bridget's cancer had been divine punishment from the universe, then this was his. With each passing day his belief in that grew stronger, until eventually, it became certainty. There was only one way to get off the Beach.

—*A gun won't help you here. But it still has a role to play.*

The revolver was buried in the sand. Humanity would go on, but a load called loneliness weighed down on Sam. The weight of it brought Sam to his knees. Steadying his trembling hands, Sam put the gun to his temple. He could feel the cold of the metal and realized that he was drenched in sweat. He held his breath and squeezed. The sound of the waves seemed distant and all he could hear was the sound of his own beating heart over the top of them. Then… clink. *Clink, clink, clink.*

Instead of his beating heart, now all he heard was the vain sound of the gun hammer striking an empty chamber.

What an idiot. Sam could hear Amelie smile sadly in his head. If he had been stuck there forever, what would he have done?

Sam continued walking down the empty hallway. He could no longer hear Die-Hardman's speech.

"Going somewhere, Sam?" Deadman asked, chasing after him. "Tired of being the unsung hero?"

"No… I'm done is all. She's gone," he replied.

"C'mon, wait. There's something I need to tell you," Deadman exclaimed, grabbing Sam's arm. At first, Deadman seemed to have realized his mistake, but his look of horror soon turned to surprise. "Huh. This doesn't bother you anymore?"

Deadman gradually pressed tighter and Sam grimaced. But they both seemed to know that it wasn't because he was having an adverse reaction anymore. Ever since Fragile had jumped him back, Sam had a feeling that he might have gotten a little better. But in the midst of Deadman's grip, he began to feel like he might have completely recovered.

"Now, wouldn't you like to know how we brought you back from the Beach?" Deadman asked.

Sam didn't know what to say. He'd be lying if he said he wasn't curious, but it wasn't going to help him anymore even if he did know.

After he threw that useless gun back to the ground and

began to wander the beach once more, he heard a voice. Familiar voices were calling out his name. He could hear Deadman, Heartman, Mama/Lockne, and even Lou's cries. They led him to the sea.

—*See, you are connected*, Amelie whispered. Then someone grabbed him by the legs and dragged him to the ocean floor.

"We were going to use the doll, but we didn't have one handy. Which was when I remembered something else."

Deadman fiddled with his cuff link and projected a hologram.

"That what I think it is?" Sam asked.

"Yes. What could be more connected to Amelie's Beach than President Strand's umbilical cord? Heartman thought that was why she left it with me in the first place. Unfortunately..."

"It didn't work," Sam guessed.

"Yeah, she'd already cut her Beach loose." Deadman looked at his feet. "It was just... gone. We didn't know if that meant she'd dragged you into the great beyond with her, or sent you to some other Beach... We were really racking our brains. Heartman and Mama split up and started searching every Beach you might feasibly have washed up on. We looked for a month with absolutely nothing to show for it."

Sam thought about the disparity between the passage of time in this world and the passage of time on the Beach. How long had he been there? It had felt like a lifetime to him.

"In the end, this is what led us to you." Deadman reached inside his jacket and pulled out the revolver. "Just when we were about to give up, Die-Hardman reminded us about the revolver. So, we tried to follow it, and it led us to a far corner of your own Beach…"

Sam once again found himself face to face with the gun that killed him and Cliff. The gun that started everything. Amelie had admitted that it was she who had killed them, so who was the gun connected to in this world? It must have been John Blake McClane, the president's aide. He had been the one to build a Bridge to the Beach by thinking of it.

"Bingo—there you were. Mama made visual contact first. She was able to see you from her vantage point on the other side. She informed Lockne via their connection, and Heartman confirmed your location during his subsequent near-death experience. The plan was for Fragile to, in essence, 'slingshot' Lou and me to your position so we could rescue you."

So, it was Deadman who had grabbed Sam's legs and brought him back? No, it was all of them who saved him. All of them had continued the search. Sam felt like his voice would waver if he tried to say anything, so he just nodded instead.

"But it's not so easy to send multiple individuals to another person's Beach for an extended period of time. And that's where the umbilical cord came in. We wove these from President Strand's DNA. They serve as a single knot that binds us all."

Deadman puffed out his chest with pride and showed Sam the new symbol of Bridges—a *quipu*. It was intertwined with the proof that Bridget had lived.

"The president must have known all of this would happen. Ironic, isn't it? The gun that set this whole mess in motion ends up being the key to saving you."

"Amelie—she said it had another purpose," Sam told Deadman.

"Not a weapon, but a lifeline. A stick that became a rope? I suppose that's one way of putting it…" he mused.

Sam was suddenly engulfed by something that felt like a soft, warm bed.

"Oh, Sam, you have no idea how long I've been waiting to give you a hug!" Deadman's arms reached around Sam's back. He felt warm. It was like being wrapped up in a blanket when he was a kid.

"Got something else to tell you. Top secret," Deadman whispered into Sam's ear. "It's about Cliff. His BB's mother's name was Lisa Bridges. Cliff's common-law wife. And…"

Deadman lowered his voice and looked down.

"Cliff was killed by a man identified in the records only as 'John.' Former US Special Forces. Quite good at it, by all accounts. Later appointed as an aide to the president, who used him for most of her wetwork. The records go on to state that he vanished after Cliff's death. A warrant was put out, but he was later found dead. Turns out some people 'die' harder than others, though. Dear 'John' donned a mask and reappeared with a new identity."

Sam nodded silently to indicate to Deadman that he already knew. Amelie had told him so. John had also had to sacrifice his past as another sacrifice on the altar of America.

"I don't trust him," Deadman blurted out. "But I'll work with him if that's what it takes. We'll talk later."

Deadman shook himself free and took off at a trot down the hallway. In his stead appeared the new maskless president. He was too close for Sam to pretend that he hadn't noticed him, and it would have been awkward to walk away. Hopefully, Die-Hardman would just pass by, pretending not to see him.

It was the president who spoke first. But he wasn't talking to Sam. It was like he was talking at himself.

"I don't expect you to forgive me..." Die-Hardman's voice was already trembling. "But would you hear me out? I killed Captain Clifford Unger."

He didn't mention killing Sam. That's how Sam knew he was telling the truth.

"I would tell you I did it for America. For love of country. But I didn't. I did it for her—because I loved her with all my heart. She was everything to me. Everything. Now, I'm not trying to make excuses. I just want you to know, that not a day's gone by when I haven't thought about it. Time didn't help. Or the mask."

Die-Hardman couldn't have forgotten about the past. It lived on in that mask. Weighed down on him. All he'd done was bury it. Sam could sympathize with that. He had done the same. That's why he couldn't stay there anymore. But as Sam tried to leave, Die-Hardman stopped him.

"Please—let me finish. The captain saved my life."

Sam didn't believe that confessions were ever for purification's sake. They were to offload a burden for someone else to deal with later. The one who took care of that burden was the savior or human to be sacrificed. If only that role was divided more equally among everyone, then there would be no need for a savior or a hero. A society that cries out for a savior is a society that's fundamentally broken.

"You know why they call me Die-Hardman? Because he wouldn't let me die. He brought my sorry ass back home every time. And I loved him as much as I loved her."

Die-Hardman always needed someone to believe in, something to give up everything for. Sam was the same. Just as Die-Hardman sought Cliff, Bridget, and America, Sam sought Lucy, Lou, and Amelie.

"And when he stared me down, that ghost, I knew. He was here to kill me. To make it right. And why shouldn't he? Why didn't he? He couldn't save his kid. His BB. And that's what brought him back. I guess, when he saw I was trying

to do my part for America, he remembered who he was...
and he forgave me."

Die-Hardman cried loudly, falling to his knees. It was
like he could no longer bear the weight of Cliff's forgiveness.
"God! But I don't deserve it, goddammit! There is no
atoning for what I've done!" he cried. The man who had let
his guard down and was openly weeping was no longer the
president, but John again.

"Dammit!" he yelled, pounding the floor with his fist. He
kept hitting it and hitting it, not even aware that the
pounding had broken his skin and that blood was splattering
on the floor. There wasn't a shred of beauty or dignity in the
man before him, but neither did he seem pitiable or small.
Sam grabbed John's arm and helped him back to his feet.

"But maybe... maybe this is the next best thing. Maybe he
brought me back from the Beach for a reason... one last time.
He wanted me to do this. To keep on being Die-Hardman."

"No, he didn't," Sam cut in.

John blinked.

"Nobody wants a president who acts like they're immortal.
If you're not scared of death, how can you value life?" Sam
said, shoving the gun against the president's chest.

"And yeah, the old ways die hard, but that's what's gonna
have to happen... if we're gonna come together and build a
better America. 'That gun won't help you here.'"

The president slowly received the gun with both hands.

Guns had been around since their ancestors first came to America. They were used for protection, killing, and upholding justice. But now, in the president's hand, a gun was becoming something else.

"Her words, not mine," Sam added.

That gun had been a bridge to Sam. The president stowed the gun in the inside pocket of his jacket and wiped the tears from his face.

"Thank you, Sam."

Sam walked away as those words echoed behind him. He was heading outside. From the underground hallway to those fields shining with light.

"Hey, Sam. Been waiting for you." Deadman had been standing outside like a guard. The strong shutter that stood at the beginning of the slope leading outside was down. It was exactly where Sam had set out all that time ago to incinerate Bridget's body. Where it all began. Deadman looked up from his feet. In his arms was the BB pod.

"Lou!?" Sam didn't even have to check. That pod was already a part of him.

"The decommissioning order finally came through." Deadman's voice was cold. He sounded nothing like the man who had embraced him earlier. "Poor thing was never truly alive. Not in this world, at least. I know you have a connection with Lou, but Lou doesn't belong here anymore. Can't risk necrosis. The body can't stay here. I thought you might want to take care of it. You could try taking Lou out of the pod just to see what happens, but that would be in direct contravention of an executive order."

Lou was floating in the amniotic fluid, eyes closed. Sam could barely tell whether Lou was sleeping or dead.

"And there are laws about that kind of thing now that we're a nation. I just couldn't bring myself to do it. But if the alternative is defying the president… I can't do that, either. Not me." Deadman was cradling the pod with both arms like anyone else would a baby. "I'm sorry, Sam, I—"

"Alright. I'll go to the incinerator," Sam told him.

That was the incinerator where Sam first connected to Lou. As he handed over the pod, Deadman tried to act casual and wiped away the tears from his face. At the same time, he removed one of Sam's cufflinks.

"I just took your cuff links offline," he explained.

His tears were probably real, but while he pretended to wipe them away, he accessed Sam's cuff links using his own.

"In that state, there'd be nothing to stop you from removing them. If you did, the UCA wouldn't know where you were or how to find you. You'd be invisible. When you use the incinerator, you'll be reconnected to the network automatically. You can't use it offline. I trust you'll remember what I said?"

"Right. Absolutely." Sam took the pod. "Thanks for everything."

Before he ended his sentence, he turned around and hugged Deadman. That man who had first burdened Sam with Lou behind his back was now openly entrusting him with the BB. The weight and significance of the action was completely different from last time.

The shutter went up with a creak. Pale light streamed into the room and a shadow of a person was cast over the floor of the entrance.

"How's the weather?" Sam asked. Fragile turned around.

"Don't think you'll be needing an umbrella," she answered.

She had made a complete recovery. It seemed to Sam like her smile had become softer than before. There were no longer any gloves covering her hands as she put the umbrella away. She had stopped hiding her scars.

"I decided to follow my father's dream after all. Don't worry. I won't get mixed up with any terrorists this time. UCA's got my back. We're the first private delivery company to get official approval," Fragile explained.

"Sounds like you're moving up in the world. Congratulations," Sam told her.

At her chest, over her brand-new uniform, hung a *quipu*, exactly the same as those worn by Deadman and the others.

"Thanks. Wait. There's something I have to tell you." Her smile turned into a more serious look. "I didn't shoot Higgs. Couldn't pull the trigger. So, I let him choose. Death or eternal solitude on the Beach."

As she bit her lip slightly and looked at her feet, it was difficult to tell from her face why she was telling Sam this. Did she regret not getting her revenge? Did she regret exacting her revenge on him, the same way he did her?

"Fair enough. You never did like breaking things."

"That's right. I find and fix what's broken and reconnect it. I'm Fragile..." Her tone and expression lightened up a bit. "But..." She looked Sam in the eye. Sam nodded and opened his mouth...

"...but not that fragile!" they said in unison.

"Wanna come work for me? Could use a man like you." Fragile asked the same question she had asked back in the cave so long ago. Sam had to play along.

"The world's still broken. The same as before."

"Come on. You put America back together, didn't you?" she countered.

"Doesn't mean there's a place for me. I've got no ties to anyone or anything. I might as well be dead. I felt like that when we first met in the cave, and I still do."

Fragile put her hand on Sam's shoulder.

"Don't act like you're the same person! You've learned how to touch. To feel. You've connected with people—with us!"

She was right. Ever since she jumped him back from the Beach, he had begun to get better. Yet he still couldn't bring himself to be openly happy.

"Everything I touch, I lose," Sam told her.

Fragile's hand left Sam's shoulder. Both her warmth and the weight of her hand disappeared.

A ray of light pierced through a gap in the thin cloud cover. It was a sight that no one had seen for a while. Fragile squinted up at it.

One day, a woman like her might be able to go beyond the clouds. He secretly hoped that she would.

"C'mon, Lou. One last delivery," Sam muttered to himself as he began to climb the slope.

EPILOGUE

The ground underfoot was frozen and hard. But the blades of grass that covered it were soft, like they were newly grown. A young Bridget had said that the sand on the beach she dreamed of when she was young was made of the corpses of coral and shells. But this ground was made up of the rotting corpses of living creatures, too. After the Big Bang, the small amount of matter that remained that didn't come into contact with antimatter came together to create this world. If it had come into contact, it would have disappeared. This world existed because something didn't reach out in return.

Sam crossed a river that froze him to the bones, circumvented a cliff that looked like it was about to collapse, and struggled up the slope of a hill. Cryptobiotes wriggled out from the shadow of a rock and floated idly in the air. If it hadn't been connected to the world by the Beach, this strange creature would never have been discovered. It would never have been preyed upon by humans, either.

Right in front of him was something that Sam had never seen before. He stopped. It was a dull white, rod-shaped object. Slender like a stick. It didn't look human. No matter how humans died, it was unlikely they would leave bones behind. Whether it was a voidout or incineration, no trace of humans was ever left behind now. They weren't returned to this world. Nor were they eaten by animals, other than the BTs. They were completely erased from the circle of life on this planet. Eventually, all trace of them would wither away and they would disappear.

Sam licked the bone. It tasted of dusty earth. Humanity didn't return bones to the cycle of life and death, instead they remodeled them into tools of aggression and destruction. Humanity had made its own system and become the rulers of this world. But that too was about to end.

If I survive until that time comes, will I see her again? Will she be there waiting for me on the Beach?

It was impossible.

Sam flung the bone away as hard as he could. Being so light, the bone didn't even follow a curve, it just dropped to the ground. It felt like someone was telling him that it was never going to reach beyond the clouds. It was of this land, of this earth.

As Sam reached the top of the hill, the incinerator came into view.

The inside of his nose began to hurt and his eyes began to water.

This wasn't an allergic reaction. They were tears of mourning. Tears that the living shed in tribute for the dead—for they could not lay the dead to their eternal rest where they belonged, but, for their own protection, had to incinerate them into nothingness. Sam understood that now.

He was still outside the facility. To enter, he would have to verify his identity.

Should he go in? Should he go back?

The inside of the pod was dark. Sam couldn't tell what kind of condition Lou was in.

Not knowing whether he was doing the right thing or not, he pulled out the cord and connected to Lou.

His mind exploded.

—*This child's special.*

—*This child will be the bridge that connects us all.*

Sam heard a muffled voice and opened his eyes. Everything around him was blurry when someone's face swam into view. No, that's not right. Water flooded into his mouth as he tried to open it. It tasted like the sea. It ran down his throat and filled his lungs. But he wouldn't drown. He hadn't been born yet. He was still a creature of the sea.

—*This is all my fault. I should… I should never have put you in that prison.*

Even from within that pod filled with amniotic fluid, he could distinguish Cliff's voice.

—*And the second all this is over, I'm gonna take you wherever you wanna go.*

"Don't hesitate, sir. This is the only chance you'll get."

This wasn't the first time Sam had seen the revolver that Cliff had just been handed. It was the gun that Amelie had given him on the Beach. The gun he had tried to blow his brains out with after he lost all hope. Cliff checked the cylinder. This time it was fully loaded. John silently left the room. He only had five minutes.

Cliff opened the cabinet and took out one of the stacked towels, wrapping it around the gun. Then he found a cushion and turned toward the bed. This bed was no ordinary bed. It was a manmade cocoon composed of light metals and reinforced plastic and electric circuitry. Or a manmade coffin. The sleeping woman within was half-dead.

"I'm sorry, Lisa." Cliff pressed the cushion to Lisa's face and the gun into the cushion. "Don't worry. I'll take care of him. I promise you."

As he bent down to kiss her, he saw the black and blue

bruises. The marks that had caused her brain death in the first place. Cliff didn't know what had driven her to do such a thing. He had shut those memories away.

"I'm sorry."

How many times have I said those words to her now? And how many times am I doomed to repeat them in the future? Cliff wondered as he squeezed the trigger. He turned his face away and heard two muffled gunshots. The instruments connected to his wife hid her death and carried on spoofing vitals as if she was still alive. He had five minutes to get everything done.

The face got closer and closer to Sam as Cliff cradled the whole pod in his arms.

"BB. Can you hear me?" Cliff asked. Sam's world shook, but it didn't feel unpleasant. "Can you hear me? It's Daddy."

Cliff opened the door to the room and exited into the hall without making a sound. Even though Cliff had walked these corridors plenty of times before, tonight they felt like a labyrinth. But this Orpheus wasn't trying to take back his lover. He was trying to reclaim his son.

There should still have been a little time before the guards made their rounds. Cliff advanced straight toward the end of the hall, looking left and right as he went. As he took a left toward the entrance, alarm bells went off in his head. Several soldiers were headed his way from the right. But they hadn't spotted him yet.

Cliff immediately went back the way he came and held his breath.

Three soldiers passed by silently. He couldn't go after them. He had to stick to the plan. Cliff headed to the right, the direction from which the soldiers had come from. He had three minutes left.

He decided to sneak into a separate building from the adjoining hallway. But the door was locked and made of reinforced glass.

He gave up and considered his options. Should he use his original escape route? Or take a detour and head straight for the exit? Before he could decide, one of the options was taken off the table. He could hear voices at the end of the hall. They were getting closer. It sounded like a doctor and their staff.

If he acted casual, maybe they would just walk right past him. It was still one minute until the alarm alerting them of Lisa's death went off anyway. His temples were covered with sweat. Cliff realized he was nervous. His hand that gripped his gun and his arm carrying the pod were both trembling slightly. This had never happened to him before. He had always managed to give any kind of danger the slip. He wasn't afraid of death. But once his son was conceived, death became much more of a worry. Even if he wasn't afraid of death himself, he still couldn't allow himself to die.

That in itself had dulled Cliff's judgment and forced him to resign from active duty.

It was no longer Cliff but the impending alarm that decided his next course of action.

The doctors were heading back in the direction they had come, but from the opposite side came the sound of several sets of footsteps.

Cliff put his hand to the door in another attempt to open it, but from the other side of the glass came several guards with their guns at the ready.

"Freeze!"

The laser sight attached to the soldier's gun was dancing around Cliff's chest area. Cliff held up his own gun in his right hand and pressed it against the pod. The sound of the gun scraping along the side of the pod traveled through the amniotic fluid, but Sam wasn't scared.

"Drop it!"

The call for Cliff to put his gun down was echoed throughout the hallway. But Cliff made use of his trump card and kept the BB hostage. The soldiers backed off as he glared at them. Then, the commotion from the other end of the hall grew louder.

"Stand down!" a soldier shouted, but Cliff was already off running in the opposite direction. He heard a soldier fire on him.

His left shoulder grew hot. Lukewarm blood dripped

down his arm. The pod was also covered in it and Sam's view of the world was stained red. It was the same red that he saw in the sky and in the sea on Amelie's Beach.

Sam had unconsciously yanked the cord out of the pod.

A pain blew through his shoulder like he'd also been shot. His body was covered in sweat. It was that vision again. In it, Sam had played the part of both Cliff and the BB. But Cliff was already gone and Lou had grown extremely weak. Why was he seeing that now? Something had made him see it. Maybe Lou was trying to reconnect with him. While one part of him hoped that was the case, another more logical part of him knew that he shouldn't get any more attached. It was the same logic that knew that Lou shouldn't be kept in the gap between life and death forever.

That pushed Sam forward.

The incinerator gave off the same sour scent of decay as always. This place was the end of the road. It was where all traces that someone's body existed in this world disappeared. To the living, this was the world's end.

Sam remembered when he first met Lou. How Igor had entrusted Lou to him, and how he had repatriated from the Seam. He remembered going against the command to incinerate Lou, and the first time he tried connecting to

Lou. He and this kid had come a long way together.

If it wasn't for Lou, Sam never would have made it to the other side of the continent and back. Even though Lou had exceeded the usual one year of service life, Sam had relied on Lou to keep putting one foot in front of the other. Of course, Sam was mad that the Bridge Babies were used as communications mediums and that they were sacrificed as the cornerstones of American reconstructionism, but Sam had done the same to this child.

Had Sam really thought about what was best for Lou? He'd just blindly believed that because Lou was a kid, still just a baby, the BB needed protection and guidance.

But he was the one who had been protected.

The incineration apparatus rose from the floor.

The reason why it resembled an altar to Sam was because he wanted to remember the months and years he had spent with Lou as something special. For Lou, he wanted to transform the incinerator from a place of simple erasure to a place where he could preserve those memories for all eternity. This was to be a ceremony just for them, not for the American nation, so he removed his cuffs links.

—*In that state, there'd be nothing to stop you from removing them. If you did, the UCA wouldn't know where you were or how to find you. You'd be invisible.*

Sam decided to trust in the help that Deadman had given them.

He put his cuff links on the altar. He was going to erase the Sam that belonged to Bridges.

He put the pod on there, too. To free Lou.

Sam could hear thunder. The sky suddenly darkened and the smell of rain filled Sam's nostrils. If Sam dealt with Lou here, then at least Lou wouldn't be cursed to wander around with the rest of the dead. If the kid couldn't live in this world, then the least he could do was send Lou on to the next.

—Want to go home?

The one who was asked and replied with a no was a young Sam.

Then this kid—

The altar groaned as it began to sink back into the floor.

"I screwed it up. I've ruined everything."

Sam was looking down on Cliff. He was squatting down on one knee with his back to him. The blood pouring out of his left shoulder was staining the back of the jacket a dark red. Cliff stood up with a groan.

"I'm sorry, Lisa…"

Muttering Lisa's name in what sounded like delirium, Cliff turned back toward the door, leaving bloody footprints as he stepped forward. With a firm grip on the pod, he closed the door behind him and shot at the security panel twice to break it. Then he turned toward Sam. Cliff's face was flushed as though he was suffering from a high fever and his eyes were welling up, but he didn't see Sam. The only other person there was Lisa, under a blood-soaked cushion. Cliff passed straight through Sam and clung to the bed. Sam realized that the only part of him there was his *ka*. He was the only one aware he was stood there. No one else seemed to notice.

Sam could hear a noise outside the door.

"In here!"

Someone banged on the door violently. The dull thuds echoed around the room. They pounded again and again and again. Eventually, the thuds turned into the sound of metal on metal. Together with the metallic grinding sound of the engine cutter, the door began to groan.

Cliff seemed unaware as he sat slumped in front of the bed.

Are you going to give up here? But Sam's thoughts didn't translate into words. They never reached Cliff.

"BB. Don't worry. It's okay. I'll always be with you," Cliff reassured the BB, trying as hard as he could to make sure that he was hearing his message.

"This room is off-limits. No one goes in."

Sam could hear a voice behind the door clearly trying to get the situation under control. He knew that voice. It belonged to John. The sound of the cutter stopped.

"But he's in there, sir. I saw him!" a man protested.

"You saw wrong. Now, check the other way. Go!"

John dismissed any resistance from the young soldier and sent him on his way. The commotion withdrew like the tide. Sam heard John breathe a sigh of relief on the other side of the door. *Now's your chance. Run.* But Sam's wish and John's actions didn't help Cliff.

"No. Open it up. He's inside."

The command came from the President of the United States of America, Bridget Strand. John and the guards scattered. Special forces followed Bridget's commands and broke down the door, surging into the room.

Bullets flew through Sam as he opened his arms wide in a bid to cover Cliff. They simply ignored that he was even there and flew straight into their target. Cliff's body was thrown to the ground, where blood began to pool beneath him. Yet he still continued to talk to his BB.

"When I found out I was gonna be a father... I was so scared. Scared of what it would mean... I had to be there for you and your mom... no matter what. I couldn't just go off and get myself killed anymore..."

Images flashed in the back of Sam's mind. A smiling Lisa rubbing her large belly. Cliff's back as he walked away. And Lisa tying a piece of rope around her neck with trembling hands.

"I couldn't leave you all alone. I couldn't," Cliff murmured.

The soldiers stood still, guns still pointed in Cliff's direction.

"Get off of him! Now!" John commanded as he broke into the ring of soldiers that had surrounded Cliff. In his hand was the gun that Cliff had dropped under the soldiers' fire.

"I had it all wrong... all wrong." Cliff was exerting so much effort to take each and every breath. Yet he still talked to his BB. "Being a father... didn't make me scared. It made me brave. I'm sorry... sorry it took me so long..."

"Captain, look at you."

Cliff noticed John and lifted his head. His bangs were dripping with blood and sticking to his forehead. He pushed them out of his face and cast his gaze downward once more.

"Don't make the same mistake. Be yourself... Be free," Cliff finished.

As though his last ounce of strength had finally left his body, Cliff's beloved pod rolled to the floor.

Before John even had time to reach out for it himself, a special forces member rushed over and scooped it into his arms. This was the end. All Sam could do was stand and watch, dumbfounded.

John was crouching down in front of Cliff. It was like he was protecting Cliff, despite the fact that he no longer had any value to them now that the BB had been retrieved. That's when Bridget shouted.

She was cradling the pod the soldier had passed her when her face turned pale and she stared at Cliff. John gasped and the soldiers became nervous. There was nothing in the pod.

"Captain—I need you to hand it over," John pleaded, his voice trembling. The naked BB was cradled in Cliff's arms. A puddle of amniotic fluid was dripping down from the pod and spreading across the floor.

"Let it go—please," John repeated, pointing his gun at Cliff's head. Cliff looked between John and the gun and grimaced. Or maybe it was a smile. Sam couldn't tell.

"Shoot him, John," Bridget commanded coldly. But Sam could sense some quivering in her voice, too. Sam tried to protect Cliff. He crouched in front of him, opened his arms wide, and covered the end of John's gun with his hands.

"Shoot him!" Bridget commanded again.

John's arms were shaking. Sam was glaring at John, but all that was reflected back in John's eyes was the face of a blood-soaked Cliff.

He couldn't do anything here. He couldn't control anything. He was so powerless. It must have been the same as how Amelie felt, only having a soul. He was overwhelmed with frustration at only being able to stand there and watch.

"I gave you an order! Shoot him!"

John's trembling finger squeezed the trigger.

"They told me your name was Sam Porter..." Sam heard Cliff's voice behind him. He turned and Cliff nodded. He saw Sam. "But you're Sam Bridges."

All Sam could hear was Cliff's voice. Everything had stopped. John's finger was still on the trigger. Neither Bridget nor the special forces operatives moved. The only ones moving in the midst of this frozen scene were Cliff and Sam.

"My son. My bridge to the future." Cliff cradled the baby and stood up. He staggered a little, but he seemed to be full of energy now. He was looking Sam straight in the eye. "Without you, I was just like any other cliff. A dead end. No way forward. Nothing but an obstacle—looking on at the world that people like you were trying to build. Dividing people was the only thing I was ever good at."

Sam was still crouching by Cliff when Cliff reached out to him.

"But not you, Sam. You bring people together. You're their bridge to the future... and mine. Come on, Sam. Stand up."

Cliff's hands were covered in scars and wrinkles. They were the hands of someone who had been through war. They were both strong but delicate. Even though they were stained with blood, they weren't dirty. Cliff passed the baby he was cradling in his arms to Sam. It was so small that it looked like it would fit inside the palm of his hand. It was soft and warm. Sam could feel its heart beating. Its little heart was beating away strongly. It synchronized with Sam's own heartbeat.

"Is this me?" Sam asked.

Cliff nodded and hugged Sam. Sam could smell cigarettes and blood. It was the smell of a father.

It was only slight, but Cliff squeezed his arms around Sam a little more tightly.

The paused time began to play again.

Sam heard two gunshots. And Cliff's body twisted twice.

His grip loosened. When Sam looked, the baby had disappeared. All that was left in his hands was blood spatter. Cliff was staring into the distance. Sam was no longer reflected in his eyes. So much blood was pouring out of the right side of his chest. The baby he had been holding was covered in it, too. The heartbeat that had just synched with Sam's was no more.

"Oh God, not the BB too." How could John play innocent like that? Sam looked up.

John was holding the gun, but Bridget's overlaid hand had pressed his finger on the trigger.

Cliff's body slumped to the ground like a puppet whose strings had just been cut. The baby's body rolled to the ground alongside him.

Bridget ran over to the baby screaming something and scooped it up into her arms. As Sam stared at his own dead body, all he could do was stand there.

Sam watched the lid to the incinerator casket close and the whole thing sink into the floor. It was burning his cuff links. His connection with America was burning away. Now that his right wrist felt lighter, he used it to pick up Lou. A puddle of amniotic fluid was spreading out across the floor.

The cross-shaped scar on his abdomen burned. That same mark that had formed when Sam Bridges was brought back to life before he was even born, that had been left behind when Amelie had restored Sam's *ka* on the Beach, was throbbing violently.

Sam hadn't been able to burn Lou, after all. Sam knew that his talk of returning this child to the land of the dead and doing what was best for the child's wellbeing had all been bullshit. Just a lie he had told himself. He knew that from the start.

He just wanted to feel this child's skin. Just like Cliff had held Sam as a baby, how Amelie had held him on the Beach, Sam wanted to hold Lou. Maybe it was a one-sided cruel love. Sam couldn't promise Lou what that love would bring. But Sam knew that he couldn't burn Lou without a hug.

Now his wish had come true—no, he made it come true. But Lou didn't respond.

Lou felt warm. But the breaths and heartbeat that Sam felt were shallow and weak.

"Lou!"

His persistent calls for Lou were just like those Cliff had made.

"Lou!"

Sam rubbed Lou's back and tried to massage arms and legs that were so thin they looked like they could snap. Sam had no idea if he was doing it right, but Sam kept calling Lou's name, hugging Lou close and rubbing the small body to stop the *ka* from separating from Lou's *ha*.

—*Want to go home?*

Where had Amelie meant when she asked me if I wanted to go home?

Where had Cliff tried to take me when I was a baby?

Where am I going to take you, Lou?

Where do I want to show you?

It's too early to go to the world of the dead. You haven't even been born yet. Let's not head to the realm of the past where everything is settled and finished, but toward the future with infinite possibilities. But right now, the only choice that lies in that future is for you to come into this world. So wake up, Lou. I'll anchor you here.

A vague umbilical cord of particles formed at Lou's abdomen. It was a sign of necrosis.

So, this kid would never be born into this world after all.

If I'm not with you, Lou, I can't begin anything either. Even if you don't want to live with me, I want to live with you.

Even as Sam's tears dripped onto Lou's face, Lou was still trying to return to the world of the dead.

No, Lou.

Sam closed his eyes so that he didn't have to look at Lou's umbilical cord. As he stood there holding Lou, unable to do anything but cry, he knew that he was the stupidest man in the world.

The dreamcatcher that hung by his chest caught on

something. Sam looked up. Lou's eyes were open. In Lou's right hand was Amelie's *quipu*.

Lou had returned.

Before Sam had the opportunity to shed any more tears, Lou began to cry out loudly.

Lou screamed out to the world: "I'm here."

Lou was crying, trembling all over, to shake off the border between life and death and tear away the shackles that bound the BB between them.

"Welcome back, Lou. Louise."

As Lou screamed her lungs out, Sam kissed her on the cheek. He felt her tears on his lips. They were the tears of a living, breathing child.

Sam left the incinerator to find that the rain had cleared. A rainbow drew a beautiful arc over the ridge. It wasn't the upside-down rainbow Sam usually saw.

The blowing winds brought with them a scent that Sam had never smelled before.

Sam looked back over his shoulder toward the incinerator and began to walk back the way he had come. But what lay before him now was a new place that he had never been to.

Let's go home.

Sam heard a familiar voice that he knew from long ago, somewhere before.

For more fantastic fiction, author events,
exclusive excerpts, competitions, limited editions and more

VISIT OUR WEBSITE
titanbooks.com

LIKE US ON FACEBOOK
facebook.com/titanbooks

FOLLOW US ON TWITTER AND INSTAGRAM
@TitanBooks

EMAIL US
readerfeedback@titanemail.com